D0901241

"Life's a mosaic of laughter and tears. Nowhere is this more powerfully seen than when families are challenged by the care needed for aging loved ones who can no longer live independently. This reality is powerfully fictionalized in *Harmony Hall*. Although a well-written novel, it accurately portrays the emotions of this real life experience. Entire family systems are exposed and affected as the caregiver responsibility is faced. This is a warm and engaging story of a place where these needs are met in a community of loving care. The reader also experiences both laughter and tears as the story unfolds and we see "harmony" come to life."

> James Vandiver, Director
> Harpeth Hills Resource Center on Aging
> Brentwood, TN

"*Harmony Hall* skillfully captures life's ups and downs in a small, private non-profit retirement home for ladies of limited means and various needs in Lexington, Kentucky. Drawn from her own experiences in a similar community, the author's story reveals with humor and empathy that extended families can thrive in a congregate, congenial environment. It subtly underscores the importance of charitable donations to insure that affordable, loving, secure homes remain available to our greatest generation and those that follow."

> Timothy L. Veno, President
> Kentucky Association of Homes and Services for the Aging

"This memorably insightful first novel explores in compelling detail the experiences of aging parents, their children and friends who face the often inevitable move from home to retirement community. Populated by a charming cast of mothers, daughters, residents and staff, the book has plenty to say about loss, aging, humor and grace as we come face to face with life and its challenges in the sunset years. This timely novel brings everything to the table: a crisp dialogue, lovely wit and enormous sympathy for the men, women and children who populate this story. It strikes at the heart of how we come to grips with caring for our elderly relatives and friends, and the value and dignity of communal living at its very best."

> Florence Huffman, Editor-in-Chief, The Clark Group,
> Lexington, Kentucky

"An affirming view of the challenges and opportunities for older women—thank goodness this fiction is based on fact."

V. McHenry-Hepner,
Manager of Outreach Services
Lexington Public Library

HARMONY HALL

HARMONY HALL

Ric McGee

iUniverse, Inc.
New York Lincoln Shanghai

Harmony Hall

Copyright © 2006 by Ric McGee

All rights reserved. No part of this book may be used or reproduced by any means, graphic, electronic, or mechanical, including photocopying, recording, taping or by any information storage retrieval system without the written permission of the publisher except in the case of brief quotations embodied in critical articles and reviews.

iUniverse books may be ordered through booksellers or by contacting:

iUniverse
2021 Pine Lake Road, Suite 100
Lincoln, NE 68512
www.iuniverse.com
1-800-Authors (1-800-288-4677)

ISBN-13: 978-0-595-37104-4 (pbk)
ISBN-13: 978-0-595-81504-3 (ebk)
ISBN-10: 0-595-37104-3 (pbk)
ISBN-10: 0-595-81504-9 (ebk)

Printed in the United States of America

Contents

Acknowledgements

This book is dedicated to Lt. Colonel Ed Weissinger, Commander of Operation Dogwood, who shared my dream of a retirement home sitcom and agreed that _Harmony Hall_ should be its moniker. Perhaps one day that dream will materialize.

The weekly support, review and suggestions of Palmoneada Brown, Laura Hatfield, Hattie Johnson, Nelle Johnson, Vivian Mark and Mildred McKeown kept this project alive. Dot Roach and Barbara Gray, no longer at Ashland Terrace, _Harmony Hall's_ model, are remembered and thanked for their enthusiasm and interest. I am indebted to all residents, present and past, for sharing their lives with the rest of us, and helping to create our characters.

Early on, the encouraging words of Virginia McHenry-Hepner of the Lexington Public Library, and later, those of Diana Martin, Shih Tzu connoisseur and Lexington Community College professor, instilled confidence that we were on the right track. Later, Joyce Ockerman and Florence Huffman, current and past board members respectively, fueled our optimism with kind and glowing reviews.

Alan Sullivan, Brian Hill and Susan Roemer of CMW were generous with their time and expertise, as was Fred Wholstein of Milward's Mortuary.

Dr. Jack Perry, a physician with an uncommon concern for the elderly and a true friend of our retirement community, was helpful and reassuring.

Lynn Keith, beloved sister and editor extraordinaire, was tireless in her search of misplaced commas and uneven indentions.

And always, I am indebted to my husband, Jim, who generally suffered in silence as I spent sleepless nights at the computer and large blocks of our vacation time with pen and pad.

CHAPTER 1

MAGNIFIQUE

MAY, 1998

The normalcy of the morning before all normalcy ended was what she later recalled. The cleaning lady was due at 9:00 and it was 8:45. Still in a short, threadbare robe, frantically straightening the house, it occurred to Faith Greene that she'd not called her mother, who would be wondering, as she always did, if a stroke had taken her daughter out. Also, the dog poop out back needed retrieving. Handling that job daily was the only New Year's resolution she had managed to keep the last five months. As she raced down the deck steps, long legs taking them two at a time, her faithful cardinal flashed past, voicing his irritation at the empty feeder. She rushed back through the house to the garage for his breakfast, vowing for the hundredth time to move the birdseed to the backyard shed. She whistled for the cardinal as she filled the feeder, cleaned up after the dog, and ran back through the house to the closet—hoping something in there looked as if it were ironed.

Billie Jo, Faith's cleaning lady, had been referred by Faith's dearest friend, Skipper, who found her through Pam, a mutual friend. Pam knew Billie Jo when she worked as a sales rep at a now defunct neighborhood magazine. Skipper, Pam and Faith were adamant about one thing—housecleaning was not part of their agenda—and all three were glad to pay Billie Jo twice what they'd pay themselves to do the same job. They loved Billie Jo for simplifying their lives, but complained to each other endlessly about her slovenly house-cleaning. Still, as Pete, Faith's boyfriend, was fond of reminding her, Billie Jo's cleaning was better than nothing.

"How'ya doin', Faith?" Billie Jo asked as she started bringing in her cleaning supplies through the front door.

"Couldn't be much better, kiddo," Faith responded, noticing that Billie Jo had brought along her copy of *People* magazine to read during lunch, on the deck swing. "If Mom calls, tell her I'll call her from work. I've got five errands between here and there, and I'm running behind."

"No problem, hon," Billie Jo said.

Faith and Babe, her pointer/Jack Russell mix, headed for the car. Faith carefully watched her shoes for deodorant powder dust clouds. Babe scouted the yard for birds. Even spring was a problematic time for middle-aged women suffering from hot flashes. Pantyhose, once a daily prerequisite of dressing, she now reserved for cooler weather. Faith thought of her mother, marveling that Mimi used to iron her husband's shirts in Miami, without air conditioning, sweat running down her neck, all the while smiling at her daughter and cracking jokes with the neighbor's kids. *She is a better woman than I.*

As Faith wove through morning traffic to her shop, Skipper called to report that her daughter, Lauren, had been sent home for wearing her pants below her navel and exposing way too much skin. "We've talked about this a thousand times," said Skipper in exasperation. "Why don't they just decide on uniforms so at least these kids will be decent at school? I know she's taking off everything but her thong at the mall, but they can prevent it at school." Faith had always thought Lauren was given too much rope as a child, and wanted to tell Skipper to get tougher, but she clucked sympathetically. At sixteen, Lauren was just getting started.

Opening the door to *Magnifique* always gave Faith a thrill. She'd worked for years in jobs she thought she loved, until laid off in 1986 and forced to reflect on priorities. After working part time at *Boutique Magnifique* for a year, she bought it from the aging owner for $15,000 with Pete's help, and never looked back. Running a consignment shop might seem like small potatoes, but to Faith it was a major accomplishment, an ongoing challenge and a job filled with fascinating possibilities and interesting women. She appreciated nice clothes and hated to spend money, knew that women universally loved a good deal, met the upper crust in Lexington when she took in consigned articles, and frequently met the desperate and nearly destitute when the same clothes sold. It made her day to watch a young career girl walk out of *Magnifique* with a $200 suit and change from a twenty-dollar bill, or a tired mother light up in a fashionable pantsuit. Even better, she called the shots now. There were no system design committees to deal with, no office politics to consider in working with a hierarchy of managers, no sullen employees to coddle. She could bring her dog with her; she could have a cage of finches behind the counter. It was a perfect fit. She loved her work.

❧   ❧   ❧

"You OK, honey?" Mimi asked, at 11:30. Her call caught Faith in the middle of straightening sale rack merchandise, alone in the shop.

"Great, Mom, just got too busy this morning, and Billie Jo was coming, so I had to clean up the house. I was going to call you here in a sec."

Mimi chuckled, and wondered how Faith turned out to be a neat freak, remembering her bedroom back in Miami. They usually touched base about 8:00 A.M. At eighty-one, Mimi lived alone in one half of a duplex that Pete owned. At Faith's urging, she had moved from Miami in 1992, six years before, after her husband died.

"I'm going to lunch with Joyce today—can you come along?" Mimi asked. Sometimes Faith had help at the store, sometimes not.

"Sorry, Mom, I'm on my own today. You all have a wonderful time. Tell Joyce to behave. Have a martini for me, if they serve them."

"We're going to Bob Evans, Faith, but I'll think about a martini while I drink my coffee."

Joyce, the second occupant of the duplex, was a perfect running Buddy for Mimi. Always willing to go anywhere, do anything, and laugh at the ridiculous, Mimi soon influenced Joyce, who was seventy-five and without family, to adopt her as an older sister figure. They wandered back and forth to each other's half of the duplex in their robes each morning—sharing coffee and Danish, the morning paper, gossip about Pete and Faith, and delight at the chipmunks that scurried across the lawn. Joyce played bridge; Mimi gardened. Twice a week they'd climb into Joyce's '82 Cadillac and eat breakfast or lunch out. Faith cringed at the thought of either driving, but was relieved that Joyce did most of it. She had convinced Pete to disconnect the starter in Mimi's Volkswagen several years after her mother's move to Lexington and Joyce became their designated driver. Mimi's old VW sat unused in the carport.

How lucky we are that they found each other. She remembered moving her mother into the duplex, thanking God that Pete had offered it for a ridiculously low rent because he knew they couldn't afford much. Mimi was exhausted, and not entirely convinced that she'd made the right decision to leave her small concrete block home in Florida. Although many of her peers were dead, she still had her tennis group there, and a few good neighbors who looked in on her occasionally. She knew, though, that Faith would be a constant irritant if she stayed in Miami. Besides, it was very exciting to throw caution to the winds and start a new life in a new city. She could still play tennis, and she loved the idea of being close to her only child.

As Faith hung up the phone, Skipper and another woman entered the shop. Skipper was wearing her latest consignment purchase from *Magnifique,* a two-piece knit number by St. John that looked as if it had been poured over her. Skipper wasn't the least bit ashamed of her body. Faith found her friend's lack of modesty hilarious and wished she had a little bit of Skipper's exhibitionism.

"Well, she's gone back to school with a few more inches covered," Skipper said.

"Was she disciplined?" Faith asked.

"Hell, no," said Skipper. "Unless you can call changing clothes punishment. You can bet she's got a pair of tear-away pants on as we speak."

Skipper was Faith's best friend. Neither could remember exactly how they met, but it had something to do with a tailgate party at a University of Kentucky football game while they were both still married. Now single, they could travel together, get soused together, even share the same roof on bad nights. Faith loved to look at her friend's photo albums kept under the island in the kitchen. They were filled with pictures of Skipper in exotic locations on cruises, with a red-haired fellow from Montana, holding an elk's lifeless head in her lap, swimming with dolphins in Florida and wearing a huge boa constrictor around her neck in Colombia, where she'd once dated an ambassador. It was pretty obvious that Skipper or her family had some money, because she never worked—just volunteered, and knew everyone in the city, many of whom she eventually took to lunch or to bed. For the last year or so, between engagements, Skipper would visit Faith at work, fascinated at the stream of customers who relied on *Magnifique* to pull them through an uncomfortable night at the boss's house or a daughter's hastily arranged wedding.

"I went out with Peaches last night," Skipper said. "Guess who we saw at the movies!"

"George the Hunk Clooney," said Faith.

"No," said Skipper. "Guess who was *at* the movies."

Since Skipper knew most of the eligible bachelors in town, and in some cases was responsible for their single status, she was highly touted as Lexington's hot scoop queen.

"Oh, let's see…how 'bout Pam?"

The solitary customer gave Faith the "I'm ready to try these on" look. As Faith turned to help her with hangers in the dressing room, the phone rang. At this hour in the morning it was sure to be a consignor calling, wanting Faith to look over her latest closet-cleaning victims. It was always a kick to find out what would soon hang on the shop racks.

"*Magnifique,*" Faith said, picking up the phone with a smile.

❀

CHAPTER 2

CATASTROPHE

Scott Bently was a certified EMT who worked days for the Lexington Fire Department. When the 911 operator rang the fire station with the location of the day's first accident, he and the truck were on the street in twenty-eight seconds. It took three minutes to reach the intersection where a large truck and hapless car were blocking four lanes of traffic. He could hear the ambulance racing toward them, and knew at once that the morning would be long.

❦   ❦   ❦

"Faith Green?"

"Speaking."

"This is Ellen Sandusky at Sacred Heart Hospital. I'm calling about Emily Johnson. Are you a family member?"

Faith's knees began to buckle. Gripping the counter, she closed her eyes and began to pray.

"Yes, I'm her daughter."

"I'm sorry, there's been an accident. Ms. Johnson is here at Sacred Heart. Are you able to meet her?"

"Can you tell me anything about her condition?" The tears were starting; she could barely speak.

"No ma'am. It's a little too early to tell."

"I'll be there in ten minutes."

Skipper, auburn curls momentarily stilled, put her hand on Faith's. "I'll mind the store," she said, and walked toward the waiting customer.

🍁   🍁   🍁

At noon, the Sacred Heart emergency room was nearly empty; half the staff was at lunch taking advantage of a slow day. Through the entrance windows, Ellen Sandusky, at the admissions desk, watched as a tall blonde woman raced across the parking lot and entered the admitting area.

"I'm Faith Green," she said breathlessly. "I think my mother, Mimi Johnson, is here."

Ellen noticed that Ms. Green had been crying; a smudge of mascara under her right eye flawed a lovely, thin face. Her hazel eyes were brimming. Ellen clicked in *Johnson.*

"Emily Johnson?"

"Yes, Emily Marie."

"You say you're family?"

"I'm her daughter," and the tears spilled over. "I'm sorry. I just heard she was here. I…I don't know what's happened."

Ellen gave Faith several release and consent forms to sign, then reached over to pat the daughter's hand. "Let's see if we can find her."

Dear God, please let her be OK. Please, please, please.

Minutes passed. A nurse appeared around the corner. "Ms. Green?"

"Yes.. my mother…?"

"Your mother is in radiology. She's going to need a procedure or two; we're trying to determine how badly she's been injured. She's unconscious."

"No!" Faith cried.

"It's not unusual. Can you stay in the ICU waiting room until we know more?"

"Can't I see her?" This was too horrible. Her poor mother—alone and hurt.

"I'm afraid not, at the moment. As soon as we get her to ICU we'll come get you."

Faith could not think. Ellen, familiar with the horrific, gently held Faith's elbow.

"Let's get some coffee. I'll show you where to wait."

At midnight, twelve hours after bursting through the emergency room entrance, Faith began to doze off. During that interminable period she called Pete, who stopped at Magnifique to pick up Babe and feed the finches. He took

Babe home and packed and delivered an overnight bag to Faith, who was spending the night on the longest ICU couch. Faith also called Skipper at the shop, who sounded surprisingly upbeat, and offered to open Magnifique the next morning, Saturday, and stay all day.

"I've been writing *everything* down, Faith, 'cause I can't get the hang of this frickin' cash register. You've sold a bundle, darling. I talked a gal named Gina into buying eight outfits and six pairs of shoes for her cruise—and they all look great! How's our Mimi?"

Faith wondered foggily if Gina was Gina of the bounced checks.

"She's alive, Skipper, but I haven't seen her yet…I haven't seen the doctor, either."

"Why the hell not? I'm coming over there…"

"No, stay put. If I need you here, I'll call. Bless you, Skipper—what would we do without you?"

"You'd do great without me, darling, but I couldn't do without you. Call me in the morning. All will be well."

Will it? Will my wonderful, healthy, life-loving mother ever recover from this? If I hadn't talked her into coming to Kentucky she'd still be OK, and Joyce would be alive. What have I done?

A large, swarthy man called her name. Faith awoke, dazed, wondering where she was.

"Yes?"

"I'm Dr. Santana. Your mother is in ICU now."

Faith rolled off the couch to her feet.

Mimi lay swathed in bandages, her hospital gown askew. Faith absorbed her condition in slow motion, zombie-like after twelve hours of fear and worry, and the recent knowledge that Joyce was dead. Her mother's best friend was struck full force by the truck, which lost its race with the red light. Mimi regained consciousness just before the surgeon began stitching up her right temple, which had gone through the passenger's window. A lung was collapsed, punctured by one of three broken ribs. Her pelvis was broken. Mimi's pride and joy, her carefully colored red hair, was gone but for a few wisps that poked below the cerebral bandage, now stained brown with old blood. She looked through Faith and the doctor, eyes half-opened, face swollen.

"Your mother is in wonderful shape for her age. She'll be OK, I think. Just remember that the healing process takes time," explained Dr. Santana.

"How long, do you think, before she can go home?"

"I'd say several months. She'll need rehab at a nursing home for some time after she's discharged from Sacred Heart."

A nursing home! Not my mother.

Three weeks later Mimi was transported to Lady of Grace nursing home for rehabilitation. Skipper, Faith, Lauren, and Pete followed the transport vehicle in Pete's car.

"They say this rehab stuff works wonders," Skipper said, trying to sound optimistic. "This is just temporary, Faith. Your mother and I will be hitting tennis balls in no time."

"You don't play tennis, Skipper."

"I'm going to learn—maybe now I'll have a chance of winning a game or two."

Pete, beautiful balding head glistening, spoke of the phenomenal success a business associate's mother once had at Lady of Grace. Lauren sullenly worked on her split ends, furious that Skipper had demanded she remove her eyebrow ring before they left. Faith was Lauren's godmother—a relationship she'd reveled in during Lauren's first decade. It looked like the next decade would be more difficult. All of them—Skipper, Faith, and Pete—knew better than to engage Lauren in conversation, and Faith hoped the split ends would last until they arrived at Lady of Grace.

CHAPTER 3

HOME HUNTING

JUNE, 1998

"Ms. Johnson will have two rehabilitation sessions every day but Sunday," the admissions director explained. Faith stole a glance at Mimi, whose gaze was fixed on the speaker. Mimi's gaze took some getting used to, as she had one blue eye and one brown eye. Once someone noticed, it was always a little disconcerting. Ms. Gray, the Admissions Director, suddenly noticed.

"Umm," she said, losing track of her spiel.

They had all decided to join Mimi on this introductory visit to show their support—except for Lauren, of course, who was ordered to pretend. Faith was terribly worried about her mother. Since the accident, and after finding out that Joyce was gone, Mimi seemed to shrink in stature. She was silent most of the time and couldn't concentrate. She had stopped eating, unless encouraged, and was now on appetite pills. Faith knew that pain medication did strange things to people, but Mimi wasn't acting weird—just very different, as if all the spirit had been knocked out of her.

"When can we visit?" Faith asked.

"Before 9:00 A.M. and after 4:00 P.M. would be best. And, of course, at lunch, which is between 12:00 and 1:00 P.M."

"I'll be here in the morning, before the shop opens, and at 6:30, Mom," she said.

Mimi smiled weakly, her half-shaved head now sporting a quarter-inch of white stubble.

"I'll be fine, dear, don't go to any trouble."

"I'll bring along a few of my famous double dirty martinis for before supper, darling," Skipper said, hoping to get a rise out of Ms. Gray.

Lauren leaned against the wall and fiddled with her earrings. Pete held Faith's hand and kept patting Mimi's thigh as Ms. Gray outlined Mimi's care plan.

They made sure she had everything she needed in her semi-private room, shared with a wizened little woman who reminded Faith of an aging chimpanzee, and then they headed home. That night, once she was in bed and alone, Faith cried herself to sleep.

After a month of rehabilitation, Mimi was up and walking on a walker with big wheels that swiveled. She would slowly move between the wheelchairs lined up along the walls, trying to be polite to those clutching for her clothes, or asking for help. It seemed to Mimi that she was treading water in some sort of purgatory. Conditions weren't hellish—she had food, clean clothes, and help when she needed it. She just couldn't imagine ever getting back to where she was before the accident. She would picture herself doing things she loved just two months ago, and then realize that she couldn't begin to garden or play tennis now. And everything ached—especially when she took a breath.

"Your mother should be discharged next week," said Tonya, the discharge planner.

"Really!?" exclaimed Faith, who had Skipper back at Magnifique tending to business.

"Yes, she's done remarkably well, according to these status reports."

"Well, we can't wait to get her home," said Faith.

"I don't think home is where she needs to be, just yet." said Tonya.

"Where do you think she should go?"

"Probably to an assisted living community for as long as it takes to get her weight up and insure that she's steady on her feet. I think she could use some activities during the day, too. Your mother may be a little depressed, at present."

A little? She's damned depressed, and you would be too, lady. Faith mentally chided herself—she was starting to sound just like Skipper.

"I've called every community in Lexington, and there are rooms available at three of them. Actually, there's a fourth community with a room, but it's independent living."

"Where are they?"

"The closest to your part of town is Valley View Senior Living. It's a lovely place, and all the amenities are provided."

Tonya opened a left-hand lower desk drawer and searched for a file.

"I don't seem to have a brochure," she said, "but I've got the name and number here. Would you like me to call and get you in for a quick tour?"

What do I have to lose? Skipper will be fine at the shop for another hour or two.

"Sure," Faith said, and made notes in her small, precise script as Tonya confirmed directions to the facility with Valley View's marketing director.

In twenty minutes she was parked in front of a large six-story building. Near the entry, its perfectly trimmed shrubs were mulched with red stone, an unnatural combination that made Faith wince, thinking of what Mimi's reaction would be to the same scene. Once inside, she moved hesitantly to the receptionist's desk and asked for Andrea Hatcher, the marketing director.

The receptionist nodded and hit a button on her phone. She checked her nails and the clock as Faith waited, standing, beside an impatient gentleman in some sort of motorized vehicle.

"She'll be out in a minute," the receptionist finally said, and turned her attention to the old man.

Faith sat in a large, expensive, overstuffed chair across the lobby from the receptionist. She watched the thin, old man shrug and drive off down a long hall. His gray hair was uncombed. The sleeves of his long sleeved shirt hung well below his wrists, and appeared to be unbuttoned. *Who looks after him?*

Andrea appeared and vigorously shook Faith's hand. She was forty-ish, and wore three-inch heels with open toes. Faith followed her past cubicles on both sides of the hall, and into a beautifully decorated office. Andrea closed the door behind her.

"I understand your mother needs some respite care until she's able to go back home."

"Tonya thinks so," Faith said. "My mother is recovering from a terrible accident, and is still in quite a bit of pain. Tonya is worried about her cooking and being at home alone all day…" Her voice trailed off.

"Oh, we have lots of residents in your mother's condition here. They have kitchens in their apartments, but everyone usually comes down to meals once or twice a day. Can your mother ambulate?"

"Yes…well, with her walker. Slowly."

"Is she continent?"

"Yes." **Is** *she continent?*

"There should be no problem, then. Our meals are served in a central dining room that's just been redecorated. We have fresh linen tablecloths at every meal, and linen napkins. It's very nice. If a resident wants us to bring the meal to her, there's a small fee, but that service is also available."

Andrea glanced at her watch. "It's 12:45. Would you like to take a quick tour of the dining room and see our operation?"

Faith nodded and stood up. They walked back down the hall, past the receptionist's station and down another long hall to the huge open doors of the dining room. Inside it, at tables for four, sat dozens of well-dressed men and women. Waiters in black pants and white shirts were about, delivering plates and clearing them. There wasn't much talking going on. Faith noted that most of the women had on suits or dresses.

Andrea walked briskly out the dining room's exit door and led Faith to an apartment that Valley View used as its model. Obviously decorated by a designer, it looked like a room at a luxurious resort, complete with kitchenette.

"We have a fee-for-service policy here," said Andrea, as Faith looked around the room. "If a resident needs someone to bathe her, there's a fee. If she needs help with medications, that's a separate fee. We charge a certain amount for doing laundry, providing transportation to doctors, delivering meals—or, these services can be dropped once the resident improves. We feel it's a very fair and practical way to handle things."

"It's just beautiful," said Faith. "How many residents do you have?"

"We're nearly full. This week we have one hundred thirty-seven."

They left the perfectly appointed apartment and took the elevator back down to the first floor. Andrea led Faith outside, to a sparkling pool and lounge chairs.

"How wonderful!" Faith exclaimed. "Do many of your folks swim?"

"Yes—after a fashion," laughed Andrea. "We're putting a heater in the pool this summer to insure it gets used when the temperature drops below 80 degrees."

They made their way back to Andrea's office. She handed Faith a large, glossy folder, filled with sheets of various apartment layouts and a price list of what each service cost.

"What are your mother's needs now?" Andrea asked.

"Not many, really. She should probably have someone else prepare her meals for a while. I'm not sure she can tie her shoes yet. Honestly, that's about it. Probably what she needs more than anything is enough distraction and activity to keep her from thinking about her condition and her best friend, who was killed in the accident."

"Well then, it won't be nearly as expensive for her." Andrea pulled out diagrams of each floor and showed Faith where there were vacancies.

"What about this studio apartment," asked Faith.

"With the meals and an aide one hour a day it's only $2,700 a month. That doesn't include telephone, cable and transportation, of course."

"Of course," said Faith. She could feel the sweat breaking out on her forehead, and her feet were beginning to feel wet in her shoes.

"We've called our waiting list, and it's likely this apartment will be taken soon. Would you like to hold it with a deposit?"

"Let me talk it over with Mom. She'll want to look around before I do anything permanent."

"Sure! Just let me know when you're coming and we'll arrange lunch for both of you."

"That sounds lovely," said Faith.

She found her way to the lobby and walked through it to the exit, clutching the expensive folder. The unkempt old man was back at the receptionist's station, staring angrily at the receptionist's empty chair. Perhaps the receptionist was taking her lunch break. Outside, the warm June air, normally an aphrodisiac, was stifling. The asphalt, newly applied, seemed to stick to her soles. She sensed the red rock rimmed hydrangeas pleading for water. In her car, safe from Andrea's expectant eyes, she started the engine, slammed the air conditioner control to "High" and willed the nausea to stop, her eyes closed and head resting on the steering wheel.

There's no way. My God, what will we do?

Faith studied her hands, then brought her gaze to Tonya's face. "We can't afford it, Tonya."

"What can you afford?"

"Well, mother gets $890 a month. I can chip in $200 or $300, maybe. I think she should come home and live with me."

"Think about it, Faith. Your mother can't cook, can barely walk, and would be home alone most of the time. I really think she needs some outside stimulation. Let's check out Harmony Hall."

Tonya picked up her phone, dialed a number, and chewed the end of her pen.

❧   ❧   ❧

"Where the hell is Harmony Hall? Sounds like some sappy sitcom." Skipper was a little peeved at having to miss bridge with three friends who played on Sunday in lieu of church. Tonya had been able to convince the assistant director, Terry, to meet them both at Harmony Hall for a tour.

"This is the only possible place we can afford, Skipper, except for HUD housing, which doesn't provide meals. I think this place uses a sliding scale based on income. It's not assisted living, but Tonya thinks Mom can manage here. Thanks so much for coming."

"Hrumph," said Skipper.

Faith and Skipper were about to ring the bell at the Harmony Hall entrance, off the parking lot, when the door opened. A tiny lady, smiling broadly and squinting, asked if they were there for the party.

"No, we're here to see Terry," said Faith, smiling back at her.

"Oh, Terry, now there's a nice one," said the lady. "Just go down that hall. I think he's in the office."

Suddenly a tennis ball rolled past Faith and Skipper, followed by a bounding gray poodle/schnauzer-mix dog, tail held high, who barely glanced at them. As she watched the dog, Faith saw something large crawling around the corner toward them. Skipper was fixated on it. Faith laughed when she realized it was a man, on all fours, who pretended to be chasing the dog. When he saw her, the man stood up and said, "Oh, I'm so-o-o-o-o sorry! You must be Faith. I'm Terry. Welcome to Harmony Hall!"

CHAPTER 4

TOUR TWO

The dog, anxious to play, raced back to Terry and stuck his butt in the air, looking for action. Skipper reached down and rubbed his ears. He grinned at her and ran back the way he came, expecting at least one of the three to give chase.

"He's off to the office!" exclaimed Terry. "Can I get you two anything to drink? Coffee, tea, bourbon?"

Skipper said, "On the rocks," and Faith laughed, the second time in three minutes, for the first time in a week.

Faith and Skipper sat in front of a large desk in a corner office at the far side of the building. Behind it, Terry quickly sized them up. Faith, honey-blonde hair pulled back, hazel eyes ringed with dark circles, was tall, thin and classy. Her friend, Skipper, shorter and probably younger, was one of those rare women who appeared to have it all, knew it, and didn't take herself seriously. Her dark red hair curled unmanaged around a lovely face. Sensual lips naturally curved upward. Terry liked them both immediately.

"So, who needs a home?" asked Terry. He was thinner than any man Faith knew. His head was shaved; his cheekbones extended prominently below hollow eyes. A small gold ring hugged his left ear lobe. Faith found it hard to take Terry seriously, but knew he and Harmony Hall might be Mimi's only hope. She took the plunge and began believing, as she talked, that what Tonya told her at Lady of Grace was true. Nodding empathetically, Terry's gaze drifted to the office doorway, where an elderly woman, looking distressed, motioned to him.

"Ohhh, Hello-o-o-o, Bertha! Excuse me, ladies, I'll be back in *one second!*"

Faith and Skipper exchanged glances. Terry sprang to the hall, whispered to Bertha, and returned.

"Lost her upper plate," he reported, matter-of-factly.

Skipper was fascinated by Terry. Faith knew the look…it was reserved for free spirits, the very wealthy and those Skipper hadn't quite figured out.

"Tell me, Terry, what's your function here?" she said, cupping a perfect chin in a manicured palm.

"Oh, I'm the number one universal employee," he said. "I do it *all.* I make sure we all get to meals, drive to appointments, fix toilets, help with the newsletter, cook, arrange flowers, walk Mack, clean the bird cage, and decorate for parties. It's a great job." His twinkling eyes met theirs. Terry laced his fingers and sat back in his chair.

"So, what's going on with your mother, Faith?"

"She was involved in a car accident that killed her best friend, who she was with. She's recovering from broken ribs, a collapsed lung, a broken pelvis, and a head injury. I can't begin to tell you how much this has changed her—she's just not the same. The discharge planner thinks she's depressed. I'm afraid she may be right."

"Is she on an anti-depressant?"

"Yes, fifty milligrams of Zoloft."

A dark-eyed woman with silver hair appeared in the doorway.

"Oh, oh, excuse me…I didn't know…"

"It's OK, Sarah, what's up?" asked Terry.

"He found them."

"Oh, *NO.* Are you sure?"

"Yes, I'm going to try another place," she said.

"OK. I'll be up to see you in a minute."

He turned back to Faith. "So, has it helped?"

"Has what helped?" said Faith, confused.

"The Zoloft."

"Ummm—maybe a little."

"Well, let me tell you what we provide here, and you tell me if it's what your mother needs, after we take a little tour. First, we ask all residents to come to all meals each day in the dining room, and we check on them if they don't show.

We have activities every day and housekeeping once a week. We also provide bed linen and towels once a week, and, of course, we have Mack," he said, bending down and kissing the dog on his small black nose. "Because we're an independent living community, we can't provide help with what's been defined as the Activities of Daily Living: continence, transferring, toileting, bathing, dressing and eating. They probably drilled you on the ADLs at Lady of Grace." He glanced out the window briefly. "Our main concern here is that residents are appropriate for our environment and happy. You can't have one without the other."

"What is your rent?" asked Faith. There was no need to continue the tour if rates here were anything like Valley View's.

"It's based on monthly income," said Terry. We have a minimum monthly rent of $700, and everyone pays 65% of her monthly income. So, if your mother's income is $1200 from social security, income from investments and any pension, her rent will be $780."

"How can you charge so little?" asked Faith.

"We're endowed," said Terry. "And blessed. Years ago a philanthropist gave Harmony Hall money that was wisely invested. Since then, we've been able to pull funds out each month to help meet expenses and basically subsidize everyone who lives here. We're *very* non-profit."

"Can it last?" asked Skipper.

"We hope so," said Terry.

"Do you have a room we could look at?" asked Faith.

"OH, YES! Let's call someone." Terry dialed a number from memory. "Minnie? It's Terry. Can I come see you and bring two *lovely* girls to see your room?" Terry smiled at Skipper, who, used to ignoring more lascivious male attention, smiled back. "Okay, we'll be right there."

The three of them took the elevator to the second floor and walked a short distance to Minnie's room, opposite the laundry room. Terry started to knock on a door adorned by a huge stuffed rabbit with the name "Ms. Nibbles" written on a large card that hung from a thread around its neck. Minnie Potter opened the door before he knocked. Bertha of the lost plate was sitting on the bed in Minnie's room. She smiled, still plateless, as they entered. Minnie, a tiny slip of a lady with a thick white moustache, extended both hands to Faith and Skipper, and introduced them to Bertha, who, in a way, they already knew.

"We're looking for her plate," said Minnie. "Take a look around. I don't think it's here, but you never know!"

Terry moved fluidly across the room, pulled two dead roses from a vase on Minnie's television, and gracefully leaned over to pick a pair of underwear off the floor. "What's *this*?" he asked.

Minnie whooped, grabbed the underwear, and punched Terry on the arm.

"I can't *make* them keep their rooms straight," he said, in mock frustration.

The room was the size of an average bedroom, with two windows, a closet and a bathroom. Filled with very old, worn furniture, the room could have originated in the early 1900s, like its occupant.

"How do you like living at Harmony Hall, Ms. Potter?" asked Faith.

"I couldn't be in a better place," said Minnie.

As Faith completed an application for Mimi, Bertha interrupted Terry to advise she had placed her plate, by accident, in someone's leftovers in the laundry room refrigerator. Sarah, the lovely hunchbacked, dark-eyed woman, saw them to the door with Terry—he kidding her all the way down the hall and through the seafoam green lobby about dragging her walker behind her. "She gets in a tizzy and can't remember whether to push or pull."

Next to the inside lobby door was a framed copy of the Harmony Hall mission statement:

> *The employees and Board of Directors of Harmony Hall, a community based retirement home, are dedicated to providing loving attention, superior housing, meals, activities and the opportunity to flourish to all residents at the most affordable price.*

Faith read it carefully.

"Notice it doesn't say anything about assistance," Terry said. "If your mother needs help, Faith, she'll need to hire it, just as if she were at home."

"Just think, darling, she has you and me to do it for free!" Skipper winked at Terry and they stepped out under the portico.

"Stay back, Mack," warned Terry. "Good-bye, girls." He waved at them and turned to chase the gray dog back down the hall.

Faith and Skipper were silent as they walked across the parking lot. Faith started the car and let it idle.

"What do you think?"

"She'll have a ball there."

"No, really, Skipper. Doesn't it seem a little…*unprofessional?*"

"Get real, darling. It's like a big sorority house. Mimi will love it. Life's too short to be professional."

CHAPTER 5

TOUR THREE

The now familiar, slightly sweet odor at Lady of Grace enveloped Faith as she hurried toward Mimi's room.

"Mother?"

Mimi was asleep in her chair, a walker in front of her, its basket filled with a box of Kleenex and mail. Mimi's roommate, Claudine, was gone; her bed was neatly made.

"Mother, it's me." Faith patted Mimi's knee.

Mimi's brown eye opened, then both focused lovingly on Faith.

"Hey, honey, how's it going?" she asked groggily.

"Great! Skipper and I visited a place today that may have an opening soon. I want you to see it."

"Why?"

"Well, they tell me you may need a little interim stay somewhere before you go home…"

Mimi's half smile faded.

"I don't think I need an interim stay, Faith. I think I need to go home and try to get back to normal."

She looked out the window, its sill crowded with Get Well cards.

"Mom, you can hardly walk and your balance is bad. I can't see you cooking. This is an independent living community—all ladies—and we can afford it. I can't let you stay by yourself yet, and even if you came home with me, you'd be alone all day. Won't you at least look at it? I promise we'll do something else if you don't like it."

Her mother's voice trembled, "I don't think I'll like any place that's not home, Faith."

"It's nothing like this, Mom," Faith said, gesturing at her mother's cramped space. "It's lovely and bright, and we can rent by the month. The fellow I spoke with said they don't want anyone there who doesn't want to be there, so if you don't like it, they *want* you to leave."

Only silence from her mother.

"This is a place for independent gals, Mom."

"If they're so independent, why are they there?"

She's not going to budge.

"For better nutrition or more security, Mother. Think about going home. Joyce is gone. There's nobody there to talk to. You can't play tennis or garden yet. You can't lift anything."

Mimi held up her hand, as if to stop Faith, at Joyce's name. They both began to weep.

"OK, dear, I'll try it," murmured Mimi.

Faith left a brochure and an activities calendar with Mimi, who agreed to visit Harmony Hall on Wednesday. According to the brochure, Harmony Hall started out as a home for destitute cholera victims in Lexington, and evolved into a home for elderly women. It was renovated and expanded in 1997, and now housed 35 women. The brochure listed the amenities offered by the community. Mimi glanced at the services: Housekeeping, three meals, transportation, activities, a beauty shop, basement storage and an accessible garden. It sounded nice enough, but there was nothing that could take the place of home.

Billie Jo asked about Mimi, then clucked sympathetically when she heard that Faith's mother was depressed.

"Where's she going to stay once she leaves Sacred Heart, honey?"

"I hope she'll stay at Harmony Hall for a few months…we're due to go for an interview tomorrow."

"Harmony Hall!"

"Yes…why?" Faith braced herself for some sort of awful story.

"That's a great little place. How'd you get in?"

"We haven't. Skipper and I met the assistant director Sunday, and Mom and I are interviewing with the director tomorrow. What do you know about it?"

"I've known folks who've lived there and loved it. They have a great garden, too, and the public can pick flowers and walk around in it. I'm so happy for you!"

Faith silently apologized to Terry for accusing him of being unprofessional.

"Do you need help moving? Jackson has a truck we can borrow."

"Oh, Billie Jo, that would be wonderful. Pete said he'd help. Are you sure Jackson wouldn't mind?"

Jackson, Billie Jo's live-in, was a huge hulk of a man who ran the produce department at Kroger.

"He'd love to help. Just tell me when."

Faith left for *Magnifique*, a definite spring in her step.

"I'm just glad she's willing to try it," said Faith, leaving Skipper last minute instructions at the shop. Faith was taking Mimi to her hairdresser for a permanent and a rinse. Tomorrow they'd visit Harmony Hall.

"She'll be a new woman with a new hairdo—trust me," said Skipper. "The only thing better is a mini-face tuck."

"How do you know?" laughed Faith.

"Street talk," said Skipper, looking over her reading glasses at a customer, and smiling.

Why am I so nervous? Surely she'll like the place. Faith pulled into a space in the small parking lot behind Harmony Hall. It was 9:30. Their appointment was for 10:15, but Faith wanted Mimi to see the garden behind the parking lot. As Mimi painfully exited the car, Faith steadied her walker. Suddenly the frantic barking of a dog destroyed the morning calm.

"Goodness!" said Mimi. A squirrel shot past the arbored garden entrance, followed unwillingly by an elderly lady at the end of a leash. Mack was trying his best to get to the squirrel. The lady was barely hanging on. "Hel-l-l-l-o-o-o-o-o" she said, as he pulled her along.

"Hello!" yelled Mimi, to her back.

"That's the house dog, Mom. His name's Mack."

"Looks like he has a thing for squirrels."

They followed the dog walker through the entry, past a sign that read "U-Pick," a price list, a small locked moneybox and three pairs of scissors hanging from a hook, all anchored on a large post. Dahlias and daisies grew behind a bank of obedient plant on their right; on their left were calendulas and globe amaranth. As the walkway curved, they passed snapdragons, and suddenly Faith noticed dozens of rose bushes in a staggered row, along the walkway to her right.

"Look, Mother…smell this!"

Mimi leaned over a perfect pink rose. To her left were six raised beds, three on each side of a dense grade aisle. The beds were filled with herbs and cucumbers. As they moved toward a large cedar tree they passed masses of daisies and zinnias. A woman and two small girls, picking zinnias in the middle of the bed, waved at them. Rounding a curve, the sound of splashing water startled Faith. A large pond appeared on their right; two teak benches faced it to the left of the path.

"Oh, Mother, let's sit here a minute."

Mimi's eyes were bright; her face glistened with perspiration. She lowered herself gingerly to the bench, never taking her eyes off the pond. Four huge koi chomped hungrily at the pond's edge before gliding away and resurfacing below the waterfall. Ringed by hostas and hydrangeas, daylilies and hemlocks, the pool seemed far removed from civilization. Mimi was mesmerized. Faith was enchanted.

At 10:00 Faith helped her mother up from the bench and they began to make their way slowly from the garden exit at the edge of the parking lot. At the same time an old faded station wagon pulled up in front of the building. The tall, thin man behind the wheel hopped out, opened all four doors and the rear storage compartment door, and began helping four women get settled in the vehicle. All four were on walkers. The words *Harmony Hall* were written on the driver's door, though the *H* in *Hall* was nearly gone so that the moniker looked like *Harmony all*. As Mimi and Faith approached, the driver loaded three of the walkers in the back of the dilapidated wagon. The fourth he fastened to the top of the car with a bungee cord. The four ladies inside the car all seemed to be talking at once, until they noticed Faith and her mother. Then all talking stopped, and Faith could feel their eyes taking in every detail. Mimi stood up just a little straighter.

❦   ❦   ❦

This time Terry met them at the door.

"Faith! How *are* you?!"

He grasped her hand and squeezed it, looked at Mimi and said, "I'll bet you're Mimi!"

In the old days Mimi would have said, "How *much* you wanna bet?" but now she simply nodded.

"I'm Terry. Faith," he said, "where's that Skipper?"

"She's minding the store, bless her heart," said Faith.

"Well, come on in. Let's meet Dot."

Dot Turner was seated in the same office Faith and Skipper sat in on their first visit.

"How nice to see you," she said to Faith. "Terry told me all about you. And you must be Mimi. I'm Dot Turner, the director here. How are you doing?"

Barely taller than Mimi, thin and sinewy with tanned arms and short dark hair, Dot was beginning to gray at the temples. Green eyes took in everything. She seemed very interested in Mimi's answer.

Faith held her breath. Mimi looked at Faith.

"How *am* I doing?" she asked.

Faith told herself to relax, then said, "She's doing great, considering what she's been through. She's able to dress herself and transfer, and is getting over the effects of the accident. We all just think she needs a place to stay for a while until she gets stronger." Her eyes locked on Dot's. *She really needs to be here. Sell her on it.*

"Mimi, how do you feel about coming here?"

Her mother seemed less subdued than she was when they left Sacred Heart, an hour earlier.

"I think Faith's right—this is probably what I need until I get my strength back. I just hate the thought of not going back home."

Her mother's voice began to crack. Faith started to say something, then thought better of it. *Shut up, your mother's being interviewed—not you.*

"I can certainly understand that. Everyone here—thirty-five ladies—would rather be at home. All of them know, though, that they're safer, for one reason or another, here. This is a perfect place for folks who aren't driving and feel vulnerable living alone. For most of us, it's a hassle to cook, and we need some social interaction. We don't admit ladies who have dementia, although the entire staff is demented."

It took a second for the words to sink in, then Mimi chuckled.

"We allow our residents to have pets, if they can care for them," she continued, "so if you're allergic to cat or dog hair or bird feathers, this is not a good place to live. If you're a loner, and you can't stand the thought of coming to the dining room three times a day, it's also not a good place for you. We pretty much expect our residents to be cordial to each other."

Mimi nodded. She had been voted Miss Congeniality sixty-three years earlier.

❦   ❦   ❦

On this tour, Dot accompanied Mimi and Faith. Mack had returned from his walk in the garden, and joined them.

"Mack is from the Humane Society," explained Dot. "He's a Schnoodle—part schnauzer, part poodle. He's about three—and thinks he's in charge here. We're all gaga over him."

Mack made a quick detour into someone's room. "MACK!" resounded, and he reappeared in thirty seconds. "Like everything that seems to happen here, it was providential that we found him."

They stopped at room 22, and Dot knocked on the door. A large woman, introduced as Kitty, showed them her room. Kitty told them she was from Eastern Kentucky.

"Well, how yew doin'? Are yew goin' to come live 'ere?

Mimi murmured, "Maybe."

"Well, this 'ere's a great place," said Kitty, showing Mimi her room. When they left, Kitty hugged Mimi, which seemed a little forward to Faith, but didn't seem to bother her mother.

They passed a small library, filled with six or seven residents, and Terry, who waved at them. All were intent on what one of the participants was reading.

"This is our journaling group," said Dot. She stepped out on a balcony that overlooked the open central courtyard and its fountain. Below, three women were snapping beans into large pots. "We'll have those at supper tonight."

By the time they returned to Dot's office, Mimi had been introduced to eight residents, none of whose names she would remember. All seemed delighted to meet her and happy at the prospect of having her join them at Harmony Hall. Dot promised to let Faith know when a room would be available—possibly within days. Faith was charged with getting medical reports to Dot, confirming that Mimi was appropriate for independent living.

As they exited the building the Harmony Hall wagon pulled up. Mimi's eyebrows rose slightly, and she smiled. The three walkers originally stashed in the back of the car, apparently displaced by groceries, now also rode atop it, tied securely with cord. The driver began unloading the walkers, grinned at Faith and Mimi, and said, "They bought out the store."

"What do you think, Mom?"

Mimi was silent as she fastened her seatbelt. Faith pulled away from the portico and headed down the exit driveway to the street.

"I'll try it—for a while."

CHAPTER 6

THE MOVE

"Skipper, where in the world do we start?"

"Let's have a glass of wine and think about it."

They were at Mimi's duplex. Sunlight streamed through the mini blinds, falling on Mimi's modest collection of miniature critters—frogs, snakes, salamanders and turtles—all carefully placed on her coffee table. Faith looked at the pictures arranged on one wall: Mimi with her husband, Brad, dancing at a nightclub in Miami; Faith and her girlfriends at college; Mimi and Faith and their great brindle boxer, Scout, in front of their old '59 Dodge in Miami; Mimi at the center of a dozen middle-aged women, all in tennis garb, on a court somewhere in Florida, obviously victorious; graduation shots; prom shots. Mimi was so proud of her friends and family. Faith started with the pictures. She supported them in a large box with Mimi's favorite afghan, crocheted many years earlier by a beloved sister-in-law, now dead.

"I can't believe this is happening to my mother, Skipper. She went through so much downsizing when she came here from Miami. Now we're at it again."

"This may not be downsizing—just moving out and back in—quit worrying about it, darling; what will be, will be." She handed Faith a large glass of Merlot. "All I could find. At least it's not from a box."

Lauren rang the doorbell, opened the door and slouched in.

"Hey, honey, come in!" Faith tried to sound cheery.

"Need some help?" Lauren asked, ignoring her mother.

"Sure! Let's put her bathroom stuff in this box, and I'll pack her dresser drawers in this one. How've you been?"

"Freakin' fabulous. I'm flunking math, my boyfriend just kissed me good-bye, and I have eight zits. How are you?"

Skipper said, "The zits don't look bad, darling, and the boyfriend was a jerk. Math's the only problem we need to address."

Lauren refused to meet her mother's eyes. "Yeah, right," she said, and started throwing Mimi's toiletries into the box.

❦   ❦   ❦

Early on the last Friday in June, Jackson drove the truckload of Mimi's belongings to Harmony Hall.

"How you gonna get all this stuff in there?" he asked Faith, from the hall outside Mimi's room.

"They've got some great basement storage, Jackson…we can overflow into it," Faith said, hoping the overflow could be contained in the storage unit. Pete, for once, looked impatient. Billie Jo, Skipper and Lauren were all talking at once. Jackson and Pete would carry the heavy items to the room with a huge "WELCOME" sign on its door, and stand there, waiting for the final decision on placement. It all took much longer than Faith expected.

Thank God she's not here. This would put her over the edge.

Two residents Faith had never seen strolled by, asking about Mimi.

"Is she your grandmother?" asked one of Lauren, looking hard at her pierced navel.

"No, she's my great godmother," said Lauren.

"Oh…," the resident said.

"She's my mother—I'm Faith. This is Lauren, my goddaughter."

"And I'm Lauren's evil mother, Skipper," and Skipper shook hands with Harriett and Virginia, who both looked at Lauren again, with great interest.

Pete and Jackson introduced themselves, and Harriett and Virginia asked if they could help.

"Good Go…" Pete began, and caught Faith's eye. "No, thanks very much. I think we have plenty of help here." Faith could tell that the thought of two more women giving advice would put *him* over the edge.

In the end, it all worked out. Mimi's chest of drawers and bed and night-stand, her Florida motif recliner, the 24" T.V. and stand, her critter collection and the rattan chair Faith had curled up in so many times, were placed attractively in room 26. Pete climbed down the ladder, stepped back, and critically eyed the valances.

"Good. I think we're done."

Billie Jo was scratching Mack's butt. He had wandered in, checked out each of them and Mimi's furniture, and decided to stay awhile.

"I suggest we all go get pizza and beer—on me," announced Skipper.

Lauren said, "Great!"

"You can have O'Doul's, darling."

Faith put her arm around Lauren on the way to the lobby. "Thank you so much for helping; we needed you."

"No problem," said Lauren, snapping her gum. She kneeled down and kissed Mack on his soft cheek before following Faith out the door.

CHAPTER 7

INTRODUCTIONS

I wonder what they'll think of this damned walker...

Mimi slipped on the old lady shoes Faith had bought her. They had Velcro closures. She slowly stood up, using her walker to help. It took an hour to dress. With all of her belongings gone, the room at Lady of Grace looked antiseptic. The sink and mirror she shared now gleamed. Faith, always anxious to leave a place in better shape than she found it, had polished both. Claudine had moved to the Alzheimer's unit. Mimi stared at herself a moment in the mirror.

Just another chapter, kiddo. You'll be back home before you know it.

On the way to Harmony Hall, Faith was silent. Mimi knew her daughter was as nervous as she was about the move. Minutes after Faith left her, there was a gentle tap on her door. Mimi slowly got up and opened the door.

"I'm Harriett, Mimi. I'm your official Buddy for the next few days until you know your way around."

Mimi looked at the small hunched woman, wondering how in the world *she* got around. Harriett's hair was salt-and-pepper; her gray eyes twinkled.

"I live in room 30," she continued. "If you need anything, just come see me. I never lock my door."

"How nice of you to be my Buddy," said Mimi. "Won't you come in?"

"Thank you. I'd love to. What a pretty room." She sat gingerly on Mimi's bed.

"I had nothing to do with it, Harriett. My daughter and her friends moved me in while I was still at the nursing home."

"They did a lovely job."

"I know. I'm forever indebted." *They're going to love moving all this back to the duplex.*

"How did you happen to come to Harmony Hall, Harriett?"

"Providence, I think. My son put me on the waiting list two years ago. They called several times and I refused to budge. One day I got out of bed and collapsed on my way to the bathroom. I lay there twelve hours. It was a heart attack, and I broke my leg when I fell. I have a pacemaker now. While I lay on the floor, I promised myself I would come here if I lived—and I did. It's been over a year."

Terry stuck his head in.

"Mimi! How *are* you?" He was beaming. Mack cavorted at his heels, then looked at Mimi and seemed to grin.

"Hey," said Mimi to Terry, feeling like she'd known him all her life. Mack put his soft poodle paws on her knees, and she rubbed his ears.

"That's the dearest dog I've ever seen," said Harriett, getting up to go. "I'll be back at lunch time, Mimi, and we'll go down to the dining room."

Terry sat in Mimi's rattan chair. "How's it going? Do you need anything? Do you know enough to know what you need," he said, laughing.

"I think I'm fine, dear."

Dot stuck her head in. "Mimi! You're here!" She stepped in, looked at Mack, and said, "I see your welcoming committee is doing its job." She walked over to Mimi and hugged her. "We put the office phone number on a sticker on your phone. Will you promise to call us if you need anything?"

"You're both too kind" said Mimi. "I think I'm in good shape."

Dot turned to leave, and then added, "Terry, I've got two interviews this afternoon. Can you watch the phones?"

"I promise they won't get away," said Terry.

"You rotten dog," Dot said to Mack, and headed for her office.

Mimi walked to the dining room, Harriett leading the way, both exhausted by the time they reached Mimi's table. Four lined faces looked up as she maneuvered her walker to a spot where her chair could be pulled back. Four lovely smiles greeted her.

Harriett tried her best to introduce Mimi to the four ladies at her table. Eloise Brown was legally blind, and looked through Mimi as she shook hands;

Bertha Green, whose upper plate was in today, flashed her a grin; the lady she'd seen Mack walking, Camille Everson, raised her eyebrows and smiled lopsidedly; and Minnie, whose room Faith had seen on the tour, gave her a thumbs up. Everyone began talking at once, and Mimi felt overwhelmed but thankful that she seemed accepted. Two of her tablemates had walkers; Harriett's and Bertha's were somehow placed out of the way. Mimi wasn't sure where to put hers. Terry swooped in, moved it to just outside the door of the dining room, and made eye contact with Minnie. She nodded at him. "I'll get it for you after lunch, Mimi," she said.

"I'm so glad to be a part of your table," Mimi said, looking around at all of them.

"We're glad to have you, believe me," said Minnie. "It makes it so much easier to pass the bowls when all the seats are full."

Mimi, startled, couldn't believe her ears. She looked at Minnie, who was grinning and poking Camille in the ribs. Everyone started laughing. Suddenly Minnie's head seemed to change shape. Mimi realized with a start that Minnie was wearing a wig, and it was slipping.

"You know I'm kidd'n ya, doncha?" said Minnie. She reached up and centered the wig on her head. Strands of her real hair hung below the page boy at her neck.

"Absolutely!" said Mimi, passing the fruit salad to Bertha.

"We have a lot of fun at this table," murmured Eloise. "I'll bet we're the noisiest bunch in here."

"It sounds like everyone has fun here," said Mimi, listening to the conversations, unintelligible but vibrant, throughout the dining room.

"You ain't seen nuthin yet, kid," Minnie said, slipping off her wig and hanging it on the back of her chair. She wiped her glistening forehead with her napkin and passed the potatoes to Camille.

Mimi glanced past Minnie and saw Mack staring longingly into the dining room from the hall beyond the open doors off the corridor. He plopped down, head on paws, and inched forward. His forepaws hung over the metal toe strip separating the dining room vinyl from the hall carpet.

"How did you train him to do that?"

"We all stayed on him constantly," said Camille. "The only time he comes in here now is when he thinks no one's looking," she snickered.

"He comes in here when he knows *you're* looking, Camille," said Harriett.

"Well, now and then I forget to remind him of the rules," Camille laughed. "It's hard to discipline the cutest dog in the world."

Mack stared lovingly at Camille, who stared back at him.

"I don't know what we'd do without that little guy," she said to Mimi.

All of a sudden the swinging door to the kitchen opened, and Evie, the main Harmony Hall cook, entered the dining room with a tiny birthday cake, candles ablaze. Dot followed with a camera, and sang in a loud baritone voice, "HAP—PY BIRTH—DAY…" Immediately the whole dining room erupted into the birthday song, and the little cake, with Dot following, moved to the other end of the dining room. A resident there looked up at Evie, beaming, and the fast flash of the camera caught her as she blew out the candles on her cake. Mack stood up, anxious to join the celebration, but sank back to his belly as Dot headed his way.

"She's ninety-six today. If I didn't know better, I'd think she was sixty," said Dot, grinning at Mimi.

She picked up Mack just outside the dining room, held him like a baby over her shoulder, and walked toward her office. Mimi caught his delighted grin, next to the back of Dot's head, as he was carried to a treat in honor of the day's birthday girl.

CHAPTER 8

❀

INTERVIEWS

Dot looked around her office and began straightening the piles on her desk. At 1:00 she'd start the first of two interviews.

🍁　　　🍁　　　🍁

Julie Painter would graduate in December from the University of Kentucky with a degree in Family Science. Julie was from Pikeville, a coal town in Eastern Kentucky, where disputes were too often settled at the end of a gun, and where most folks were fabulously wealthy or miserably poor. Raised with six brothers, the only daughter of a minister, Julie was both spiritually and experientially rich. She had no idea how refreshing she was to the ultra sophisticated, nor how attractive she was. She was determined to better the world, and saw things, at twenty-two, in black and white. She weighed ninety-eight pounds soaking wet, and looked a little like a young Kim Bassinger, without the curves. Her friends called her Buzz, short for buzz saw, because they said she always cut through the crap. Julie read her Bible every day and led a Bible study group. Everyone knew she would go far. To graduate, she needed to intern for three months at a worksite that had something to do with her major. Julie was interviewing at a small, independent non-profit community for ladies of limited means near the campus in downtown Lexington. She couldn't wait.

❈   ❈   ❈

"Tell me a little about yourself, Julie," Dot said. *She looks too young to be in college, much less graduating. And she's so little.*

"Well, I just love senior citizens. One of my best friends is over at The Evergreen community, and he's ninety. We have lunch together once a month. I'm hoping to graduate with a degree in Family Science in December—and someday do something like what you're doing here. I've heard so much about Harmony Hall from a few friends of mine who've volunteered here—it sounds like a wonderful place to work."

"Have you had any office experience?"

"I worked at a bank over the summer last year in Pikeville. I can type and use Word on the computer. I love office work, too."

Dot laughed at Julie's enthusiasm. "Fortunately, we don't spend a lot of time in the office here. I can hardly find time to visit my office, much less work in it! All of us here, Julie, regardless of our official titles, are really universal workers—we do everything that needs to be done. For example, I may be speaking with a prospective family member one minute, and serving coffee in the dining room the next. Terry may need to fix lunch and that afternoon may call bingo. You're applying for a position of part-time activities director, but you might be called on to clean the terrace doors, or wash dishes or pick tomatoes. Or, I might need you to review all the resident files and update each information sheet on the computer." She paused, watching Julie's fresh young face carefully. "What do you think?"

"I think I can learn to do anything you need to have done," Julie gushed. "It sounds like every day will be different, and I'm *real* flexible."

She's probably too good to be true. We'll soon find out.

They discussed schedules and salary, and agreed that Julie's first day would be the following Wednesday. Harmony Hall was about to get its first part-time activities director.

At 3:30 Dot introduced herself to Jim Atkinson, who had taken early retirement at sixty-one from IBM's middle management level, when layoffs looked imminent and he'd had all he could take of corporate intrigue. Gray-haired and mustached, slightly rotund, he reminded Dot of a kindly grandfather.

Harmony Hall needed a new maintenance man. Phil Brown was leaving in a week—a mutual agreement. Jim was the only applicant for Phil's advertised position, which paid less than similar jobs in larger communities. In keeping with the Harmony Hall philosophy of universal responsibilities, the maintenance job involved a substantial amount of driving.

"Have you had any experience working with the elderly, Jim?"

"Well, my mother was elderly when she died, and I took care of her for years."

"I'm sure you're aware that employees in this industry need a great deal of patience," Dot said, looking again at his resume. "Most of it is needed in dealing with our ladies, who don't always feel well or may be lonely or frustrated or depressed. Sometimes, because we're a non-profit, we have to have patience by making do with things that a big, successful corporation would replace in a heartbeat. Our car, for example, is quite old, but we just don't have the funds right now to buy another…" Her voice trailed off.

"I've got plenty of patience, Dot. I just want to get out of the rat race and do something that makes a difference. I'm sure you can understand that."

Dot smiled. She had fallen into the job at Harmony Hall twelve years earlier, and realized later that *she* was out of the rat race and making a difference.

"This is probably just the place for you, Jim."

After he left, Dot pulled up the board meeting agenda on her computer and updated the section under Personnel. The meeting was a week from Monday. Harmony Hall's CPA would be present. In addition to personnel, Dot would also be discussing the need for a small van.

CHAPTER 9

SARAH

"Terry, have you noticed how much weight Bertha's been losing?"

Dot had just finished the end-of-the-month weigh-in. Bertha was down eight pounds from the previous month.

"She's down again. I'm going to call her daughter. Her bottom plate may need a new liner."

Dot picked up her phone and dialed Bertha's daughter's workplace.

"Suzie, it's Dot—there's no problem here, but your mom's lost eight pounds since last month. I'm wondering if her dentures may be part of the problem."

Suzie, who worked as a waitress, couldn't get off work to take Bertha to the dentist.

"I'll take her in as soon as I can get an appointment. We'll let you know," said Dot.

As Dot placed the telephone in its receiver, Minnie came to the door. Terry put his head between his knees and covered it with his arms. Minnie sidled over and tried to blow in his ear. They both burst out laughing.

"Dot, I'm worried about Sarah. She's starting to talk funny when she thinks no one's listening. Think it may be too much medicine?" Minnie's moustache moved up and down when she talked, a phenomenon no longer noticed by the staff and residents. They also accepted her as Harmony Hall's self-proclaimed diagnostician, though she was usually dead wrong.

"I don't know, Minnie. When does this happen?"

"Usually on her way to supper or back to her room."

Terry and Dot exchanged glances. "Let us check it out, Minnie," said Dot. "Thanks so much for your concern."

Sarah Stevenson had been a beautiful young woman growing up in Lexington. She loved to tell the story of the day workmen watched her walk to her flower shop and yelled to her, "Are those real?"

"Now look at them!" she'd say, and look at her chest and chuckle. Childless, Sarah depended on a nephew and his wife after her husband, Seymour, died. When she broke a hip, at home alone, they decided it was time for her to move. Her silver hair was always swept back; her longish, straight nose gave her an aristocratic look. She had inherited her mother's heavy metal walker, and refused to use any other. She pulled it behind her when she hurried. Brilliant, she would outplay everyone at the group crossword game, blurting out each word before Terry could find the answer on his answer sheet. Dot, Terry and Minnie all loved Sarah and tried to protect her. It was becoming a difficult assignment.

"Sarahh! Are you there?" Terry knocked on her door, then pushed it open when he heard her voice.

"He's at it again. Look!" She led him to the windowsill, moving the mini blinds so he could look behind them. Nothing was there.

"What was here?" Terry asked.

"My medicine! I put a decoy there, and he came out of the closet last night and took it. He's driving me crazy!"

*Our dear, lovely Sarah. You **are** crazy.*

"Tell you what…" Terry said. "Let's put something you think he'll want in a hiding place—and then I'll check on it every time I'm upstairs. How's that?"

Both black eyes glittered, and Sarah shook her head. She was smarter than that. "He'll know we're trying to trap him. He's up there listening. I hear him at night."

"Sarah, there's no one up there. Here, let's look in the closet again."

He opened the metal sliding door. Sarah's closet floor was piled high with clothes. The built-in shelves were disorderly, one shoe here, one there. If her closet was an indicator, Sarah was very confused.

"Sarah! Look! It's nearly 5:30—time for dinner!

"Oh, Oh! Let's go!" she exclaimed joyfully. She was out the door, dragging her walker, heading to the elevator, her nephew and his malfeasance forgotten. Terry leaned against her doorjamb. Sarah's nephew was visiting her more often, and she wasn't sleeping. He pictured her rattling around all night, frantic, hiding, then moving, her underwear, her medicine, her jewelry—God knew what else. Sick at heart, he followed her to the elevator.

CHAPTER 10

LUNCH

"Mother, it's me. I think Skipper and Lauren are coming with me to have lunch. Is that going to be a problem?" Faith couldn't turn Skipper down when she'd asked to be included, and for once Lauren seemed interested in joining her mother. This might be an opportunity for them to bond a little.

"I don't know, dear. Do you want me to ask Dot?"

"No, I'll call her. See you at 12:30."

Faith hung up and called Dot. She had some reservations about asking Billie Jo to mind the shop for a few hours, but since Mimi's accident her reserve about a lot of things had diminished.

"Dot, I hate to bother you, but my dearest friend and her daughter, my god-daughter, would like to join me for lunch with my mother. Is that OK? We'll be happy to pay."

There was a slight hesitation on the other end.

"I'm sure we can find a spot for them, Faith. Just check with me when you get here."

It was 11:30. Dot headed for the dining room, hoping there was enough chicken to go around, and that she could sweet-talk three of Mimi's tablemates into moving temporarily.

Harriett, Eloise and Bertha agreed to sit at other tables for lunch. Dot steeled herself for the inevitable. She knew Bertha, now at Kitty's table, would forget that her lower plate belonged on her lower jaw, and in front of her new, less hardened tablemates, would take it out and put it in her pocket, wrapped in a paper napkin—probably during dessert. She'd found a spot for Harriett at

Virginia's table; Eloise would be sitting with Sarah. Dot found herself wishing that Eloise were deaf rather than blind, in case Sarah started in on her nephew and his home in her closet.

❋   ❋   ❋

"Mimi, darling, it's so good to see you," cried Skipper, hugging Mimi at the table. Faith and Lauren followed Skipper into the dining room, slightly intimidated by the stares of all the residents seated there.

"Hello, Mother," said Faith, kissing Mimi on the forehead.

Lauren stared at Minnie's wig and sat down at the far end of the table. Her own hair, a very new do, stuck out from her head in spikes, formed with a great deal of mousse. Mimi was immediately reminded of a porcupine.

Skipper must have dragged her along. Oh well, she'll warm up.

Mimi said, "Camille and Minnie, this is my daughter, Faith, and her best friend, Skipper, and Skipper's daughter, Lauren."

"I'm delighted to meet you," said Faith.

"Are you two keeping her in line?" asked Skipper.

Lauren was silent, watching her tomato aspic as if it were alive.

Minnie took in Lauren's eyebrow ring and looked at Camille. "You know," she said, turning to Skipper, "we try to stay out of line around here. How 'bout you?"

"I've never stayed in line in my life," said Skipper. "I'm afraid that's a trait that's passed on from generation to generation."

Camille said, "Not in my family. My parents were in line, but I'm not." She looked at Lauren. "Do you know that I refused to wear a bra until I was in my twenties?"

"Why?" asked Lauren.

"I wanted to be the son my father never had," said Camille. "I finally met my husband and decided I'd better get some bosom—ha!"

Lauren giggled and looked at Faith, who was smiling at her over her coffee cup.

"It's hard to get Lauren to wear a bra," said Faith. "Fortunately, she can still get away with it."

"A lot of *us* get away with it, too," said Minnie. "We just can't get the damn things on any more."

Terry whooshed into the dining room, stopped at their table, and straightened Minnie's wig from behind. "Faith! Skipper! How *are* you? And who is *this*?"

Lauren sat, frozen, staring at Terry's shaved head.

"She's my daughter, Lauren," said Skipper. "Sometimes she forgets how to talk."

"Love your *hair*," said Terry. "Do you need anything?"

"Do you have Coke?" asked Lauren.

"The drink?" asked Terry.

Lauren choked. Terry winked at Skipper and headed to the kitchen. Mack grinned from the corridor at Lauren, and inched forward, ears akimbo, until his chest rested on the toe strip. Camille began talking to Lauren about Mack's last grooming, Skipper and Minnie compared notes on wigs, Mimi and Faith caught up on news of *Magnifique*. It was a lovely lunch.

That night, her fifth at Harmony Hall, Mimi closed the door to her room, undressed, slipped her nightgown on, and slowly settled into bed. She could barely hear Harriett's television next door. As was her habit, she reviewed the day, marveling at the speed of its passing: Breakfast at 8:00, exercises at 10:15, Bible study at 11:30, lunch with Faith, Skipper and Lauren at 12:30, bingo at 2:00, Book Club at 4:00 and supper at 5:30. She had wandered out onto the veranda after supper and sat there with Sarah for an hour. Sarah was a little odd, but beautiful and witty. Mimi fell asleep quickly, dreaming of dancing walkers bowing and turning in a brightly lighted hall.

CHAPTER 11

THE PICK UP

JULY, 1998

"Jim, I've got a special assignment for you."

"What's that, Dot?" He stopped collecting her trash. It was the fourth day of his first week on the job. It seemed as far removed from the corporate world as one could get.

"There's a resident at The Evergreen who's interested in coming to live here, but she doesn't drive and doesn't want her friends to know she's checking us out. They've raised the rent over there again and she can't afford it any longer. She's got a doctor's appointment at 10:00 tomorrow, and I told her I'd send you over to pick her up, take her to her doctor's appointment with Dr. Clarke at Broadway Medical Center, and then swing her by here for an interview before taking her back home."

"Sure. Where do I go?"

"She's in the independent living section on Main. She should be in the lobby when you get there. If not, just ask for Maybelle McCardle."

Jim pulled into the parking lot at The Evergreen. The temperature gauge on the 1989 Caprice was way past mid-point. He looked longingly at The Evergreen's late model Cadillac, its signage unblemished, at the curb.

A portico connected two large buildings, and he entered the first. Several residents were sitting in wheelchairs in the lobby. A flustered certified nursing assistant asked if she could help him.

"I'm here to pick up Maybelle McCardle," Jim said.

"Oh, just a minute. I'll have to go get her."

The CNA rushed off. Five minutes later she returned, pushing a woman in a wheelchair. "Here she is!" she said, and rushed back the way she came.

"Ms. McCardle, I'm Jim Atkinson."

Maybelle began talking to Jim about her Easter eggs. Jim wheeled Maybelle out to the car, and discovered she couldn't stand on her own. With some difficulty, he got her in the front seat and managed to get her wheelchair in the back of the station wagon. He headed for the doctor's office on Broadway, feeling certain that Dot would determine, after their interview, that Ms. McCardle was not appropriate for independent living at Harmony Hall.

"Is this Dot Turner?"

"Yes?"

"This is Maybelle McCardle from The Evergreen."

"Hello, Mabelle!"

"I was just wondering when your driver would be here. I'm late for my appointment."

Dot looked at her watch. Jim had left at 9:15; it was now 10:15.

"Maybelle, I can't imagine where he might be; he left for you an hour ago. Let me make a few phone calls and I'll get right back to you."

Damn! Where the hell is he?

Dot's intercom buzzed. Irritated, she punched it.

"YES?"

"Line two's for you. I think it's Jim," said Julie. It was her third day at Harmony Hall, and she was acting as the receptionist until bingo started, at 2:00.

Dot hit the second button and said, "Dot Turner."

"Dot, it's Jim. I think we've got a problem. I'm at Dr. Clarke's office. He's never heard of Maybelle and she doesn't know her doctor's name…in fact, I don't think she knows she *has* a doctor. She keeps talking about her Easter eggs. Oh, another thing—she can't walk. Don't people have to be able to walk to live at Harmony Hall?"

Dot's eyes closed. "Where did you pick her up, Jim?"

"At that building on Main—the first one you come to when you make the turn off Central."

"Can you hold on?" Dot asked.

"Sure. I've got her in the lobby of the medical building. She's not going anywhere."

Dot picked up line three, called The Evergreen, and asked for the Director of Nursing at the nursing home. A harried voice picked up. "This is Sue. May I help you?"

"Sue? It's Dot over at Harmony Hall. Fine. How've *you* been?" *You're not going to be fine in about fifteen seconds.* "Listen, my driver was supposed to pick up Maybelle McCardle at your independent living section, and I think he may have picked up someone from your nursing center by mistake. Could you check it out and call me back?"

There was a long silence. "Is she in a wheelchair?" Sue asked.

"Yes."

"Hold on."

In seventeen seconds Sue determined that Mable McKenzie, one of her nursing home patients, had been taken to the lobby and offered up to Jim Atkinson. Sue was panting and sounded frantic when she returned to the phone. "Is she OK? Where is she?"

"She's fine. My driver has her in the lobby of the Broadway Medical Center. I'll get her back to you A.S.A.P. Sorry for the confusion, Sue," said Dot. She picked up line two. "Jim, we've got the wrong girl. Just take her back to the same place you picked her up. Then come on home. We'll get the real Maybelle McCardle over here later in the week."

"I may be a little late getting back," Jim said. "Somebody needs to look at the radiator in the wagon—we're overheating."

Dot called Maybelle and explained that they'd run into a problem and asked her to reschedule her appointment. As she was hanging up from the call, Julie appeared in the doorway with the Health Department inspector. Apparently their unannounced six-month kitchen inspection would be performed today, and Evie, the head cook of nearly three decades, was on vacation.

When it rained, it poured.

CHAPTER 12

HELPING HANDS

Julie was delighted when Dot asked her to accompany Bertha to the dentist for a check-up.

"Just ask him to check her liner, Julie. She's been losing weight, and I think it's because she's having trouble chewing."

"Will she be able to pay for it?" the always practical Julie asked.

Dot's crow's feet deepened. "He'll bill her daughter."

She paged Jim and explained that he could drop off Julie and Bertha on his way to Home Depot.

"Good luck!" Dot said, and patted Julie's shoulder.

Julie jumped from the station wagon and pulled Bertha's walker from the back. She rushed to the passenger's door, unbuckled Bertha's seatbelt and held her charge's hand as she struggled to her feet. They walked slowly to the door of Dr. Berkley's office, entered the waiting room and settled down. Together they looked at a copy of *Better Homes and Gardens*.

"Ms. Green?" Dr. Berkley's assistant smiled at Bertha, who looked back at her and said, "Heh?"

Julie helped Bertha up and headed her in the right direction.

"Bertha, the dentist is going to look at your liner—it'll just take a minute," Julie said, squeezing her arm.

"My what?" said Bertha.

"Your teeth," said Julie.

"I don't have any teeth."

"Your plate…your false teeth."

Julie tried to keep her voice low. Everyone in the waiting room was watching them.

"Oh. OK," said Bertha, picking up speed.

It was 2:05 P.M. At 2:06 P.M. Dr. Berkley entered the waiting room and motioned to Julie. She sprang to her feet, wondering if this was a problem she'd have to call Dot about. They moved behind the door separating the waiting room from the patients' chairs.

"Are you from Harmony Hall?" asked Dr. Berkley softly.

"Yes, I'm Julie. Is Bertha OK?"

Dr. Berkley took in the blue eyes, blonde hair, too-thin body and obvious consternation.

"She's doing fine. However, it's obvious why she's losing weight. These aren't her teeth."

"What?" said Julie.

"She's wearing someone else's plate," explained Dr. Berkley.

"How can that happen?" asked Julie.

"I'm sure I don't know."

"What should we do?"

"We've got her impressions. I'll have to make another set if hers don't show up," said the dentist.

Terry and Dot were poring over menus when Julie returned to Harmony Hall.

"Whose plate could she be wearing?" asked Julie.

"Should I put out a memo, Dot?" Terry snickered. "How 'bout, 'Lost your choppers? Want 'em back? See Bertha Green, the plate pack rat!'"

Dot chuckled, looked at Julie, and shook her head. "Who else is losing weight?" she asked.

Red-haired and hot-tempered in her younger days, Camille Everson at eighty was now more mellow. Years before she was something of a fashion plate; now she was less concerned with keeping up appearances. In hot weather she would don shorts and sandals and stroll to her seat in the dining room, leg wrinkles shaking with every step. As Mack's official day walker, she exercised more than the other residents, and seemed in better shape than her contemporaries. She had learned early that the secret to happiness was to help others, and those at Harmony Hall in more precarious health than she took advantage of that philosophy.

Jim looked at the handwritten work orders on his clipboard. Harriett's sink was draining slowly. He grabbed his snake, a bucket and a towel, and headed for her room. "Harriett?" He knocked again, louder this time.

"Just a *MINUTE*," came from behind the door.

Harriett's voice was high and distinctive—almost shrill. This voice was lower and sounded slightly frantic. He waited, bucket in hand.

"Harriett?"

"Hold *ON*," the voice said.

Suddenly the door opened a few inches. Camille, a lock of hair over her right eye, peered at Jim.

"Oh. Hi, Jim. What's up?" She glanced over her shoulder.

"Harriett's got a slow drain. I thought I'd work on it…"

"Not *now*," said Camille. "Harriett's not feeling well."

"OK. I'll come back later," Jim said.

Camille's eyes narrowed. "Is Dot here?" she asked.

"I think so. Do you need her?"

"Harriett may need her. Do you mind sending her up?"

"Not at all."

Jim went back down to Dot's office.

"Dot, Harriett's got a problem, and Camille's with her. She's wondering if you can go up."

"Sure. Should I take anything with me?"

"I don't know—she didn't say."

Dot ran through the possibilities: Incontinence, sudden, unexplained weakness, nausea, trouble with a hearing aid battery—it could be anything. "Watch the phones, would you? I'll be right back."

Harriett was in room 30 on the second floor. Dot took the stairs two at a time. Ten years before she was forever changed when she told an ailing resident she'd be back soon, and returned fifteen minutes later. That resident, Patsy Beauchamp, was in the last throes of a massive heart attack when Dot re-entered her room. Could Patsy have been saved if she'd returned ten minutes earlier?

"Harriett?" Dot knocked loudly on the door to room 30.

"Dot!" Camille opened the door. Over her left shoulder, Dot saw Harriett in bed. She was lying on top of the spread, face to one side, her knees drawn up near her chest, her bottom in the air.

"Anything wrong?" asked Dot.

"Harriett's constipated," said Camille, never one to mince words.

"Harriett, what can I do?" asked Dot.

Harriett's muffled voice replied, "Show her how to do it."

"Do what?"

Camille looked abashed. "I can't get this thing to work" she said, holding up a Fleet enema.

"What are you doing?" asked Dot.

"I'm putting it in, and nothing happens," said Camille.

Dot took the bottle from Camille and studied it. "Camille, did you take the cap off?"

"What cap?"

"This one," Dot said, pointing at the tip of the bottle. "This needs to come off before it's inserted."

"Oh," said Camille.

"Thank God," said Harriett.

CHAPTER 13

SETTLING IN

Faith's goldfish, spawning in the warm water below the deck, magnified the splashing sound of the waterfall in her garden pond. Skipper watched them, wondering how the eggs and sperm ever found each other.

"How's Mimi doing—really?" she asked Faith.

"I think she's OK. I called three times yesterday and never got her in her room, so I finally checked with the office. All three times she was busy doing something. I finally got through to her last night. She told me she was going to church with Eloise today."

"Church? Your mother doesn't go to church."

"I think Eloise asked her to go—she's almost blind, you know. I'll bet Mom was going along to help her."

"That sounds like your mother...and like she's adjusting."

"I hope so. I'm having breakfast with her tomorrow—we'll see. It bothers me that she hasn't talked to me about things, Skipper. We used to talk about everything. Now I can't pull anything out of her."

"She doesn't want to say anything negative and worry you," Skipper said. "Give it some time. She'll talk when she's ready."

Faith pitched a ball into the back yard for Babe, who scurried down the deck steps to retrieve it.

"I'm getting the silent treatment from Lauren," Skipper added, "but for a different reason." She laughed bitterly. Lauren had refused to speak to Skipper since her grounding for the latest—and very visible—tattoo. "I'm surrounded by silent women," Skipper murmured, watching the fish. Then looked at Faith and smiled, "Except for you, darling."

"Oh, Skipper, Lauren's a teenager. Everyone goes through this with teenage girls."

"Maybe so…but I've got a silent mother, too."

Skipper rarely mentioned her mother, though Lauren on many occasions had reported to Faith that her mother and grandmother were at odds.

"What's her problem?" asked Faith.

"She hates me," said Skipper, sounding amazingly like Lauren.

"Oh, Skipper, she does *not*."

"Yes, she does. Nothing I've ever done was good enough; everything I've ever bought was too flashy and too trashy. None of my friends—except you—are classy."

"When did you talk to her last?" asked Faith.

"On my birthday—April. We got in a fight on the phone. I could hear that wimp husband of hers mewling in the background. What a jerk."

Faith could tell Skipper's Bloody Mary was beginning to kick in. "Why don't you invite her home from Connecticut to visit? Maybe the three of you could hole up at Shakertown and just talk and walk."

"I can see the headlines now," said Skipper, squinting and rolling her eyes. "Daughter, mother and granddaughter die in unusual three-way murder/suicide during bonding session at Shakertown."

Faith laughed and kicked her under the table. Skipper drained her glass and got up to fix a refill. "I'm serious, Faith. They *both* hate me."

With some effort, Mimi made it up the three low steps of the *Mary Magdalene* bus, behind Eloise. Mimi's walker was stowed at the back of the bus. The driver, a church member, promised he'd retrieve it for her when they reached the church. This was her first trip outside Harmony Hall without Faith, and the start of her second week at the home.

"You all right?" asked Eloise. They sat next to each other at the back of the bus.

"Great," said Mimi, beginning to perspire. "How far to the church?"

"It's only five minutes away. That's one of the reasons I came to Harmony Hall—it's so convenient to my old neighborhood. Where did you go to church?"

"I hate to tell you this, Eloise, but I didn't attend church. I used to get my spiritual needs filled in the garden, when I *could* garden."

Eloise's sightless eyes seemed to light up. "I'm so glad you're coming with me. You'll love it!"

"I'm sure I will. I've never been to a Catholic service."

"Well, there's a lot of kneeling—if you can kneel. If you can't, just stay on the pew—that's what I do."

At 12:20 the bus pulled back into the Harmony Hall parking lot. The driver helped Mimi and Eloise to the front door. Mimi started to unlock the door with her key, but it was pushed open by Minnie, who greeted them, wig in hand.

"Mimi, can you help me with this dang thing?" she asked. "I just got it, and I can't figure out which end is which."

The wig was chestnut, curly all over and looked like a limp animal in Minnie's hands.

"Doesn't it have a tag?" asked Mimi, taking it from Minnie.

"I took the price tag off."

Other ladies were beginning to move toward the dining room. Mimi and Minnie sat in the lobby, and Mimi examined the wig. She carefully pulled it down over Minnie's forehead and ran her finger under the bottom edge, pushing white strands of Minnie's hair back under the edge of the wig. "Let's see, Minnie," she said.

Minnie jumped up and turned to face Mimi. "Am I gorgeous?"

"Yes!" Mimi said, laughing.

"Let's go!" said Minnie, pirouetting toward Mack, who was lying in his usual place at the entry to the dining room.

Mimi followed Minnie. Church had made for an interesting but exhausting morning. She had to get back in a garden.

That evening Lauren rang the bell at Harmony Hall. It was 6:30. At 6:00 she had finally broken her silence and asked Skipper if she could go see Mimi, swearing she'd be home by 8:30. It was a twenty-minute walk. Reluctantly, she'd changed into her running shoes, leaving the five-inch sandals at home.

Carmen, the beautiful security employee who lived at Harmony Hall, answered the door.

"How *are* you, Meese Laura?" she asked. Carmen called all the ladies at Harmony Hall "Meese."

"I'm good. I'm here to see Mimi."

"Wonderful!" said Carmen. "Meese Mimi weel love to see you."

Mack, hearing Lauren's voice, came bounding around the corner of the lobby.

"Watch, Meese Laura!" Carmen pulled a tiny treat from her pocket. "Mack! Seet!"

Mack sat, wriggling at Carmen's feet. "Mack! Roll over!" Mack grinned at both of them, hesitated, and rolled over. He jumped up and took the treat from Carmen, then put his paws on Lauren's knees.

"Mack! You're awesome!" said Lauren.

"He ees the *best* boy!" said Carmen, laughing, as she headed to the kitchen.

Lauren took the elevator to the second floor with Mack. Harriett, Mimi's Buddy, was sitting in her room with the door open to the hall.

"Lauren! How are you?" she called. Lauren stuck her head in Harriett's room.

"I'm good. I just saw Mack roll over."

"Isn't he wonderful?" Harriett said, as Mack sniffed around her room. "I think we need to teach him Get Set, Ready, Fire—that's what my mother taught our dogs when I was a girl."

"What's that?" asked Lauren.

"Well, you teach the dog to sit, first. Then you put a treat on the dog's nose and make him stay still when you say, "Get Set." After a few seconds you say, "Ready," and then when you say, "Fire," he tosses the treat in the air and catches it. It's very impressive."

"I bet Mack could learn that," said Lauren.

"Why don't you and I teach him?"

"Cool!" Lauren looked at her watch. "I came to see Mimi tonight, but I'll be back another time to work with him."

Harriett wrote her phone number on a slip of paper.

"Here's my number, Lauren. Any time you want to come by, let me know, and I'll try to have Mack rounded up and some treats ready."

Lauren and Mack stopped at Mimi's door. Lauren knocked several times and put her ear to the door. There was no sound within, and it was locked. She walked back to Harriett's door.

"Harriett, do you know where Mimi is?"

"You might check the balcony, honey. Oh, maybe she's with Sarah on the veranda. If not there, you might try out back in the garden."

Mimi wasn't in the home. Beginning to worry, Lauren left Mack inside and headed for the garden. As she entered the walkway beneath the arbor, a garter snake slithered across it and was out of sight immediately. Lauren gasped, and ran to the vegetable garden behind the shed. Surprised, she saw Dot picking squash.

"Hi, Dot. What are you doing here? It's Sunday."

Dot's sleeveless jean shirt was soaked with sweat. "Hey, Lauren. I consider this play time…and it's a great stress reliever."

"Have you seen Mimi?"

"No. Have you checked down by the big pond?"

"No, but I will. Thanks. By the way, did you know you have a *snake* in this garden?"

"I hope so," laughed Dot. "They're death to slugs."

Lauren turned down the walkway toward the big pond. She saw Mimi between the raised beds, cutting flowers and putting them in a small vase, her walker behind her.

"Mimi!"

"Lauren! Come give me a hug!"

Lauren's spiked hair felt hard against Mimi's face, and she seemed much shorter today.

"I'm so glad you're here! Is your mother with you?"

"No, I walked."

"You're kidding! That's great! Come sit by the pond with me."

Lauren carried Mimi's vase and they made their way to the benches facing the koi pond.

"You're walking so much faster now," said Lauren.

"I know. Isn't it wonderful? I think I'll be done with this dern walker soon. How goes things?"

"I'm OK. I'm grounded again, but Mom let me out to see you."

"What did you do to deserve a grounding—or can you talk about it?"

"I got this," said Lauren, showing Mimi the butterfly tattoo, high on her left arm.

"It's kind of pretty, actually," said Mimi.

"I know. Mom told me not to get any more, though, and I did."

"Well, then you deserve to be grounded, I 'spose," said Mimi. "Eighteen will be here before you know it, and you can do whatever you want then. 'Course, by then you'll be smarter, and some of the things you want to do now you won't consider doing."

"I guess," said Lauren. "How are *you*, Mimi? Do you like it here so far?"

"I have to admit I do, honey. I'm beginning to think of this as home. Isn't that funny?"

"I love coming here," said Lauren. "Everyone's so laid back and friendly."

"They are," agreed Mimi. "It's a little like a big house for a bunch of sisters. It's nothing like I thought it would be."

They sat silent for several minutes, watching the koi. Two starlings landed at the top of the waterfall and began bathing. A squirrel chattered somewhere in the distance. Blackie, the outside cat, joined them and curled up beside Lauren on the bench, eyes fixed on the koi. An Oriental couple with a baby stroller passed them, headed for the parking lot. Frequent visitors, today the diminutive mother held a vase of daisies. The baby cooed at the fish and waved her tiny fist at them.

As long shadows began to fall across the walkway and the sun sank behind the cedar tree, Lauren rose to start for home.

"Give your darling mother my love," Mimi said.

"I will," promised Lauren, for once feeling good about walking home.

CHAPTER 14

BINGO

As Faith parked the car, she noticed an older man working between the raised beds in the garden. He waved at her as she turned toward the parking lot door. It was 7:55...almost time for her first breakfast with her mother at Harmony Hall.

"Hi, honey!" Mimi opened the door before Faith could unlock it.

"Mother, you look great!"

"She *is* great," said Harriett, on her way to the dining room. The trio headed in that direction.

Camille was out of town, and Faith sat in her spot. The other four residents at the table were wearing robes. Her mother wore a pantsuit.

"I spent some time with your goddaughter yesterday," said Harriett.

Faith couldn't believe her ears. "What?" she asked.

"Lauren was over last evening. She seems like such a nice girl."

Faith looked at Mimi, who nodded.

"She spent some time with me in the garden. We had a lovely visit."

Terry moved between them, pouring coffee and delivering hot water decanters for tea.

"Well, I'm delighted!" said Faith. "I didn't know Skipper was letting her get out yet."

"She knew Lauren couldn't get into any trouble here," said Minnie.

"I don't know about *that*," said Terry. "*You're* in trouble all the time, Ms. Minnie."

Minnie thumbed her nose at him. Her wigless head was nearly bald. She looked vulnerable and unprotected. Her new wig, already too hot, hung from the back of her chair.

"She *walked* here, Faith," said Mimi. "Can you imagine?"

"Not in those *sandals!*"

"No, she had on sneakers. I didn't know Lauren owned sneakers," chuckled Mimi.

Eloise said, "Speaking of sneakers, my great-grandson is said to have some that light up when he moves. What will they think of next?"

Bertha looked questioningly at Minnie.

"Sneakers," said Minnie loudly. "We're talking sneakers, Bertha."

"Oh…I see." said Bertha.

"Mother, look what I've got you," said Faith, changing the subject. She pulled a new cell phone from her purse and handed it to Mimi.

"Faith! Thanks so much! I've never used one of these. How do they work?"

"We'll have a training session right after breakfast" said Faith. "You'll love it."

❧   ❧   ❧

"You have plenty of quarters for bingo, Julie?" Dot was looking at Monday's scheduled activities on the Week-At-A-Glance calendar. Bingo was at 2:00.

"There are six," said Julie, checking the quarters cup.

"C'mon. I'll show you where to get more." Dot walked to the key box between her office and Terry's, and showed Julie which cash keys to take to the washers and dryers on both floors. They walked together to the laundry room, and Dot deftly extracted the contents of the cash box from each appliance.

"We've got a great source of quarters, and it never runs out," Dot said. "Everybody just recycles what they win at bingo when they do their laundry."

Julie took the box of bingo cards from the lobby closet and started upstairs. Terry walked up with her on his way to Sarah's room. Sarah's nephew was pilfering from her again.

"Do you want a cup of coffee before you begin?" he asked, grinning. "An alarm clock, perhaps, to wake you when you start sawing logs in the middle of the game? How 'bout some smelling salts for when you pass out?"

Julie laughed. She found bingo exciting, in a way. The ladies loved it, and she liked watching them win.

"You're crazy, Terry," she said, as the first of sixteen residents began filing into the parlor. It took several minutes to align the walkers and find suitable chairs.

"Has everyone put in a quarter?"

"Virginia hasn't," said Camille, adding in a low voice, "she never does."

"Virginia, do you have a quarter?" asked Julie.

"Oh—let's see," said Virginia, digging reluctantly in her change purse. She brought up a dime and fifteen pennies. "This is all I have to my name."

Camille rolled her eyes.

"Thanks. That's fine," said Julie, smiling around the table. "Are we ready?" she queried.

"Yes!" A dozen voices answered.

"Let's do it!"

She sat next to Eloise, who needed help covering the numbers on her card.

"B-3," Julie said.

"What?" Virginia asked.

"B-3," repeated Julie, holding up the card for all to see, and closing Eloise's B-3 cover on her card. Several silver heads nodded, "Yes", several shook "No." Monday's bingo game was in full swing.

Mimi's therapist walked around the upstairs hall with her. "You're doing fine. Actually, you're doing beautifully."

Mimi stopped, her walker wheels squeaking.

"Can I get rid of this thing?" she asked, shaking the walker.

"Not quite yet," said the therapist. "Keep up the walking and the exercises we've reviewed. It's very likely that by next week you'll be on your own."

At 2:30, the end of her half-hour of therapy, Mimi looked in on bingo. She decided it was too late to start, and she headed for the garden with her new cell phone. It was turning out to be a pretty good day.

Lauren was on the computer when Skipper got home from lunch with Pam and a three-hour volunteer stint at the blood center.

"Hello, honey," she said to the back of Lauren's spikey head.

"Hi," said Lauren, not turning around.

There was something new in Lauren's voice—just the barest lilt, as if she were slightly interested in what she was looking at on the computer, and didn't mind if Skipper knew.

"Whatcha got?" asked Skipper. She looked over Lauren's shoulder at the monitor. There, staring back, was a snake.

"Just reading about snakes, Mom," said Lauren.

Skipper headed for the kitchen and her wine. This snake thing could be serious.

Pete parked his car in front of *Magnifique* at 6:05, just as Faith was locking the front door. He joined her there.

"Hi, honey," she said, giving him a hug.

Their beginning tennis class five years before had brought them together, and neither had ever been happier in a relationship. Together they had settled Mimi into Pete's duplex, at his insistence. Both products of unhappy and dissolved unions, neither Faith nor Pete felt compelled to marry. That decision delighted Mimi, who over the years had many friends in less than ideal marriages. She knew she could live without grandchildren. "You two have it made," she'd tell Faith. "Don't spoil it."

They walked arm in arm to *Annie's*, Faith's favorite neighborhood restaurant. Annie always had great specials on Monday nights. Pete held Faith's hand and looked at her over the checkered tablecloth.

"Tell me about Mimi. Is she liking it at Hominy Hall?"

Faith had given up getting Pete to call her mother's new home Harmony Hall. His first and only experience there had convinced him that Harmony was not a description of what went on in the place Mimi now called home.

"I think she is, Pete. It's amazing, but in no time she started acting like she'd lived there forever. Oh—she'll probably be off her walker in a week! She called me on her new cell phone to give me the news." Faith's face was glowing. "Lauren loves the place. I had breakfast with Mom this morning and found out that Lauren *walked* from Skipper's to Harmony Hall yesterday."

"No way!" laughed Pete.

"Honestly!"

"How *is* 'ole Skip? I haven't seen much of her lately—*or* you."

"She's nuts. She called this morning to tell me that Lauren may be getting involved in some sort of satanic ritual stuff with snakes. I don't know if either are going to survive these teenage years."

"They can be tough." Pete thought briefly of his own teens, and knew that without the military at eighteen he probably wouldn't have made it to his twenties.

"Mine really weren't," Faith said. "Aside from arguing with Mom about tennis—which I refused to play back then—I can't remember any problems. I guess I was a teenage milquetoast. Skipper must have been awful—and they still can't get along."

"I hope that changes before it's too late," said Pete.

"Me too. It's unimaginable to me that a mother and daughter their ages won't speak to each other. It would kill me to have that kind of relationship with Mom."

Faith fiddled with her napkin.

"Pete, we need to talk about the duplex. May I pay you a month's rent and can we hold it open just a little longer?"

"Don't worry about it, Sweetie. I've got Joyce's half rented—to a pharmaceutical sales rep—and there's no mortgage on the place. She can just store her stuff there until she gets back."

"Pete, we've got the money and I know Mom thinks I've already handled it. Please take a month's rent."

"No. That's final." The military man was beginning to show through.

"Darling, how can I ever repay you?"

"Just keep giving me the pleasure of your lovely company," Pete said, squeezing Faith's hand.

CHAPTER 15

DOWNSIZING

AUGUST, 1998

At 6:30 Skipper dropped off Lauren in the parking lot at Harmony Hall and headed for Faith's. Lauren promised to walk home right after she finished visiting with Mimi, who was feeling celebratory about finally getting off her walker. Skipper and Faith were going out. They were feeling celebratory about a lot of things. The store was doing well, Lauren was beginning to act almost human, Mimi was starting to move like her old self, and Skipper had run into a fellow who appeared to be single, interesting and interested. It was Friday night. For the first time in forever, all was well with the world.

Lauren first checked the garden for Mimi, watched the koi churn the water in the big pond and headed for the building. It was still hot, muggy, and bright outside. Camille and Mack were leaving as she entered—Mack was biting his leash, excited to be walking and determined to show it.

"Hey, Lauren," Camille said, wrestling with Mack and the leash, "Whaddya know?"

"Just checking on Mimi," said Lauren. Mack growled at the leash and rolled his eyes at her.

"I think she's with our new resident," said Camille.

"Who's that?" asked Lauren.

"Maybelle McCardle. She just moved in this morning. Mimi's her Buddy."

"Her Buddy? Where does she know her from?" asked Lauren.

"Oh, nowhere," said Camille. "She's been appointed Maybelle's Buddy until Maybelle can get around on her own." She and Mack lunged out the door, each pulling on the leash.

Lauren walked up the wide staircase to Mimi's room. The door was open, but Mimi wasn't there.

"Harriett, have you seen Mimi?" Harriett was listening to a book on tape.

"No, but I think she's Maybelle's Buddy. Have you checked room 24?"

"Thanks. I'll do that."

Lauren knocked on the door to room 24. "Come in," said a weak, high voice.

Lauren opened the door. The room was a shambles; half-opened boxes lay everywhere. The bed, mattress exposed, was covered with clothes on hangers. Mimi sat in a corner chair, and smiled at Lauren. The occupant of the room, Maybelle McCardle, looked at Lauren, and said in a piteous voice, "Are you my home health helper?"

"No ma'am," said Lauren. "But I'll be glad to help you."

"Maybelle, this is Lauren, my great-goddaughter," said Mimi.

"She's *what?*"

"She's my daughter's goddaughter, so that makes her my great-goddaughter."

"So glad to meet you," said Maybelle. "Do you need some work?"

"Sure" said Lauren, who had never had a job of any sort, but was finding that extra money could come in very handy for tattoos, hair appointments and special vegetarian diets.

"Help me put this stuff away," said Maybelle, "and I'll give you $5.00 an hour."

Mimi raised an eyebrow, but was silent.

"OK," said Lauren. "Where should I start?"

"How 'bout the closet?" said Maybelle.

"Honey, I'm going to take a little walk outside. Come see me when you're through for the night," said Mimi, getting up to go.

"OK," said Lauren, wondering if she'd hurt Mimi's feelings.

"Maybelle, don't hesitate to call me if you need anything later on. I'm right around the corner."

"Thanks, Mimi. If I ever get this hellhole organized, it'll be a miracle" said Maybelle.

Lauren began lining up shoes in the closet.

❧   ❧   ❧

Mimi headed for the garden, a glass of wine in her left hand, a cane in her right. Friday was wine night at Harmony Hall, and she'd saved hers for reflection and thanksgiving in her favorite spot at the koi pond. Rounding the curve past the roses, she nearly ran into a tall, gray-haired gentleman in long shorts and a Kentucky Wildcats tee shirt. He was leaning on a hoe and watching the koi. His closely cropped moustache was white. His arms and hands were tanned, and he wore running shoes and a baseball cap with *Costa Rica* across the front.

"Aren't they beautiful?" asked Mimi, breaking into his reverie. She slowly sat on her favorite bench and laid her cane lengthwise in front of her.

"Yes, and they look hungry!" said the stranger. "Do you feed them?"

"No, but one of our residents does," said Mimi. "I just love to watch them and listen to the waterfall and the birds out here."

"It's a great place," he said. Mimi didn't know if he was talking about Harmony Hall or the garden.

"I'm Henry Caldwell. I volunteer in the garden."

"I'm Mimi Green. I live here temporarily."

"You look too young to be here," said Henry.

Mimi laughed. "Well, I'm not. I dye my hair. That makes a big difference!"

Henry looked at her closely. He had noticed her eyes.

Mimi took a sip of her wine. "How long have you been volunteering at Harmony Hall?"

"About three years. My aunt used to live here, and I couldn't stand to leave it when she died. Dot talked me into working in the garden, and I'm here two or three times a week."

"What a wonderful gift to this place. Are you a flower or a vegetable man?"

"I love all of it, Mimi. Do you garden?"

"Oh, yes. Well, actually I used to. I'm trying to mend—and bend again! It shouldn't be long before I can hike a hoe with the best of them!"

Henry laughed, and looked at her quizzically. "Are you from here?"

"No, not originally. I moved here from Florida in '92 after my husband died, to be near my daughter. How 'bout you?"

"I'm a native. I spent some time in New York and California, and couldn't wait to get back to Lexington. This is a great little town."

Mimi wondered if her hair were flat and wiped the sweat off her upper lip with her index finger. Henry looked longingly at the bench.

"Would you like to sit a bit?" Mimi asked.

"Sure," said Henry. He sat down at the far end of the bench. "Look!" he said. A striped snake was making its way to the pond's edge, not ten feet from them. It stopped when it reached the water, lowered its oval head, and drank. Mimi and Henry sat motionless.

"Isn't he something?" she said.

"Yes—snakes are remarkable. Imagine having to get around and fend for yourself with no hands or feet—forever at the mercy of the thermometer. I've always been fascinated by them."

Suddenly Camille and Mack appeared, and the snake moved out of sight under a large hosta. Mack was still tugging on the leash. Camille looked worn out. Her hair was plastered to her forehead and sweat rings were showing on her sleeveless blouse.

"I'm getting too old for this," she said, raising both eyebrows at Mimi. "Hi, Henry."

"How are you, Camille?" asked Henry.

"I'm about ready to kill this sweet dog, I'll tell 'ya," said Camille. "He's running me ragged."

"Would you like me to take him around the block for you?" Henry asked.

"Sure! I'll sit here with Mimi and get my breath back."

Henry took off with Mack, and Mimi and Camille watched his tall frame move quickly from the parking lot to the driveway and down the sidewalk.

"He seems like a nice fellow," said Mimi.

"He's a champ," said Camille. "I knew his Aunt Flo. She was 103 when she died, and he was the best nephew you ever saw. His wife died two years ago, and I don't think he'll ever get over it. They used to travel all over the world together after he retired."

"Does he live alone now?" asked Mimi.

"Far as I know. He doesn't talk much—probably afraid we'll pounce on him if we know too much."

"We should invite him in for lunch on days he works here," said Mimi. "I'm sure Dot wouldn't mind."

"Hell, *she's* asked him a hundred times," said Camille. "I think it makes him sad to come inside—too many memories of his aunt and his wife. She used to come with him to visit Flo."

Lauren appeared from nowhere. She looked stricken. "Mimi, I think you need to come talk to Maybelle. She's crying, and I don't know what to say to her."

"Oh, no!" said Mimi. "I'm coming, Lauren. Camille, I'll see you at breakfast, if not before." Mimi reached for her cane, steadied herself and started toward the doors at the back of the building.

Maybelle McCardle had a son named Carl who was very much interested in making money and spent little time with his mother. Maybelle's rent at The Evergreen had been raised annually since she'd moved there fourteen years earlier. Carl was not happy about the inevitability of helping his mother pay her rent, and convinced her that a move to Harmony Hall, at a third the monthly cost of her present rent, was an excellent idea. He didn't consider the fact that Maybelle had three times the space at The Evergreen, and that at her advanced age of 89 her only friends lived there. Maybelle, anxious to please Carl, whom she rarely saw, agreed to move. He handled her finances, and if he said it was a wise move, she knew it must be so.

Mimi and Lauren knocked on Maybelle's half-opened door. Mimi could hear sniffling coming from the bathroom.

"Maybelle? Are you O.K.?"

"No! I'm awful. What was I thinking about when I moved here?"

Mimi pushed the door open. Maybelle, with red eyes and wild hair, tried to move to her bed and thought better of it. She sank as far as she could into a chair piled high with sweaters.

Mimi noticed that Maybelle's closet was full. Lauren had done a good job of hanging things so that all the hangers faced the same way. A dozen pairs of shoes were lined up below on the closet floor. Unfortunately, it was hard to tell that anything had been moved from the room to the closet.

"Maybelle, we've got to get some of this stuff to your storage unit in the basement," said Mimi.

"Who's going to do that?"

"Can't your son come help you?" asked Mimi.

"He's going out tonight with his banker," said Maybelle.

Mimi looked at Lauren, pulled her cell phone from her pocket, and dialed Faith's number.

🍁   🍁   🍁

"Mother? Is that you?" It was noisy in the restaurant, and Skipper was laughing and flirting with the waiter when Faith's phone rang.

"Faith? Can you hear me?" It sounded to Mimi like Faith was at a party.

"Yes. Are you OK?"

"Honey, I'm fine. I'm worried about Maybelle, my new Buddy. Lauren and I are here with her, and she's in a real state. We need some help moving her things and getting her organized tonight."

Faith tried to gauge Skipper's mood. If she were having too good a time it would be awful to suggest they leave for Harmony Hall to help a disgruntled resident on a Friday night.

"Let me talk to Skipper; hold on, Mom."

Skipper had quit flirting. Her eyes narrowed. "What?" she asked.

"Mimi's Buddy is having a bad time of things," said Faith. "Mom wants us to come help her and Lauren get Maybelle situated."

"Where's *her* freakin' family?"

"I don't think they pay much attention to her," said Faith.

Skipper gave the waiter, now across the room, a last long glance, and folded her napkin. "Well, nuts. Let's go."

🍁   🍁   🍁

Faith and Skipper checked with the Friday night security employee, Tammy, and got permission to borrow two carts from the kitchen. They took the elevator up to Maybelle's floor and raced their carts to her room. Maybelle looked exhausted. She was still crying.

"It's Friday night, Maybelle, you should be putt'n on the dog," said Skipper, as she entered the room.

"I need to be put in a grave," said Maybelle.

"Oh, shush," said Skipper. "This room's going to look 100% better with 90% of this crap downstairs."

She began piling clothes on her cart. Faith started picking up boxes and checking with Maybelle about their usefulness. Mack dropped by to visit, but backed off when Maybelle threw a rolled up pair of socks at him. Nothing personal, she told them, but she hated dogs. Lauren said, "C'mon, Mack, let's go practice," grabbed him, and headed for Harriett's room.

By 10:00 P.M. the room was transformed. Mimi adjusted the air conditioner and reminded Maybelle that breakfast was from 8:00 to 10:00 A.M. She gave Maybelle her cell phone number. Skipper pulled the comforter back on the now-made bed, and crooked her finger at Maybelle.

"You need to get some sleep, kiddo."

Faith, her blonde hair gleaming in the light of the bedside lamp, leaned over and hugged Mimi's unhappy Buddy. Maybelle's thin arms squeezed her back.

"Thank you both so much," she whispered. "You've saved my life."

Faith chuckled. "It will all look better in the morning."

Lauren poked her head in and waved at Maybelle.

"Your money!" said Maybelle.

"I'll get it another time," said Lauren. They turned off the light, gently closed the door to Maybelle's room, and walked to the stair landing. Mimi hugged each of them.

"I'm sorry I ruined your evening out," she said to Skipper and Faith.

"We had a great meal before you called, Mother. This was fun. Just don't hurt yourself trying to make everything right. Some people can't be happy, you know."

"Yes, dear," said Mimi, winking at Lauren.

It was later, as she turned out her own light, that Mimi thought of Henry Caldwell and how nice he looked in the bright, reflected sunshine of the koi pond.

CHAPTER 16

ANGELS

Thursdays were busy days at Harmony Hall. Angel, the beauty shop operator, was in at 8:30 A.M. and worked non-stop until mid afternoon on nearly half the residents who wanted their hair done in-house. Mimi thought Angel looked like Dolly Parton—blond, beautiful and buxom. Angel often wore tee shirts that said things like, "I'm Saved" and "Follow Him." Over the years she had learned to be extremely polite and accommodating, but not to take anything from ladies who felt they needed to throw their weight around. It was a paradox; residents who felt most helpless were most likely to demean and demand.

By Wednesday afternoon Julie had posted the next day's appointments on the *"Angel's Salon"* door. Angel greeted Bertha, her first customer, with a smile and a hug, and Mack flopped down on the couch to watch and snooze. By 10:00 both dryers were occupied, and Angel was washing Camille's head. Harriett was waiting on the couch, Mack beside her, when Terry looked in. His eyes made a quick sweep of the room. He bent over a nodding Minnie, under the dryer, and asked, "Hot enough?" laughing when she opened her eyes. Bertha, under the other dryer, had her lower plate in her lap. Angel and Camille were snickering when Maybelle, still in her robe and slippers, entered the beauty shop.

"Where's one supposed to sit around here?" she asked, looking distastefully at Mack.

"Why don't you sit in that cutting chair?" asked Angel. "Do you want me to lower it for you?"

"No, I came in here to get my hair done. How long's the wait?"

Angel stifled the urge to remind Maybelle that she was early, and her appointment wasn't until 10:15.

"About fifteen minutes, Hon," said Angel, rolling Camille's strawberry blonde hair.

"FIFTEEN MINUTES? I've never!" Maybelle turned on her heel and left the shop, followed by Mack. Angel raised her eyebrows and said to Camille, "Don't you ever get like that, Missy!"

"Believe me, when I get like that you can ship me off to the nursing home" said Camille, chortling.

Dot poked her head in. "Angel, is Maybelle on your list?"

"Yeah, she's due in fifteen minutes."

"Oh, great. I'll let her know," said Dot.

"She knows—I just told her." Angel grinned at Dot in the mirror. Dot disappeared and Julie came in.

"Angel, Maybelle, our newest resident, has an appointment at 10:15."

"I know. She was just in here," said Angel.

Julie looked confused. Angel knew the process. If you're disgruntled, tell everyone you can about it and raise a stink. Maybelle was working the first floor like a master politician.

"She'll be OK, Julie—this is her first time in here, and she's just not used to waiting, I guess."

At 10:10 Maybelle reappeared. She was crying. Terry followed her in and put his arm around her shaking shoulders.

"Maybelle, honestly, Jim was yelling at Mack—not you."

"What happened?" asked Angel, securing the last roller at the base of Camille's head.

"Maybelle was coming through the dining room at the same time Jim was yelling at Mack to get out of the dining room. Poor Maybelle thought Jim was yelling at her."

Angel laughed, thinking how great it was that, sooner or later, people get what they deserve. "Maybelle, I've been working here three years, and I've never heard anybody ever yell at a resident."

Maybelle sniffled. It had been a horrible morning. Tomorrow she'd have been here a week, and she still wanted to go back home to The Evergreen. Carl hadn't been by to see her, and his wife had hung up the phone without so much as a good-bye yesterday when Maybelle called to talk to him. She didn't like the ladies at her table—one of them was practically blind, and one was deaf. The lady on her left kept forgetting to pass food to her. When she complained about things to her Buddy, Mimi acted like they weren't important. She felt alone and friendless.

"Harriett's going to let you go ahead of her. Are you ready?" Angel flashed Maybelle her biggest smile and patted the wash chair. Maybelle headed for it, tripped on the mat under the chair, and pitched forward into Angel's arms.

"Wow, you *are* in a hurry!" said Angel.

Harriett jumped up and grabbed Maybelle's hand, "Are you OK?" she asked.

Camille raised the dryer and came over to check on Maybelle, her head bristling with rollers.

"I'm OK," said Maybelle. "Thank you for letting me go ahead of you, Harriett."

"No problem, dear. I've got all the time in the world."

Angel settled Maybelle in the chair and lowered her head to the wash basin. "You're going to feel a lot better with a clean head," she said, and turned on the water.

❧   ❧   ❧

Dot stared out her window at a sparrow intent on catching a moth on the sill. There were times, albeit few, when she wished someone else called the shots. On Monday she'd learned that Maybelle was left high and dry in her room by her son the previous Friday, the day she had moved in. Maybelle had recounted on Monday how appreciative she was of Mimi's family, who helped her finish moving. Twice since then Julie had left messages for Carl to call her and verify information on Harmony Hall's emergency contact sheet. It was now Thursday, and he had yet to respond. Maybelle seemed miserable, and was crying off and on; a slap in the face for Dot and the rest of the staff, who tried non-stop to make everyone happy. Dot finally managed to cajole Carl's wife, Betty, into giving her Carl's cell phone number. Something had to change Maybelle's attitude, and Dot was betting that Carl was the one person who could do it—with some encouragement.

"Carl? It's Dot, at Harmony Hall."

Usually when Dot called a resident's family she immediately prefaced her conversation with, "There's no problem here." Today she simply waited for Carl's reaction.

There was a brief silence. "Is Mother OK?" he asked.

"I think she's physically OK," Dot said, "but she's a mess emotionally. She's not liking it here, Carl, and I'm not sure if it's Harmony Hall or some other issue that's creating the problem. Do you know if she has a history of depression, or if she's lost a good friend lately, or anything else that would be responsible for this sadness we're seeing?" *Like maybe no attention from her son?*

"Hmmm," said Carl. "I can't imagine what it could be. She seemed happy to be going there."

"Have you been by to see her since she moved?" asked Dot.

"No, actually I've been up to my eyeballs at work this last week."

Dot knew Carl was a successful real estate agent, and that he had more flexibility at work than many of the other family members who were tied to desks during the day. She also knew he lived within two miles of Harmony Hall. She could feel her face flushing with anger; the sweat was beginning to pop out on her forehead.

"Well, there may be a few things we can try to improve Maybelle's mood. You can make an appointment with either her doctor or a psychologist to talk about the crying and maybe get a prescription for an anti-depressant, if she needs one. The other thing you can try is spending a little more time here with your mother during this initial adjustment period. If it's hard to get away in the evening, I'd suggest you just drop by for lunch. We serve it at 12:30, and you could be out of here by 1:00." *I know it's a real hardship to carve a half hour out of your important schedule, you jerk.*

Carl cleared his throat.

Dot continued, "I know it's early in the game, Carl, but when one resident is unhappy in our little community, others become unhappy. It's like having one rotten apple poisoning a whole barrel. I haven't talked to your mother yet, but if she's not feeling better about being here in the next few days, I'll have to suggest to her that she leave for a more appropriate environment. I'd hate to see that happen, because I really think we're the best place for her."

"I do, too, Dot." Carl said.

"Would you like to stop by today? I can have Evie set a place for you at Maybelle's table."

There was a longish pause. "Sure. That'll be fine. At 12:30?"

"Why don't you make it 12:25—I'll let your mother know you'll be here," said Dot, using her palm to wipe the perspiration from her brow.

Dot arranged with Evie to set out a plate for Carl next to Maybelle, and entered *"Angel's Salon"* just as Angel was settling Maybelle under the dryer.

"Hey, how's it goin'?" asked Dot.

Maybelle's glasses lay beside her on the table between the two dryers.

"Is she talking to me?" Maybelle asked Angel, the dining room incident still fresh.

"Yes," laughed Angel.

"Maybelle, guess who I just talked to," said Dot, putting her hand on Maybelle's.

"Who?"

"Carl!" said Dot. "He's going to stop by and have lunch with you today."

"My son? With me?" asked Maybelle.

"Yes—he'll be here about 12:30," said Dot. "I've got him set up right next to you in the dining room. Is that OK?"

Maybelle suddenly felt like hugging Dot, but she couldn't get out from under the dryer on her own. She squeezed Dot's hand and simply nodded. Angel turned on the heat, and Dot left the salon. Before she dozed off in the cozy beauty shop under the dryer, Maybelle thought how right Angel had been. She felt *so* much better now that she had a clean head.

Carl parked his BMW as far away from the other cars in the Harmony Hall lot as he could get it, straightened his very expensive tie, and checked his watch. It was 12:20. He wanted to talk to his mother for a minute before lunch about how important it was for her to straighten up. There was no way he and Betty could—or would—subsidize her rent at The Evergreen; she was just going to have to accept things at this new place. Carl took the elevator to Maybelle's room, but it was locked. He took the stairs to the first floor, and heard his mother's voice ring out as he entered the dining room.

"Carl! I'm over here!"

She was with three other women, all silver haired, who peered at him with great interest. Terry showed Carl to his chair next to Maybelle, and took his drink order. His mother introduced him to a Sarah, a Virginia, and a Kitty, all who seemed extremely friendly and eager to talk. Carl noticed how pretty his mother looked, and told her so.

"I had my hair done this morning in the beauty shop," Maybelle explained. "Do you like it?"

Virginia said, "What?" and Sarah repeated to her that Maybelle had her hair done.

"This shop is too expensive," Virginia said. "I go to the beauty school—it's $7.00. I went to Ethel at *Great Hair* for twenty years," she said, "and then I found out that she was charging me $1.00 more than another client. That did it. I never went back."

"What did you pay Ethel?" asked Maybelle.

"Nine dollars for a wash and set," said Virginia. She took the paper napkin from the unoccupied place setting to her left and stuck it in her walker basket next to the Styrofoam cups she'd pinched from the coffee station.

Carl asked Sarah how long she'd lived at Harmony Hall. She told him six years, and that her nephew lived with her.

"I thought all the rooms were single bedrooms," said Carl.

"He lives in my closet. He comes out at night and steals my underwear and anything else he can get his hands on. I think he knows I'm watching him now. This morning all my medical cards were where I hid them last night."

Maybelle rolled her eyes at Kitty, the large woman at the end of the table.

Kitty explained to Carl, "Sarah's nephew is very careful not to let anyone see him. Sarah, I think you're the only one who has, aren't you?"

Sarah nodded. "I had the same trouble with him when I lived at home with my husband. This is a problem nephew. He followed me here."

Carl thought it best to change the subject.

"Are you from Lexington, Kitty?"

"No, I'm from Eastern Kentucky. My folks worked for a coal company, and made sure I got away from Hazard when I could. I've lived here for sixty-five years, though. How about you?"

"Mother and I are from Alabama originally. My dad died when I was fairly young, and we moved here to be close to Mother's sister, our only relative. She died ten years ago. It's a nice town and we've been very happy here—at least up 'til now." He looked at his mother.

Maybelle met his gaze. "I'm happy," she said, and smiled at her handsome son as Evie served them her special oven baked barbecue chicken.

✤   ✤   ✤

Dot's Executive Committee was meeting at 1:30 to discuss employee bene-
fits. Julie was watching the phones in the lobby; Jim was taking Bertha to a
doctor's appointment. Bertha's granddaughter had called that morning to tell
them that Bertha was going to a new doctor. Because Bertha was so hard of
hearing and was beginning to have trouble seeing, Dot asked Jim to walk her
into the doctor's office and help her with the New Patient Information form.

✤   ✤   ✤

Jim parked the station wagon after dropping Bertha at the clinic entrance.
He asked her to sit on the bench just outside the building, and promised he'd
be back in five minutes. The wagon's exhaust pipe had broken loose and
bounced off the road all the way to the doctor's building. He'd sworn silently as
heads turned to watch him in the oversized station wagon. When he returned
to his drop-off location Bertha was dozing in the early afternoon sun, her back
against the wall, her mouth slightly open.

"Bertha?" There was no answer.

"Bertha!!"

She opened her eyes, confused. That nice Jim was bending over her.

"Hello, Jim."

"Bertha, we've got to get to your doctor's appointment. Are you OK?" Jim
was never sure any more who was OK and who wasn't. Things happened so
fast at Harmony Hall, you just couldn't tell.

Bertha took Jim's hand and unsteadily got up behind her walker. They
slowly climbed the ramp, entered the building and reached Dr. Snelling's office
with plenty of time to spare. Jim signed the waiting room form for Bertha and
took the New Patient Information sheet on the clipboard back to his seat next
to hers. The room was full of patients—mostly younger women—who seemed
to be looking at Jim with some interest. Dot had sent Bertha's Harmony Hall
information sheet with him, so Jim had an easy time of the basic questions on
the form. He filled in Bertha's name, birth date, social security number, and
medications. Then the form began to get specific.

"Bertha, when did you have your last period?" Jim whispered.

"What?"

"Your last period. You know, your menstrual cycle," explained Jim, with a sinking heart. It was now obvious that this was a new gynecologist.

"I'm too old for that," said Bertha. Jim wrote down 1975, hoping that was close.

"Do you have any breast tenderness or soreness?" he asked softly, looking nervously at his watch. Every eye in the waiting room was fixed on Bertha, except for those behind magazines.

"What?"

"ARE YOUR BREASTS SORE?"

"I only have one," said Bertha, grabbing her left breast.

"Is *it* sore?"

"No."

Jim checked "**NO**" next to the "Are you pregnant?" question.

"Do you have any discharge?"

"I think Medicare will take care of it."

"No, DO YOU HAVE ANY DISCHARGE?"

Jim's shirt was soaking wet. He pulled a handkerchief from his pants pocket and wiped his face, not daring to look at the other patients in the waiting room.

"I can't tell," said Bertha.

Jim finished what he could of the form and thanked God that he lived in Richmond, miles away from Lexington. None of these people would ever see him again. When her name was called he walked Bertha to the door of the waiting room, and explained to the nurse that Bertha was extremely hard of hearing, and nearly blind. She grinned at him.

"Thanks," she said. "I'll take it from here."

Mimi wandered into the living room about 3:00 P.M., and walked through it to the veranda. It was her second favorite place at Harmony Hall, after the garden. Jim kept the bird feeder full, and there were two squirrels who consistently jumped from the ground past the baffle to share the birdseed with the pigeons and cardinals. The bird "spa," a bubbling birdbath, attracted critters from all over the neighborhood. Traffic from downtown Lexington was only a block away. Visible from the street, the veranda's rattan furniture with its green and white cushions beckoned those with time to kill. Today Julie was taking her break at the far end of the veranda, talking on her cell phone, and Minnie was dozing in a chair at the other end. She opened one eye and waved at Mimi, who settled down near her in an oversized chair. It was a warm, muggy August afternoon, but a soft breeze wafted up the hill, met on the veranda by moving air from the humming ceiling fans. Mimi closed her eyes and listened to the birds. In the background she could just make out Julie's conversation.

"I don't think he's dating anyone, Trish. I think I'd know—one of my ladies would tell me. He's just so nice and so funny. I've never heard him say anything bad about anybody, and he makes everybody laugh." There was a brief silence. "Why don't I ask him if he'd be interested in doubling with Bobby and me—and tell him I've got a good friend in town from Pikeville who needs to see something of Lexington? OK, OK. I'll call you back. Love you, too." Julie got up and walked toward the veranda doors. Mimi opened her eyes and smiled at her.

"How's it goin', kid?" she asked.

"Wonderful, Mimi. How are *you*?" Julie asked, sitting down in the chair between Mimi and Minnie.

"I'm sleepy, honey. This is a swell place to doze off, don't you think?"

Minnie snored lightly.

"I'm trying to fix Terry up," said Julie. "I've got the sweetest girlfriend, and I think she'd just love him."

Mimi wondered if she'd heard right. "Our Terry?" she asked.

"Yes. Don't you think he's the *nicest* guy?"

"Uh-huh," said Mimi. *Didn't Julie know?*

"My friend Trish has dated some really big, stupid football players," Julie said. "Terry would be so different from what she's used to."

You have no idea how different, kid.

Mimi wished Minnie would wake up and help her out. She thought back to the time in Miami, sixty years before, when she'd seen men with men in a bar, and how unsettling it had been. She was over that now, but was suddenly intent on protecting Julie from the same discomfort, and shielding Terry from embarrassment.

"Have you asked him if he's already taken?" Mimi asked.

"No. It's too easy to turn down a blind date. I'm going to invite Trish to the Meet & Greet, and see what happens." Julie watched a pigeon take a sparrow's place at the feeder. "I don't think he'll be able to resist her."

CHAPTER 17

MEET AND GREET

NEWS TO USE

Don't forget Friday's Meet and Greet in the living room at 4:00 P.M.! Refreshments will be served and a door prize awarded to one lucky resident or guest! Friends and family members are welcome—just let Terry or Julie know who's coming for name tags and seating!

This weekend's movie at 2:30 Saturday is "It Could Happen To You" with Bridget Fonda and Nicolas Cage.
8/27/98

Though old hat to Terry, this would be Julie's first Meet and Greet, and she was determined to make it the best one ever.

"Terry, has anyone said they'd be bringing a guest?" asked Julie, as she set up the drink table in the living room early Friday afternoon.

"Only one—Mimi's invited Henry Caldwell to stop by. His aunt used to live here and he volunteers in the garden. Have you met him?"

"No. What's he like?"

"A real nice guy. I think he's lonely. Mimi's been talking with him after breakfast the last few weeks. I think she's got the hots for him."

"Oh, Terry…I'll bet he's got the hots for *her!*"

"All I know is she invited *him*, Smarty."

"I'm so excited," squealed Julie, already envisioning an engagement.

"Well, don't get your hopes up—every resident who visits the garden sets her cap for Henry, and he always gets away."

"He's never known anyone like Mimi, I'll bet," said Julie, and left to make Henry's name tag.

"Mom, is it OK if I invite Harvey to Mimi's party?" asked Lauren, taking out her nose ring. It was now customary to remove all visible piercings before entering Harmony Hall.

Skipper hesitated, wondering if Lauren had an ulterior motive, but couldn't think of one. Harvey was Lauren's best male friend. Neither found the other romantically attractive, but each considered the other a soul mate. Skipper's only worry was that Harvey was seventeen—a year older than Lauren. As Faith was fond of saying, though, "Lauren's in her thirties when she needs to be."

"Sure, darling. Mimi hasn't seen him in ages, and he's never been to her place. Have him come."

The mood at the McCardle residence on Friday was grim. Carl had a terrible time convincing Betty she should attend the Meet & Greet, and he wasn't high on going himself, but his mother's reaction to his visit the previous day convinced him he should show up. His wife didn't feel the need.

"Why don't I just meet you at Tony Roma's at 5:30?" Betty asked, as Carl changed his shirt.

"Because you need to see how Mother's getting along. It's only an hour or so, honey."

"Your mother can't stand me, and we never get along, Carl. I don't like to put up with her attitude in front of family, much less strangers."

Carl's jaw tightened. He slammed his closet door shut and turned to leave the house. "Fine. I'll see you later."

Betty reconsidered. Not spending an hour with Maybelle wasn't worth spoiling the whole evening with Carl.

"Oh, hell—I'll come along," she said, and followed him to the Beemer.

Mimi knocked on Harriett's door at 3:30 and entered when she heard, "Come on in!" Harriett needed help with her dress, which had buttons halfway down the back. She had asked Mimi at lunch if she'd stop by to help before the Meet & Greet.

"Mimi! You look beautiful!" exclaimed Harriett.

"Oh, dear, how you do go on," laughed Mimi. Her red hair was fluffed around her face, her lipstick gleamed and her eyes sparkled. She was in a lime green pantsuit and had on sandals with low heels. She buttoned Harriett's dress and moved toward the door.

"You look pretty darn good yourself, kid. I'm going to run down and see about Maybelle. Her son and daughter-in-law are coming and she's nervous."

"Why nervous?" asked Harriett.

"I think her daughter-in-law isn't as friendly as she'd like," said Mimi. "I'm going to sic Skipper on her and see if I can get Faith to spend some time with Maybelle."

"You're such an operator," chuckled Harriett. "I'll see you at 4:00."

"Maybelle, you're a sight for sore eyes," said Mimi, entering Maybelle's room. Maybelle was sitting in her recliner, feet up, afraid to wrinkle her skirt. She was all made up, and even had on mascara. Angel's handiwork of the previous day remained. Mimi wondered if Maybelle had slept in her chair Thursday night to preserve it.

Maybelle smiled. "You think so? How about these shoes?"

Mimi looked at Maybelle's swollen feet, crammed into low heels, and hoped there was another option.

"I'd wear flats if you think you'll be standing around meeting people." She remembered suddenly that her own shoes had heels, and added, "Especially if your feet hurt."

Maybelle looked distressed.

"Let's see what you've got," said Mimi, opening the closet door.

"Oh! Look at these!"

Mimi handed Maybelle a pair of well worn Naturalizers. "I'll bet these are comfortable."

Maybelle looked relieved. She gave Mimi her heels and slipped on the flats. "You're so good to me," she said, struggling to get out of the recliner.

❧   ❧   ❧

Low music and loud voices greeted Mimi and Maybelle as they entered the living room. It was 3:50. Nearly half the chairs and both couches were filled with residents; many had their walkers in front of them. Julie and Terry were asking folks for drink orders. Mack was sniffing everyone's legs and wagging his tail. When Dot spotted Maybelle she walked over and hugged her, and then hugged Mimi.

"As our newest residents, you two are our guests of honor," she said, beaming.

Maybelle looked delighted. She nodded "yes" to Terry when he asked her if she wanted wine, and then returned a hug from Julie. Virginia sidled over to them and began talking to Maybelle about her hair, and Mimi moved to Sarah's couch and took her bearings. It was going to be a great party. She could feel it in her bones.

❧   ❧   ❧

At 4:15 a large group of non-residents arrived at the same time and moved into the living room from the hall. Faith, Skipper and Lauren descended on Mimi amid laughter and more hugs. Across the room Pete and Harvey began talking with Terry. Julie and a pretty young girl were watching the three men and whispering to Minnie in a corner. Minnie looked like she was about to fall down laughing. As Mimi moved toward Pete, Maybelle was surrounded by Lauren, Faith and Skipper. She assured them all that she was doing just fine now. Somewhere in the background noise Mimi could hear Tony Bennett singing "I Left My Heart in San Francisco," and at intervals Mack would let out a short bark, but she couldn't see him. Suddenly there was an arm around her shoulder, and she looked up into the face of Henry, who grinned down at her, his crisp, clear blue eyes looking especially friendly. Mimi had never seen him without a cap, and was surprised to find that he had a lovely head of silver hair.

"Well, you made it!" she exclaimed.

"I sure did—it looks like a happening place," said Henry. "What can I get you?"

"I'll take a glass of white wine and Sprite on the rocks, thanks," said Mimi, and Henry took off for the drink table.

Dot approached Mimi with a well-dressed couple, and introduced them as Betty and Carl, Maybelle's daughter-in-law and son.

"How good to meet you," Mimi said. "I'm Maybelle's official Buddy—or was. She doesn't much need me any more."

"Are you the one who helped her put her things away?" asked Carl.

"Well, my daughter and her friend did most of it," said Mimi. "They're always there when I need them. Oh—here's Skipper now."

Skipper flowed across the room toward them and introductions were made. She was wearing a low cut black top, tight white Capris and high-heeled black sandals. She gushed, "Oh, I heard so much about you two the night we put Maybelle's things away. It's good to put your names with your faces!" She flashed her megawatt smile at both of them, and continued, "How awful to have to leave town the same day you move a family member."

Betty and Carl looked at each other.

"Uh," said Carl.

"Um," said Betty.

Skipper motioned Faith over.

"Faith, these are Maybelle's kids, Carl and Betty."

"So good to meet you," said Faith, sensing that Carl and Betty were feeling uncomfortable. "We've so enjoyed your mother. How's she doing?"

"I think she's beginning to adjust," said Carl. "I understand it takes a few months to get acclimated."

"Maybe for some," Faith said. "I think Mother was acclimated the day she moved in. Your mother may just need a little more time." She looked around the now crowded living room for Lauren, finally finding her near the veranda doors with Julie and a nice looking older gentleman. She caught Lauren's eye and waved. Lauren said something to the tall man, and both of them began working their way toward Faith, stopping to say "Hi" to Sarah, who was grinning and nodding at everyone who passed, and patting Mack, who now sat on a footstool at her feet.

"Henry!" Mimi said as they approached.

Lauren and Henry joined Faith, Skipper and the McCardles. Introductions were in order for Henry, who hadn't met any of them. Mimi introduced him as a Harmony Hall volunteer, and added that most of his volunteer time was in the garden. Faith exchanged glances with Skipper and then Lauren, knowing her goddaughter would be fascinated by a friendship between Mimi and an older man.

"I'm so glad you've met my goddaughter, Lauren," said Faith. "She's beginning to garden since Mimi came to Harmony Hall."

"I *know* Lauren," said Henry. She's helped me pick beans and deadhead roses. She's becoming quite a naturalist."

Faith was speechless. "Really!?"

"She helps me out before she goes in to see Mimi, and usually takes her a rose."

Henry and Mimi began talking with Betty and Carl, and Angel walked up and introduced herself to Faith.

"We just love your mother. Aren't you just too excited about her new friend?" she said, under her breath.

Faith watched Henry and Mimi as they walked back to the veranda. "You mean Henry?" she asked.

"Yes! She *had* to have a rinse yesterday, two weeks ahead of schedule, because he was coming today."

Faith laughed. *Well, I'll be darned.* "I didn't know that, but I'm not surprised," she said.

"Everybody's excited for her," said Angel. "I hope it develops, don't you?"

"If it's meant to be," said Faith. Worry lines began to form as she watched her mother smile up at Henry across the crowded room.

Julie and Trish walked out onto the veranda.

"What do you think?" asked Julie.

"I think he's great," said Trish. "He's got a swell sense of humor. Is he dating now?"

"I honestly don't know," said Julie. "I meant to ask him and just got too busy. I can find out next week. Do you think you'd like to go out with him?"

"He'd be a lot of fun," said Trish.

At 5:20 Julie asked each person at the Meet & Greet to shout out a number between one and forty. The person who had the number she'd written on a slip

and given to Dot for safekeeping, or who came the closest to it, would win the homegrown flower arrangement now gracing the piano.

"Twenty-two" said Betty, Maybelle's daughter, when Julie nodded that it was her turn to guess.

"YES!" exclaimed Dot. "It's yours, Betty! Congratulations!" Betty looked shocked but pleased as she took the vase of mixed garden flowers from Dot.

"Home grown and picked fresh this morning!" said Dot.

Maybelle happily clapped with the rest of the residents and guests. Carl actually laughed as his wife took the bouquet around to show to those less lucky.

At 5:30 the Meet & Greet guests began to move toward the lobby. Mimi hugged Faith, Skipper, Lauren and Pete goodbye, thinking as she did it how dear they were to visit. Henry was having dinner with her, and together they joined Harriett, Eloise, Bertha and Minnie in the dining room. Camille moved to another table for the meal to allow Mimi and Henry to sit together. Cookie, the evening cook, came 'round to ask if anyone wanted wine, and everyone at the table, feeling celebratory with Henry present, asked for a glass. Minnie pulled her wig down tight on her head and left it there. Eloise didn't drop a thing in her lap. Bertha's plate stayed where it belonged. Harriett was charming. Henry and Mimi held hands for a moment under the table.

Julie surveyed the dining room and counted noses, listening to the chatter and eruptions of laughter. She had done it. This was, she was sure, the best Meet & Greet ever.

CHAPTER 18

AU REVOIR

It was Sunday. Babe stood on Faith's deck, half heartedly pointing at the doves making circles below Faith's backyard feeder, turning her head slightly to watch Faith's reaction.

"She's never been taught to do that," chuckled Mimi, putting her coffee down. "Isn't it fascinating that the pointing just comes out of nowhere?"

Faith smiled slightly at both of them. She had invited her mother over this morning to have breakfast, but knew that today they would have to talk about Mimi's plans for the future. Tuesday was September 1. Her mother's half of Pete's duplex was still not rented and many of Mimi's possessions remained in it. Mimi needed to move back in, or move her things out. Faith thought back to May and the horrific accident that had claimed Joyce's life and nearly killed Mimi. Remarkably, in only a few months her mother had recovered. On some days she was stiffer than others, but her old spark was back. Faith's memories of those early days after the accident were fuzzy. She marveled at how much had changed in their lives since then and how much fuller her mother's life now seemed. Did Mimi feel the same way? Did she miss her apartment and her kitchen? She had never mentioned either to Faith since the move to Harmony Hall.

"Mother, we need to talk about the duplex."

Mimi turned from watching Babe and the birds, her eyes hidden behind huge sunglasses with purple frames.

"You know, dear, I've been thinking the same thing. Seems like I've been gone from it for years, doesn't it?"

Faith nodded.

Mimi continued, "I think we should run over there and take a look at it. Do you have time?"

"Sure. Shall we go now?" Faith asked.

"No time like the present," said Mimi. "Let's take Babe and stop by the park on the way home."

Faith grabbed her purse. She wasn't sure what her mother had in mind, but at least the subject was out in the open.

"C'mon, Babe," she said, and fumbled for her keys.

Faith pulled into the driveway on Mimi's side of Pete's duplex. Apparently the pharmaceutical rep who was now living in Joyce's old apartment was away. She didn't answer the doorbell and there was no car in her driveway. It was hot, and the grass was turning brown. No one had been tending the planter that ran along the front of the building, and weeds had overgrown the azaleas that Mimi once fertilized religiously. Her old bird feeder under the kitchen window was gone, but the shepherd's crook remained, leaning askew. Two old copies of the Lexington Herald-Leader, yellowed in their plastic wrappers, lay on the small front porch. The yard, once filled with birds and scurrying chipmunks, seemed lifeless in the heat. Mimi made it up the steps easily, but had a hard time finding the proper key for her front door. She and Faith were both silent as they entered her apartment and surveyed the musty living room. Several small plants were dead in their pots on the windowsill. A few boxes remained beneath the dining room table, leftovers from the day Faith, Skipper and Lauren were there packing things up for the move to Harmony Hall. Mimi walked to the back door, opened it, and stepped out onto the concrete slab at the rear of the building. There were leaves in her two folding chairs. The birdbath was dry, and the marigolds she had planted in early May around its base were dead. The backyard looked small and rough now, unmowed and overgrown. Mimi brushed the leaves out of both chairs and sat down in one, motioning Faith to do the same in the other. They sat together without speaking for several minutes.

"It doesn't seem like the same place, does it?" Mimi asked.

"It just needs a little TLC, Mom. Remember, you've been gone for months."

Mimi was silent. Faith began to imagine her mother's day at the duplex without Joyce. Get up. Make breakfast. Watch some TV. Work in the yard.

Maybe go out with an old tennis friend. Make supper. Watch some TV. Go to bed. She suddenly knew why Mimi wanted to stop by. It was to compare the new with the old, to reassure herself that this period of her life was over. Her mother seemed too vibrant for the duplex now that Joyce was gone; she needed more outlets than Pete's place could provide. Even more important, Mimi needed to be needed.

Babe ran around the perimeter of the back yard, coming up birdless. She flopped at Faith's feet, panting in the heat. Mimi took off her sunglasses and chewed on the end of one purple sunglass arm.

"Faith, do you want me to come back here?"

"Mother, I want you to be happy wherever you are. It's totally up to you."

"Then I think I'll stay put," said Mimi, standing up and reentering the dark apartment.

"Now, where are we going to store all this stuff?" She picked an empty box off the floor, as if ready to start packing that minute.

Dot had staff meetings only when necessary. She and Terry talked off and on all day and both of them were good about filling Julie and Jim in on developments. Today, Monday, Evie had some questions, and it seemed a good time to get everyone together. Dot asked Kitty McElroy to sit in the lobby and answer the phone and take messages for about fifteen minutes, while the five of them met. Kitty would also answer the door.

"We'll make this short, guys," Dot said. "I know you've all got a lot to do. Evie, what's up?"

"I'm worried about Eloise," said Evie. "She's not eating enough to keep a tick alive."

Julie made a face at the reference to a tick, and Terry made a gagging sound.

"The other thing I'm worried about is Sarah," continued Evie. "Cookie called me at home last night. Seems Sarah came down to the dining room in her slip. Minnie grabbed her before she got to her seat and took her back upstairs to get some clothes on. When she came back down she had her dress on inside out and two different shoes on. What's going on with her?"

Dot could feel a knot begin to form in her stomach. Evie was right, of course. Sarah was becoming inappropriate for life at Harmony Hall. Minnie was covering for her. Hell, all of them were covering for her, which would have to stop before long.

"Evie, Sarah's developing some dementia. It makes her do things that don't make sense to the rest of us," said Dot.

"Is she taking any medicine for it?" Julie asked.

"Yes," said Dot. "We're giving her pill envelopes filled by her family at breakfast and supper, but she may be taking them back to her room. She's been known to use them as decoys for her nephew."

Nobody laughed. They were all furious at the apparition that would ultimately force Sarah to leave, and Dot and Terry sometimes found themselves talking about him as if he were real.

"Carmen told me she found Sarah in the lobby at 2:00 A.M. one morning last week," said Terry.

"What was she doing?" asked Dot, knowing that Terry had kept this bit of information to himself to protect Sarah.

"She was looking out the lobby doors. Carmen heard Sarah talking to herself through the walls of her apartment. She thinks Sarah was yelling for the police."

"Dammit, Terry, why didn't you tell me this earlier?" said Dot, knowing why he hadn't told her.

Julie's eyes widened. She had never heard Dot curse before, and she couldn't believe Dot was talking to Terry this way.

"I'm sorry, Dot. I was afraid we'd have to make her leave," said Terry, looking miserable.

"You know we're going to let her stay as long as it's safe for her," said Dot, "but things are escalating. She'll be wandering down Main Street if this continues, and we won't know it. Then it will really get interesting around here. I'm sorry I said 'dammit,'" Dot said, looking at Julie. "I'm going to call Sarah's niece, and let her know what's going on. Evie, when Cookie gets in, tell her I want to talk to her about watching Sarah and her medication at night. Eloise is probably having a hard time passing bowls and can't see well enough to serve herself what she likes. What do you think about plating her food?"

Dot, above all others, knew that Evie was the most indispensable employee at Harmony Hall. If the head cook wasn't happy, no one was happy. A twenty-eight year employee, Evie had seen it all. In the last ten years she'd made many changes at Dot's urging, but Dot was careful to ask Evie's opinion before varying a procedure.

"Sure—that's no problem," said Evie.

"Fine, let me talk to her and I'll get back to you. What else is going on?"

Julie looked at Terry and back at Dot.

"There was a terrible smell coming from Virginia's room today. I went in, and she had a Depends in her bathroom window. I asked her why, and she said she was airing it out so she could re-use it. Can they be used twice?"

Dot rubbed her temples. "No, Julie, they're supposed to be thrown away after one use. Virginia's just too cheap to use anything once."

Terry grinned at Dot, and said to Julie, "I swear this is true, Julie—I saw Virginia wash some paper plates once, and she used them when her ex-neighbor's son stopped by to see her."

Julie looked horrified.

"Is she that poor?"

"No," Terry said, "she's that cheap."

"So, Julie, where's the Depends now?" asked Dot, trying to get back on track.

"I told her I felt she needed to get it into a plastic bag and out of her window" said Julie. "I think she did."

"That's exactly right," Dot said. "Jim, would you check her room? If we need to buy one of those plug-in air freshener things for the short term, let's do it. I'll talk to her later today about her Depends."

Suddenly a voice came over the public address system, and they all jumped: "DON'T YOU THINK YOU OUGHT TO PUT YER DENTURES IN?"

Terry and Dot exchanged glances; he raced to the lobby. Kitty had hit the "PAGE" button in error, and everything she said was being broadcast throughout the building.

Camille came to the door of Dot's office. Mack was with her, tail held high, leash firmly grasped in his mouth. He was going for a walk.

"Hey guys, sorry to interrupt, but there's a sour smell coming from the laundry room. You might want to check it out, Jim."

"Sure, Camille, thanks," said Dot. Mack dragged his favorite resident to the door, anxious to get outside.

Terry returned, grinning. "I think she's got the hang of it now. She apologizes."

The phone rang and all five held their breath, but Kitty seemed to have answered it without hitting "PAGE."

"Sorry for the interruption," said Dot. "Jim, that sour smell is probably Virginia's Depends. I'll talk to her about buying some airtight bags—you can bet she's using something from the grocery store that ties at the top. You have anything else?"

"Someone's failing to turn off the faucet completely in the downstairs shower room," said Jim. "We've got a sign posted in there, but three or four residents on this floor are legally blind. They may be missing it."

"Julie, find out how many ladies on the first floor use that shower," Dot said. "Just explain to them how important it is to turn off the water, and to keep that handheld sprayer pointed away from the curtain—there's no real lip on the floor to keep the water in. Anything else, Jim?"

"Someone's leaving her milk in the lobby bathroom every morning. I find it when I go in to empty the trash."

"It's Camille," Terry said. "She leaves it there while she walks Mack and forgets about it. I'll take care of it." His eyes twinkled as he thought about approaching Camille with the milk.

"Anything else?" Dot asked.

They were silent.

"This probably affects Jim more than anyone else because he does most of our driving. I have good news and bad news, guys."

"We need good news," said Terry. "Good news first, Dot."

"The board has approved the purchase of a ten passenger van."

"Hurrah!" said Jim, making a fist and reaching for the ceiling.

"We can take more than six people out to eat!" said Julie.

"It's long overdue," said Dot. "The bad news is that our investments aren't making enough money to keep the endowment where it should be, and it's likely we'll have to raise rents in January."

"How long has it been since they were raised?" asked Julie.

"About six years. I'd rather pull out my eyeteeth than raise rents, but something has to give. Everything keeps going up except earnings on investments. If it happens, it will be January." Dot looked resigned. Her eyes met Terry's. "I'll let you know about my conversation with Sarah's niece. I'm sorry, guys, but she may have to move soon."

It was 7:30 P.M. The entertainers who began at 6:30 were gone, and most residents were in their rooms. Sarah pawed through her underwear drawer, looking frantically for her underpants with the wide lace edging. Not finding them there, she moved to her dirty clothes hamper, pulled everything out, and exclaimed, "No!" Muttering, she then began emptying the drawers in her little desk, moving from there to the built-in shelves on the right side of her closet.

In minutes her room was a shambles. Small piles of clothes lay everywhere, along with documents, old Christmas cards, shoes, and an assortment of empty pill bottles.

"He's done it, he's done it," she repeated, and left her room, dragging her mother's heavy metal walker behind her. In a full slip and barefoot, she nearly collided with Mimi and Minnie as they rounded the corner from the opposite direction.

"Sarah! Where 'ya goin'?" asked Minnie.

"He's done it, he's done it," whispered Sarah.

Mimi and Minnie exchanged glances.

"What's up?" Minnie asked, holding Sarah's arm.

"I've got to get help," said Sarah.

Mimi gently turned Sarah around. "Let us help you, honey," she said.

The three of them slowly made their way back to Sarah's room, and together began again the search for her underwear.

It was 8:45 A.M.; time to check on folks who still weren't down for breakfast. Dot scanned the tables, counting noses and pouring coffee. Three of the thirty-five seats were empty. Two residents were out of the building; the third empty seat belonged to Sarah, who needed reminding at nearly every meal that it was time to eat. Sarah wasn't eating much these days. Obsessed with her nephew, frantic and fatigued, she was slipping away from them. Dot told Evie she was going up to check on Sarah, and grabbed the master key from the key box next to Terry's office. She pondered Sarah's situation as she walked up the stairs. Sarah's niece had cried on the phone the previous day when Dot told her it was time for her aunt to move to a personal care home, but agreed that it had to be done. Sarah was one of the few residents who could afford a higher level of care, for which Dot was grateful. She knocked on Sarah's door.

"Sarah?"

Dot put her ear to the door, listening for a rustle or muttering, or the sound of the toilet flushing.

"Sarah, honey, it's Dot."

Dot hated to open a resident's door. She crossed the hall to the public phone on the table and dialed Sarah's number. No one answered. Retracing her steps, Dot unlocked the door and entered the room. Sarah was still in bed, the spread pulled up to her chin, her head turned away from the door, facing the windows.

"Sarah? It's time for breakfast." Dot moved to the bed and patted Sarah's hip gently. "Sarah?"

There was no movement beneath the cover. Dot walked around the foot of the bed. Sarah's eyes were slightly open; there was a half smile on her face.

"Sarah!!" Dot's voice had a desperate edge. She shook Sarah's right shoulder, then searched for her dearest resident's wrist, knowing she was too late. She grabbed Sarah's phone and dialed 911.

Terry walked in as Dot hung up. She was crying, and looking around Sarah's room for a Kleenex.

"Oh, Dot," said Terry, beginning to cry as well. He hugged her, and they sat on the bed. Terry stroked Sarah's hair softly. "She was the brightest woman I ever knew," he said.

"There will never be another like her," murmured Dot. She surveyed the room. Sarah was childless; few family pictures adorned her walls. Three tan pill envelopes were pushed between the window and the sill—Sarah's last decoy for the nephew who would no longer make her life miserable. Several bureau drawers were pulled out; clothes hung from them, half in, half out.

"I'm calling her niece," said Dot. "Do you mind waiting here until the EMS guys arrive?"

"I'll take care of her," said Terry, wiping his eyes.

Julie bounced in at 1:58 and ran to gather her bingo cards.

"Julie? Got just a second?" Dot was standing in her office doorway.

"I'm late, Dot—I'm so sorry."

"It's OK, they'll wait a minute."

"What's up?" asked Julie, breathless.

"Honey, Sarah died sometime during the night."

"What?" Julie sank into the nearest chair, eyes brimming.

"I wanted to tell you," said Dot. "The ladies all know—Terry and I went door to door this morning."

"Oh, Dot—our beautiful, smart Sarah."

"I know, Julie, it's so hard to believe." She handed Julie a Kleenex.

"How are the ladies?" Julie asked.

"As always, they're amazing. They've been through this so many times in their lives, you know. Death is less a mystery to them. Will you be OK?"

Julie nodded, wordless. Dot listened to her trudge up the stairs to the parlor.

"Hello, ladies…" Julie broke down momentarily.

Dot moved to the bottom of the stairs. Above her, there were understanding murmurs from eighteen experienced survivors, all empathizing with Julie's pain.

"I'm sorry…I'm still in shock," she heard Julie say.

There was a brief silence, a sound of sniffling, a nose being blown.

"Here's to Sarah! Are we ready?"

Dot smiled. *I love that girl.*

❦   ❦   ❦

Dot buzzed Terry at 3:00. "I'm going to the garden, unless you need me."

"We're good. Have fun."

"Thanks. I've got my cell phone if anything comes up."

She walked to the big refrigerator in the laundry room, grabbed a beer from her six pack in the vegetable crisper, stuck it in her sport bag and walked to the garden shed. As she'd done a hundred times, Dot changed quickly in the shed and threw her bag, minus the beer, in her car. She slipped the beer in a Styrofoam holder, put on a visor and garden gloves and started to weed with a vengeance. After an hour in the 90-degree heat, she sat on the bench under the entry oak and sipped on her beer. A hummingbird darted between sprays of hyacinth bean blooms that trailed up the screen between the garden and the shed. A robin landed two yards away, eyed Dot, and began searching the newly turned soil, enjoying a secondary benefit of her weeding.

I will miss you so, dear Sarah. Are you still here, flitting around our home and garden, finally connected and at peace with your family? Do you understand my relief that you died here, where you are loved and understood? Thank you for sparing us all the heartache of seeing you move, knowing you'd be among strangers who couldn't possibly understand your history and potential.

Dot watched two swallowtail butterflies trade places as they moved fluidly from coneflowers to garden phlox and back to coneflowers, remembering the times Sarah had walked the garden path, back hunched, turning her head to admire the same species. It seemed at that moment Dot could hear Sarah's exclamations of delight. She picked up her cultivator and tucked her fondest memories of Sarah in a safe place, deep in her heart.

CHAPTER 19

EMPLOYMENT

SEPTEMBER, 1998

Lauren gazed out the window, wishing she were any place but school. It was a Business Education class and so far it was a bore. As usual, Lauren had been remiss in checking out her options, and had just discovered that the class was also a work/study program. She was going to have to find a job for three months—one that had something to do with business—for eight to ten hours a week. The class would study "Interviewing Techniques" and "How to be a Valuable Employee" for two weeks, and then they were on their own. She met Harvey outside the gym and walked with him to the bus stop.

"I've got to get a freakin' job for my Business Ed. class," Lauren said, disconsolately. "What a crock."

"They're taking apps at Wendy's," Harvey said, helpfully.

"I think I have to do something in an office where I can type on a computer. We're going to practice interviewing and I have to report back to Mrs. Fatgut after every job interview."

"Well, Mrs. Farragut probably told you it's a good time to go job hunting," said Harvey. "People will want to take time off for the holidays, and you can fill in."

Lauren punched his arm. "You're so positive, darling—just what I didn't want to hear." She was beginning to sound like her mother.

❦   ❦   ❦

"Mom, I've got to get a part-time job for Business Ed. They need you to sign this authorization saying it's OK." She added hopefully, "You don't have to if you don't want to."

Skipper was doing her eyebrows—she didn't trust the salon with her eyebrows or her upper lip.

"Great! Your first real job! How exciting, darling!" said Skipper, turning from her 10X mirror and putting on her reading glasses.

Lauren's usual "I know it all" attitude seemed strangely absent. Skipper signed the form and grinned at Lauren over her specs. "Do you have any ideas?" she asked.

"No. What do you think?"

"Well, you know I'm an expert on working," said Skipper, with a short laugh. "I'd say you've got two good possibilities."

"What?"

"Faith and Dot. Both those places would be great to work in and you already know the bosses!"

Lauren looked shocked. "You're right! Thanks, Mom." Impetuously she hugged Skipper.

"I'm calling Dot tomorrow."

❦   ❦   ❦

Terry answered the phone when Lauren called during her lunch break the next day.

"Terry? It's Lauren, Mimi's great goddaughter."

"Lauren! How's school?"

Lauren giggled. Terry was so enthusiastic about everything.

"It sucks. How's work?"

"It sucks sometimes. Did you know that Sarah died yesterday?"

"Oh, no." Lauren was speechless. Sarah was the only person she'd ever known in real life who had died.

"Aside from that, work's great," Terry said.

Lauren was silent.

"You still there?" asked Terry.

"Oh, I'm so sorry," said Lauren.

"Thanks, honey. We all loved her, and we will never forget her. That's about the best that can be said for anyone who dies."

"Well, I guess I need to talk to Dot," said Lauren, with dampened spirits. She remembered Sarah's lovely smile and how she and Harvey had laughed about the dragged walker.

"Hold on," said Terry.

"Dot Turner," answered Dot, when her extension rang.

"Dot, it's Lauren, Mimi's great goddaughter."

"Lauren! What do you know?"

"I know I need a job for eight hours a week 'til the end of the year for Business Ed. You don't need to pay me, Dot—it's mostly for experience."

Dot thought for a second. "Do you have computer experience?"

"Yes."

"Can you answer a telephone?"

"Yes."

"Are you empathetic, sympathetic, conscientious, loving and patient?"

"I think so—when I'm there."

Dot laughed. "Well then, let's set up an interview and get you on board."

❧   ❧   ❧

Skipper drained her Merlot and called Faith. "Guess what! Lauren's got a job!"

"You're kidding! Where?"

"Harmony Hall! She came home yesterday with a Business Ed. authorization for a work/study program, and Dot hired her this afternoon."

"Oh, Skipper, how wonderful! Is she excited?"

"I think she is, darling. I know I am! Imagine—my daughter with a real job. It's a milestone!"

"When does she start?" Faith asked.

"Next Monday, at 3:00. How 'bout dinner at 5:30 that night to celebrate—with Lauren?"

"You're on," said Faith.

❧   ❧   ❧

"Mimi, it's me."

"Lauren, dear, how are you?"

Mimi and Henry were deadheading roses together; Mimi held her cell under her chin and continued snipping as she talked.

"Great! Guess what?"

"What?"

"I'm going to start working there on Monday!"

"What?"

"I have to have a real job for Business Ed. and Dot hired me!"

"That's wonderful! What will you be doing?"

"I don't know everything, but I'll be doing some work on the newsletter and walking Mack, for starters."

Mimi thought back to the previous year, when Lauren's only excitement was generated by a new tattoo or a pair of high-heeled sandals.

"I can't wait to see you, dear, and I'm so proud of you. Let me know how I can help."

"OK, see you soon, Mimi." Lauren hung up and went looking for Skipper. They needed to talk work clothes.

Julie checked Mack's bowl for food, and realized that for the fourth consecutive day she didn't need to feed him before she left—his bowl was still full.

"Dot, have you fed Mack this week?"

"No, his bowl's been full," said Dot, checking her e-mails.

"I haven't fed him all week, either," said Julie.

"Nuts!" Dot exclaimed. "Somebody's slipping Mack table scraps and dog snacks."

"I could barely fasten his halter yesterday," said Julie. "He's getting fat."

"Let me talk to Camille. If she's not feeding him, she'll know who is."

Dot cornered Camille later the same day.

"Camille, somebody's feeding Mack. He's gaining weight and not touching his food. What do you think?"

"Hmmm. I'm feeding him his dried food in my room—but nothing else."

"You know he can't have wet food or table scraps," said Dot, "they're bad for his teeth."

"Well, come to think of it, every now and then I do moisten his food with a little chicken broth and put just a few little pieces of chicken breast on top." Camille looked chagrined.

"Camille, we've got to stop it—he's getting too fat and before you know it we'll be having to get his teeth cleaned. We can't afford it this year. Is anyone else feeding him?"

"I don't know. You know how he is."

"Totally irresistible," said Dot. "I'll put out a memo."

ANNOUNCEMENTS

> *Our little dog, Mack, is so heavy*
> *His halter won't fit 'round his belly.*
> *If you want him to stay here,*
> *Be healthy, with eyes clear,*
> *Don't give him table scraps and jelly!*

*Ladies: Please resist the urge to feed Mack—we're endangering his life when we feed him anything besides his dry dog food—which he should **only** be eating in the office bathroom. Thanks for your help in keeping Mack healthy and happy.*

*On Monday, September 12, **Lauren Collier,** Mimi's great goddaughter, will begin working at Harmony Hall on a temporary part-time basis to complete require-ments for her Business Education class. Please welcome Lauren when you have the opportunity.*
9/9/98

CHAPTER 20

GOTCHA

Dot and Julie sat on the balcony overlooking the courtyard in the most comfortable chairs at Harmony Hall. As they swiveled and rocked the early afternoon sun began to have a soporific effect on both of them; Dot couldn't stop yawning and Julie nearly fell asleep while Dot recorded her answers to the Harmony Hall Exit Interview. It was Friday, Julie's last official day as an intern. In a few months she would graduate from college. Julie turned her gaze from the bubbling courtyard fountain to Dot.

"I would love to work here full time, Dot. I can't imagine working in Social Services now."

"Wouldn't you be serving the same aging population in Social Services?"

"Sometimes, maybe. It just depends where you're placed or what's available. Most of the folks I've worked with aren't as sweet as these ladies. There's usually a terrible problem in the family—drugs, abuse, incest, unwanted pregnancy—it's so depressing. When I walk into Harmony Hall, it's like walking into a big house of grandmothers. They may have some physical problems, but their environment and their support system is great. I think I'm spoiled, Dot."

"I'm afraid we're all spoiled here, Julie. You must know, though, that it's not always smooth sailing. I've had residents whose sons or daughters would pop in to pay the rent and never take the time to say "Hi" to them. We had a bag lady with no family who came from a house with junk piled so high that she'd made tunnels in it and slept in the backyard at night where she could stretch out. A year or so ago a woman lived here who was so jealous of Camille that she refused to ride in the car with her. Another gal threatened once to wrap her walker around Virginia's neck. It's not all wine and roses—even here."

Below them, sparrows in the Sweet Bay magnolia were softly chittering. A pair of doves floated down to pick at the pavers near the fountain. Dot and Julie were silent, each lost in thoughts of past experiences. Someone let Mack into the courtyard. They watched as he quickly chased the doves off, took a drink from the base of the fountain, and began looking for critters under the landscape plants. A minute later the courtyard door opened. Maybelle walked in and shuffled to the bench beneath the magnolia.

"Uh-oh," said Julie. "We have a problem."

"Maybe he'll steer clear of her," said Dot.

Maybelle settled on the bench, and opened a small paper bag that she'd carried in her walker basket. Mack burst from the foliage along the periphery of the courtyard and bounded toward Maybelle.

"Oh, no," Julie and Dot whispered, in unison.

Maybelle moved to the corner of the bench. Dot began to stand up to yell at Mack from the balcony when she noticed that Maybelle's left hand was patting the seat next to her. Mack jumped on the bench and stared at Maybelle. She pulled something out of the bag and he carefully took it from her and chewed, tail wagging furiously. Maybelle's thin fingers softly stroked his silver fur, and Mack finally lay down with his chin on her lap. It was obvious this wasn't their first rendezvous in the courtyard.

"Well, there you are," said Dot, settling back in her chair and smiling delightedly at Julie. "I guess she didn't read the memo."

Harvey did a double take at the bus stop on Monday morning. Lauren was wearing Chinos, loafers and a short-sleeved blouse, tucked in. Her eyebrow and nose rings were gone. Her hair, though still spiky, looked less electric than usual. He slid in next to her on the bus.

"I take it you're working today," he laughed.

"How'd you ever guess?"

"I can't quite put my finger on it, but you look different," said Harvey.

Lauren punched his leg. It was going to be a tough day at school.

❧   ❧   ❧

At 2:30 Skipper's Mercedes convertible rolled to a stop in front of Henry Clay High School. Lauren jumped in, eyes hidden behind Gucci sunglasses.

"Hey," said Skipper. "How goes it?"

"I'm OK."

"Are you nervous?"

"No…well, maybe a little. I already know almost everybody there, so it's not like I'm going to a strange place. Plus, Mimi's there. She said she'd help me if she could."

"You'll be great, kiddo. I can't wait to hear all about it."

"Did you have a job when you were my age?" asked Lauren.

"Actually, I did. Your grandmother refused to get me a telephone in my room, and I was furious. I decided to earn the money for it myself and got a job one summer working in the office of Dixon Nut and Bolt. I think I'd worked a week before I realized not only did Dixon sell nuts but he *was* a nut. I quit when he started making advances." She looked over her sunglass rims at Lauren. "I doubt you'll have that problem at Harmony Hall."

Lauren laughed. She couldn't imagine having any problems at Mimi's place.

❧   ❧   ❧

"Lauren, why don't you sit in the lobby today and just get used to answering the phones and the door." Dot explained how to answer and transfer a call, put someone on hold and use the intercom. It all looked pretty simple to Lauren.

"We don't have voice mail here because I don't want a resident who calls with an emergency to get a recording. So be sure to take complete messages. Always put the time the person called, and always ask them for their telephone number so we don't have to look it up to call back. We have a rule that every call must be answered by the third ring. If you're on the phone and no one here answers another call that comes in by the third ring, put your caller on hold and answer the ringing phone."

Dot showed Lauren the button that would unlock the door if she happened to be on the phone when someone needed to come inside. "You'll have plenty of people to talk with out here, Lauren. This lobby's a gathering place, and we have lots of people coming in and going out." Dot left Lauren a pink message pad and a directory of extensions. "Call me if you need me," she said, and headed back to her office.

Virginia Wilhoite ambled by Lauren's desk and sat in the chair near the lobby door. Minnie came around the corner and perched on the couch behind the lobby desk. Both of them told Lauren how happy they were to see her working at Harmony Hall, and Lauren flushed with pleasure. Her first call came within minutes. It was a man from the telephone company, calling to say that the Harmony Hall phone lines needed to be tested. The lobby phone, he said, was the primary test phone. He explained to Lauren that to test a line she needed to put him on hold, punch in the third button on the panel and yell "TESTING" at the top of her lungs. The telephone company would monitor the volume on that line.

"How many times do I need to yell 'testing'?" Lauren asked.

"You'll probably need to yell it three or four times," the repairman said. "Then yell 'DO YOU HEAR ME'? It'll take a few seconds, but I'll call you back right away if everything's OK."

"OK," said Lauren. "I'm going to do it now."

"Good…thanks. I'll be back in touch."

Lauren explained to Minnie and Virginia that she was going to have to help test the phones. She hit the third line button. "TESTING…TESTING…TEST-ING," she yelled, at the top of her lungs, breaking the lobby silence. "DO YOU HEAR ME?"

Virginia said, "Yes, I do, very well."

Minnie said, "If they can't hear that they're stone deaf!"

The phone rang as Dot ran from her office toward the lobby to find out why Lauren was yelling.

"Good afternoon, Harmony Hall," said Lauren, as she'd been taught by Dot.

"Telephone man here. You came through loud and clear…" The voice broke into laughter and the repairman hung up.

Behind her, Lauren could hear Minnie laughing so hard she was gasping for breath, but she was afraid to turn around because Dot was standing in front of her looking concerned. Lauren explained the test procedure to Dot.

"Oh, Lauren, I'm afraid Terry has struck again," said Dot, with a smile. "He's the biggest practical joker I know—and I think you've just been got."

Terry poked his head around the corner. "Lauren? Have you been having any trouble with those phone lines?" He and Minnie convulsed in peals of laughter.

Lauren giggled, thinking of how silly she must have sounded. "You just wait, Terry. It will all come back."

By 4:00 Lauren had opened the lobby door for eight family members and three home health workers, transferred two calls to Dot and two to the kitchen, and directed a plumber to Harriet's room. She read a memo to Eloise, who was practically blind. She changed "September" to "October" on the newsletter Dot showed her on the computer. Suddenly Mimi was at the lobby door, holding two buckets. One was full of zinnias, the other held the last of the summer's tomatoes. Her face was flushed beneath a visor that read, "Sanibel Island, Florida".

"Mimi!" Lauren punched the entry button and Mimi came in.

"Honey—how's it going?" Mimi put the buckets down and hugged Lauren. Her neck was damp with perspiration, her tennis shoes, tied loosely, were stained with garden soil.

"It's great—except that Terry played a trick on me. We've got to figure out a way to get him back," Lauren said, laughing.

Mimi looked closely at Lauren, wondering at the transformation in her over the last six months. Was Skipper's daughter simply growing up, or was her association with Harmony Hall and its extended family working a small miracle?

"I'll be thinking. We'll pull something off. Can I bring you anything out here?"

"No, I'm great. I get off in an hour, and Mom and Faith are going to take me out to dinner. Can you come?"

"I'd love to, Lauren, but I've got plans. Henry promised to take me to a movie tonight." Grinning, she hoisted the buckets and started for the kitchen, passing Bertha, who was coming down the same hall to the lobby. Mack passed Bertha at full speed and gamboled in front of Lauren. It looked like he'd just been groomed. His legs were soft little cloud pillars; his body, as Julie was fond of saying, "a silver cotton ball." Mack hated to be groomed and always acted like he'd been released from prison when he returned to Harmony Hall.

"HOW ARE YOU, BERTHA?" Julie asked, in a loud voice.

"I'm pretty OK......." Bertha's plate flew out of her mouth and landed at Lauren's feet. Mack, acting fierce, jumped on it, clenched it in his sharp little teeth and took off around the corner of the lobby. Horrified, both Bertha and Lauren started after him. Lauren heard the phone and raced back to the desk to answer it by the third ring, noticing that someone was standing at the lobby door trying to figure out where the doorbell was.

"Good afternoon, Harmony Hall," Lauren said breathlessly, trying to reach the door buzzer.

"Good afternoon, darling, this is your mother," Skipper answered.

"Oh, Mom, I'm glad it's you. Hold on," Lauren said, and punched the hold button.

She ran to the door, opened it for the visitor, who, thankfully, knew where he was going, and ran for Dot's office, looking for Mack. She passed Bertha, who had been waylaid by Kitty. "Why don't you have your plate in?" Lauren heard Kitty saying.

"Dot!" Lauren burst into Dot's office. The director was talking to a middle aged couple and an elderly lady in a pink hat. "Oh, I'm so sorry to interrupt," Lauren said.

Dot knew from Lauren's look that something was up.

"Excuse me, just for a second," she said, following Lauren out of earshot.

"Dot," Lauren whispered, "Bertha's plate fell out in the lobby and Mack grabbed it and ran off. Have you seen him?"

"No—but he's probably in Camille's room. Go back to the lobby, Lauren, and call Terry on the intercom. He'll be able to track Mack down faster than anybody. Just ask him over the intercom to call the front lobby. Call me on my extension if you run into a problem." She smiled at Lauren. "You've had a pretty exciting first day, haven't you?"

Lauren ran back to the lobby. She noticed a phone blinking and remembered that Skipper was holding. "Mom?"

"Yes, dear," said Skipper, just a tinge of irritation creeping into her voice.

"Hold on just another minute," said Lauren.

She tried to remember how to work the intercom, but had to refer to her notes. Pushing "PAGE," she leaned into the speaker section of the phone and said, "Terry, please call the front lobby. Terry, please call the front lobby." Almost immediately her phone rang. "Terry, Mack's got Bertha's plate, and I don't know where he is. Can you try to find him and get it back?"

Terry said, "Sure, Lauren. Do me a favor, though. Hit the "RELEASE" button on your phone right now. You're being broadcast throughout the building."

In her office with a prospective resident and her children, Dot wondered if Lauren's intercom message had registered with them, and if there was any way in the world to cement that damn plate to Bertha's jaw.

❦   ❦   ❦

Skipper and Faith pulled up to the door at Harmony Hall at 6:00 and could see Eloise and Lauren sitting next to each other in the lobby, laughing, as Lauren did something to Eloise's face. When she saw the Mercedes, Lauren hugged Eloise and came out to the car. Faith got out and hugged Lauren, who climbed in the back seat.

"Mom, I'm sorry. By the time I got back to the desk you were off the line. I tried to call you at home…," Lauren's voice trailed off.

"It's OK. I only held for fifteen minutes," Skipper said, rolling her eyes at Faith.

"We had an emergency, and I couldn't talk. Mack got hold of Bertha's plate and took off, and I had to get someone to help find him. By the time I talked to Dot and figured out how to work the intercom, you were gone."

"What do you mean, 'Mack got hold of Bertha's plate'?"

"Her lower teeth fell out in the lobby and Mack thought her plate was a toy or something. He took it up to Camille's room and hid it under her bed."

Faith began to giggle, imagining Mack's little mouth clenched around Bertha's big teeth. Skipper looked over at her and back at Lauren.

"I knew you'd have a ball working there," she said, and turned the car toward their favorite barbecue place, red curls glinting in the late afternoon sun.

❦   ❦   ❦

Roger's Real Barbecue was nearly empty at 6:15 when Faith, Skipper and Lauren walked in. They found a table near the back window, ordered drinks and clinked their glasses in honor of Lauren's first day on the job.

"I wish Mother could be here to celebrate with us," said Faith. "She's going to dinner and the movies tonight with Henry."

"Hell, I'd rather be with him than us myself," said Skipper, winking at Lauren.

"Oh, Mother," said Lauren, laughing.

"Faith, Mimi's finally going to have some fun—you need to quit worrying about her."

"I s'pose so," said Faith. "I just wish I knew more about Henry—I've only met him once."

"He's super," said Lauren. "I see him all the time at Mimi's, and they do lots of things together in the garden. He's a real gentleman, and they laugh a lot."

"See there, Faith? Manners and a sense of humor—you can't ask for more." Skipper glanced around for a waiter. Her eyes fixed on Terry, dressed all in black and accompanied by a good looking young man, who had just entered the restaurant. They moved to a table near the front of the restaurant and were both laughing and talking with the hostess.

"Well, look who's here," said Skipper.

Faith and Lauren turned to watch Terry and his friend find a table. Once seated, the men began talking in earnest, and all three women saw the other man take Terry's hand in both of his.

Skipper turned back to the menu, a slight smile on her face. Faith looked at Lauren, who was blushing.

"Everybody needs somebody, darling," said Skipper. "Mimi and Terry seem to have done all right—just go with the flow."

Lauren reported that Terry had been wonderful about crawling under Camille's bed to get Bertha's plate. Mack hadn't done any damage, and Terry used Bertha's toothbrush and toothpaste to clean it after he washed it with soap and water. He also pulled out a few other things from under the bed that Mack must have hidden there: One oldish slipper that Terry thought was probably Harriett's, the green and red tennis ball that Dot threw down the hall for him to chase, a baby blanket that another resident had donated to Mack when he first came to Harmony Hall, and three pairs of socks that may or may not have belonged to Camille.

"Do you remember Maybelle from the party? Terry told me today that she's sneaking Mack treats now, and when she first came she told everybody she couldn't stand dogs! Now Dot is trying to figure out how to make Maybelle quit feeding Mack, but not discourage her from spending time with him. She seems so much happier now than when she first came."

Skipper licked her fingers. "We need to find her some low-cal dog treats. I'll pick some up and drop them off to Maybelle."

"Would you pick up some tweezers, too?" asked Lauren. "Eloise needs me to pull her whiskers out, and I think someone used her tweezers to bend metal—the ends don't meet."

Skipper choked on her pulled pig, picturing Lauren pulling hairs from Eloise's chin. "Was that what you were doing when we pulled up tonight?" she asked.

"Yes, but I was using my fingers," said Lauren, and giggled, remembering how much she and Eloise had laughed at her futile attempts to grab the long, white offending hairs with her fake nails.

"Did she ask you to pull them out?" asked Faith.

"No, actually I asked her if she wanted me to—they were driving me crazy, and I figured she couldn't see them. Angel can use wax, but it costs more, and I bet it hurts."

"When I was a teenager, Mom used to wax my upper lip for me," Faith said. "It hurt like the dickens. I always insisted that she let me run my finger over the side of the wax with all the hairs still in it. It felt a little like the back of a woolly worm with a haircut."

"Well, Eloise's wax would feel like a wig—hers are so long," said Lauren, and they all laughed.

"Lauren, let's have some fun with Mr. Terry," Skipper said, eyeing their waiter thoughtfully.

"How? He doesn't even know we're here."

Lauren looked at Faith, who was watching Skipper.

"He will," said Skipper, beckoning to the waiter, and grinning.

Roommates, Terry and Miguel had been inseparable for years. Miguel's parents were from Cuba, and his dream was to one day return with them to see the places they still spoke of after forty years. He often pictured himself walking the streets of Habana, soaking up Caribbean sunshine like the roof tiles his father used to make there; smelling the salt breeze off the harbor. A certified nursing assistant, Miguel was ideal for his work at St. Catherine's Hospital, where he was beloved by his co-workers for his good humor and adored by his patients for his empathy. Sensitive, fun-loving and at peace with his sexual persuasion, Miguel was also blessed with a lovely head of dark hair, large almond eyes, and a muscular, lean look. At the Real Southern Cooking class where he had met Terry in the early nineties, women twice his age—married and single—flirted with him persistently. They still did.

Faith, Skipper, Lauren and their waiter had their heads together. The restaurant began to fill up. It was impossible to see Terry and his friend now, from where they sat. The waiter seemed hypnotized by Skipper, whose right hand, long red nails gleaming, grasped his arm. "OK, OK,…yeah, OK," he said, smiling, as she talked. He left the table, maneuvering his way back to the hostess station.

"He'll kill me," snickered Lauren.

"We'll protect you, honey," said Faith, watching the waiter's back disappear behind a crowd of new arrivals.

"I wish I had a pair of opera glasses," said Skipper, moving her chair so that she could watch Terry's table.

A tall, well-dressed, middle-aged man strode to Terry's table, carrying a bottle of wine and two wine glasses. Terry and Miguel, intrigued and interrupted, both looked up at him, half-smiles on their faces.

"Terry?" the man asked.

"Yes?" said Terry, looking at the wine bottle, and then at Miguel.

"I'm Jack Purdy, the Manager here. You have an admirer who has asked that you have this bottle of wine to enjoy with your dinner."

"Wow! Thanks!" said Terry. He laughed delightedly.

Jack placed the wine glasses in front of Terry and Miguel, opened the bottle and began to pour the wine.

"Wait!" said Terry, "Let me check it!" He took a sip of the Merlot, winked at Miguel and nodded at Jack. "That'll work," he said.

"Enjoy your dinner, gentlemen," said Jack, and he left.

"Who do we know who would send a *bottle* of wine?" asked Terry, reading the label. Then he noticed a small card taped to the side of the bottle. Prying it loose, he looked at Miguel, who was closely watching his friend's face. The card was printed. It read:

I'll never forget our time together. See you soon.

"Who the hell…?" Terry said, genuinely puzzled. He handed the card to Miguel.

"Whoa! Amigo—what are you doing with yourself while I work late at the hospital?"

Miguel's tone was light but it was clear he wanted an explanation. Terry didn't have one.

Their meal came, and they agreed, halfway through it, to take a stroll through the restaurant in the hopes of finding Terry's benefactor. At the far end of the restaurant Faith, Lauren and Skipper were planning their own stroll; one that would take them by Terry's table.

❦   ❦   ❦

Terry saw Skipper and Faith approaching and waved at them. They made their way to his table and met Miguel, with whom Skipper immediately began to flirt.

"Do you come here often, Terry?" Faith asked, the corners of her lovely hazel eyes crinkling as she smiled down at him.

"Maybe once a month, when the barbeque urge takes over. How 'bout you?"

"Skipper likes it here. It's laid back, and they have a good selection of beer on tap. She's obviously tried a few tonight," she added, as they watched Skipper and Miguel double over with laughter.

"We usually have a beer, too, but someone sent us a bottle of wine."

"Probably one of Miguel's many admirers," said Faith, looking around.

"I'd agree with you, except that he sent it to me," said Terry, ruefully.

Terry signaled the waiter after Skipper and Faith left. Suddenly, from nowhere, Lauren appeared.

"Lauren! I just saw your mother!" exclaimed Terry.

"How was she?" Lauren asked, looking at Miguel with the same interest her mother had shown.

"Your mother's great," laughed Terry, and introduced Lauren to Miguel.

Lauren seemed unusually animated and Terry, feeling slightly guilty about the telephone repair incident, asked if she'd like to join them.

"No thanks Terry, I need to get going. I'll never forget our time together, though, and I'll see you soon."

Terry's mouth gaped open. "Lauren! You little rat!"

"Gotcha, Kiddo," she said, and seemed to skip out of the restaurant.

CHAPTER 21

THE HOMECOMING

OCTOBER, 1998

"Oh, come on, Faith. Billie Jo can handle the store tomorrow—I already asked her."

Skipper leaned on the sales counter at *Magnifique,* her voice tinged with the wheedling tone that Faith had heard her use generally with men. It nearly always worked on them, and usually worked with Faith. Keeneland's Fall Meet would begin on Friday, the next day. Skipper had a box with six seats. She never missed Keeneland. It was the one event in Lexington where Skipper could do all the things that she dearly loved in one day. She could talk to old friends, exchange volumes of gossip, wear something slightly revealing but very classy with long sleeves and put on a perfect hat and feel appropriate. She could gamble, drink, make eyes at rich, good-looking men and laugh. She adored everything about the races and the folks who showed up for them, especially if the weather was good. Tomorrow's forecast was for a perfect fall day, sunny, clear, and 68 degrees.

"Oh, Skipper, you know I don't gamble," said Faith, updating her computer with the morning's sales. "Besides, I hate driving your car, and I know I'll have to drive us home."

"We can take a taxi home, darling, and I'll pick up my car Saturday. Please come—we'll have such a good time."

Faith thought back to last year's trip to Keeneland with Skipper. They sat with two couples who had obviously started celebrating long before the first race. By the end of the day they were barely able to leave the box. Skipper hooked up with some fellow Faith had never met (and that Skipper had proba- bly just met), and somehow Faith made it home with an old friend of her own who fortunately offered her a ride when they ran into each other at the restroom. Her memories of Keeneland were not nearly as pleasant as Skipper's, and she hated to be away from the store for a full day.

"Who else will be in the box?" Faith asked.

"Some fellas I gave tickets to last week at the blood center—both of them hit two gallons and said they'd love to come—with their spouses, I might add." Skipper's lips curved up higher on both ends. Faith could imagine the repartee that took place before the tickets changed hands. The old familiar desire to keep an eye on Skipper became stronger than her will to take care of the store.

"Oh, all right," she said, testily. "I'll call Billie Jo and make arrangements. What are you wearing?"

"That hot pink and black number you hate so much," Skipper said. "With my sexiest black shoes."

Faith sighed. She could never understand where Skipper got the energy.

At 3:00 A.M. Friday morning Faith's phone rang and rang, finally pulling her out of a dream that she couldn't remember the instant she awoke. She looked at the clock, wondering why the power had failed—the time had to be wrong. Slowly, still groggy, she answered the call, sure that it must be Mimi, who had always been an early riser.

"Hello, Mother?"

"Darling, it's me. I'm so sorry to call this early."

Skipper's slightly husky voice was on the other end. The laughter, usually just under the surface, wasn't there. Skipper sounded exhausted. *Lord, she's in jail and I need to bail her out.*

"What's wrong, Skipper?" Faith asked, sitting on the bed's edge. Babe stiffly walked around the bed and rested her chin on Faith's knee. Babe never got up before 7:00 or 8:00 if she could help it.

"I just had a call from my mother, Faith. Apparently at about midnight she found her husband dead in bed. I told her to call 911 to report it, but I've got to go to Connecticut and help handle things. She doesn't sound quite with it—not that she ever has."

"Oh, Skipper, I'm so sorry. What can I do to help?"

"Well, for starters, would you mind having Lauren stay with you until I get back? I hate to pull her out of school right now. Would it be too much for you?"

"Of course not. Is she awake?"

"No. I'm taking a cab to the airport in about an hour. I'll leave her a note and ask her to call you as soon as she gets up. I'll call you once I arrive at my mother's, which should be sometime this afternoon."

Faith marveled that Skipper could sound so organized at such an early hour.

"Skipper, we'll do anything we can to help. How 'bout letting *me* drive you to the airport? I can be dressed in five minutes."

"No, thanks anyway. I'm so mad at that son-of-a-bitch for screwing up Keeneland I could simply spit. I don't want you to see me like this."

Skipper rented a sedan in New York City and got directions to Greenwich from the aging rental agent, who acted as if he wanted to drive there with her. Skipper handed him her empty Styrofoam coffee cup as she slid into the car and began adjusting the seat. If all went well, she'd be at her mother's by 5:00 P.M. If all went *really* well, she'd be home by Tuesday—in plenty of time for *next* Friday's meet.

Pansy Powell had been a beautiful young girl. She had enjoyed not only good looks but doting, wealthy parents, who insured her future through trust funds, and later through coming out parties attended by the up and coming elite in Connecticut. Pansy married well twice. Her only child, Priscilla, born when Pansy was nearly forty, adopted the moniker 'Skipper' at an early age and left home in her late teens. This would be her third trip back home in twenty-two years. Pansy, who had never been close to her daughter, didn't know whom else to call when her second husband died. Most of her remaining friends were in Florida this time of year, and the ones who remained in Connecticut would be of no help to her now.

❧   ❧   ❧

Skipper's rental car rolled to a stop at 4:30 that afternoon in front of the center hall colonial home on Sound Beach Avenue. Leaves skittered across the lawn of the huge house as she lifted her suitcase from the trunk and swore at the run in her pantyhose. Her mother's second husband, Theodore Edwards, had let the house go somewhat, she noticed, as she started up the steps. Paint peeled from the porch columns, and the porch itself needed new paint. Skipper had never lived in this house. It belonged to Theodore, who had married Pansy a year after Skipper's father died. She and Theodore were never well acquainted, as it was impossible for Skipper and her mother to be civil to each other for longer than five minutes at a stretch.

Skipper noticed the mailbox was full of mail. She grabbed it, stuck it under her left armpit, and rang the doorbell. It took several minutes for Pansy to reach the front door. The house, all 4500 square feet, seemed more enormous to Skipper now than ever.

"Priscilla?" Pansy's voice was weak and hesitant as she cracked the door.

"Hello, Mother," Skipper said, handing her mother the mail as she tried to juggle her purse, her suitcase and her coat. She bent over and kissed her mother on the forehead.

"I'm here. How are you holding up?"

Pansy seemed drugged, her response slow and uncertain.

Has she had a stroke?

Entering the marble foyer, Skipper noticed that stacks of unopened mail were sitting on the exquisitely carved table to her left. Her mother walked slowly to the table with the mail, and gently set it on top of an existing pile. Pansy's hair was uncombed. The knot that she so elegantly wore as Skipper was growing up was off center, and was now gray instead of gold. At eighty, she seemed a decade older than Mimi, who was now eighty-one. Skipper found herself comparing the two, and for once, felt a tinge of envy for Faith.

"Mother, I'm sorry about Theodore. Have you heard anything from the coroner?"

Pansy leaned against the walnut doorframe leading into the huge family room. Her hand went to her mouth and her eyes closed, trying to block a torrent of tears that spilled out and down the front of her blouse. Skipper noticed the blouse was buttoned unevenly; one side hung much lower than the other. Shocked, she then noticed that her mother's shoes didn't match.

"No, I haven't heard," Pansy whispered, choking.

Skipper pulled her suitcase into the family room and looked around. Some-one had been using the family room as a bedroom. The couch was half made up with sheets and a pillow and blanket were neatly stacked in one corner. Clothes were hung on backs of chairs and other couches in the huge room. A row of shoes, she suspected her mother's, were lined up along the base of the staircase that led to the second floor.

"Mother, I think I'll stay in one of the upstairs bedrooms, if it's OK with you," Skipper said.

"Yes," said Pansy.

"Will you be OK? Do you want to come up with me?"

"I can't go up there," Pansy said. "I live here now." She sank to the couch.

"I thought that might be the case," said Skipper, and started to haul her lug-gage up the wide, long flight of stairs.

The policeman Skipper talked with at 4:55 doubted that the coroner's office would be open, but gave her the number. She managed to reach the coroner, explained her relationship to Pansy, and was advised to come in the next work-ing day, Monday, for a copy of the death certificate. Skipper could see her plan of getting home on Tuesday deteriorating. She changed into her sweatsuit and running shoes, barely noticing that in the bedroom she'd chosen, one of four, the dust lay like a translucent blanket over everything, and the top of the night-stand was covered with pill bottles.

Faith heard from Skipper at 10:00 that evening. She and Lauren cooked spa-ghetti after they moved Lauren's things into Faith's spare bedroom after work. When Skipper called they were watching the end of *Fargo* on Faith's VCR, each feeling good about the temporary living arrangement and both glad they didn't live in North Dakota.

"Faith, it's me, the prodigal daughter."

"Oh, Skipper, I've been so worried about you. What's going on?"

"Mother and I are sitting in the family room bundled up like Eskimos because the furnace isn't working," Skipper began. "She can't remember when it stopped working, and we can't get a heating guy here 'til tomorrow at the earliest. I got here too late today to get a death certificate, and we still don't know what killed Theodore. Pansy doesn't know anything about his wishes for a visitation and funeral, or if the arrangements have been made, nor does she know if Theodore left a will. The bank's not open until Monday, either. In the meantime I'll be tearing the place apart to try to find something to help us make plans for next week. She's going to the emergency room in the morning—something's not right, but I'm not sure what."

"I know you can't talk, but are you two getting along OK?" Faith asked.

"Yes, things have changed, darling. There's no fight left. How's it going there?"

"Here's Lauren. We're doing great."

Faith stopped the VCR and handed the phone to Lauren.

"Mom?"

Faith watched Lauren's face as Skipper explained the situation in Greenwich. She could only hear Lauren's end of the conversation, but it ended with, "I love you, too." How wrong Skipper had been that day on Faith's deck…or maybe things had changed, substantially, in three short months.

"Mother, we're going to see a doctor today." It was Saturday—clear and cool but sunny. Skipper buttoned her mother's blouse and tucked it into the waistband of the navy blue skirt that seemed to be all Pansy would wear. It was clear to Skipper that Theodore had had his work cut out for him, if he was dressing his wife every day and getting her ready for bed. Skipper had gone through his bedroom—neat, overall, but for a bedside table covered with pill bottles. Had he died of an overdose?

She pulled the car up to the front door and helped Pansy down the front steps. She noticed a slight smell of urine, and kicked herself for not insisting that her mother take a bath. The heating man had promised that he'd come after lunch. Skipper left her mother's key to the house under the front door mat and prayed that the guy was honest.

The Greenwich Community Hospital Emergency Room was empty. Skipper asked the young woman at the registration desk if someone could take a blood test; that her mother seemed dehydrated and confused. Within a few minutes an intern appeared, and Pansy and Skipper were ushered into a small, curtained room, where Pansy's blood pressure, pulse, temperature and weight were recorded. Blood was drawn, her pupils and ears were examined, and at Skipper's insistence a urine sample was taken.

At 11:00 a doctor appeared and informed Skipper that her mother was, indeed, dehydrated, and that her potassium was extremely low. She also had a UTI, which at her age could make her very confused. Skipper nearly hugged him. The frightening specter of Alzheimer's began to dissipate, and amazingly, she began to relish a fight with Pansy—like in the good old days.

❧   ❧   ❧

On Monday they read the coroner's report, which stated that heart failure was at the core of Theodore's death; though the balding gentleman at the coroner's office, who knew both Theodore and Pansy, told Skipper that Theodore had also been unable to keep his blood pressure in check, and was diabetic.

"Do they have friends here in town?" Skipper asked.

"Very few. Most of the crowd they used to run with is dead. The more ambulatory are probably already in Florida. The rest are in retirement homes."

Skipper took her mother's arm as they left the coroner's office, vowing never to let her own get as flaccid. She was beginning to get a chilling picture of life in the big house her mother now lived in alone. Half the night she had lain awake imagining her mother and an even older man trying to make do in a house four times as large as they needed or could maintain. She pictured her mother struggling to get up that great flight of stairs, finally submitting to gravity, bad knees and spent breath, opting for nights on the couch, separate from her husband. Did he care? What kind of shape was he in those last five months since Skipper and her mother last had words on the phone? Whom did they have to call on for help? When did either of them last see a doctor? Were they still driving?

The funeral home was only minutes from the coroner's. Skipper had called before setting out for the coroner's office, and was urged to come by as soon as possible. The gentleman on the phone assured her that he could determine if a service had been pre-arranged for her stepfather, and if not, they could help Skipper set things right today.

CHAPTER 22

ARRANGEMENTS

McCarthy's Funeral Home, somber and elegant, was directed by Kevin McCarthy, a third generation mortician, who ushered Skipper and her mother into a well-appointed office. Once seated, he solicitously asked if they would like to talk about what had happened to Theodore.

Pansy glanced at Skipper, and said, "Ted had been ill for several weeks. He was staying upstairs and for the first time in our twenty-five years of marriage he failed to come down to tell me good night. I finally got up the stairs to his room—I have difficulty climbing stairs now—and he was gone."

Mr. McCarthy shook his gray head from side to side and said, "What an awful shock. I'm so sorry. Mrs. Edwards, I believe you and I met nearly five years ago with Mr. Edwards, right here in this office." He looked sadly at Pansy through thick glasses.

"How nice," said Skipper's mother.

Nice is an understatement. Skipper breathed deeply. *Thank God! They've made the arrangements.*

"I believe we know of all Mr. Edwards' wishes. We'll just need to update the obituary and decide on a time for the visitation and funeral. Normally the deceased is viewed for a period of time the day before the funeral, but we can arrange for both parts of this process to occur on the same day."

Thankfully, Pansy seemed slightly clearer today. She had managed to take a shower on her own, and had even agreed to pass on the navy skirt. Today she wore a crumpled but clean pantsuit that Skipper pulled out of the back of an upstairs closet. It was not her mother, though, that Skipper accompanied to

Mr. McCarthy's office, but rather a submissive, reconciled woman who seemed to be daydreaming. In younger years she would have been slightly haughty and a tad overbearing, very opinionated and quick to correct. These days she was leaving most conversation up to Skipper, who for once could have used some assistance.

Skipper turned her great green eyes on her mother. Pansy was looking at her shoes, which matched today.

"Mother?"

"What?"

"Would you like to have the visitation on the same day as the funeral?"

"What day is that?" asked Pansy.

"Whatever we decide. I'd say the sooner the better, wouldn't you, Mr. McCarthy?"

"It all depends on when your family can get here," he replied. "I would suggest Thursday afternoon for the visitation and Friday for the funeral and burial at Serenity Gardens. The obituary should run tomorrow or Wednesday at the latest."

"Sounds good to me," said Skipper, studying her nails.

"Well, then, let's see what we need to update the obituary. How about next of kin? Has anything changed?"

"What have you got?" Skipper asked.

"Why don't I read the entire obituary, and you tell me what to add or change?"

"Fire away."

> *Theodore Edwards, former trust officer at Greenwich National Bank, died unexpectedly at his home in Greenwich on October 1. He was 87. Mr. Edwards, a sixty-year resident of Greenwich and an employee of Greenwich National Bank for thirty-two years, was active in the local Lions Club and Calgary Christian Church. He was a member of the Greenwich Country Club and the Original Oldies Band.*
>
> *Born in Stamford, Connecticut May 5, 1911, to George and Helen, Mr. Edwards moved to Greenwich after graduating from Yale University in 1934. He is survived by his wife, Pansy, a stepdaughter, Priscilla "Skipper" Collier, and a granddaughter, Lauren Collier.*

Mr. McCarthy looked up inquiringly at Skipper, then Pansy. Both were silent, each lost in thoughts of Theodore's past.

"Does that still sound accurate?" he finally asked.

Skipper sighed. "Mother, what do you think?" Her eyes filled with tears; she fumbled in her purse for a tissue. *Why am I suddenly feeling so blue?*

Pansy finally focused on Mr. McCarthy. "Ted always wished we had more family…Skipper and Lauren are all we have. What shall we do about the service, Mr. McCarthy?"

"I've talked with Reverend Atchison. He's prepared to meet with you any time between now and Thursday and do the service, if you'd like. I know that Mr. Edwards loved poetry, and picked a poem to be read at some point in the service. Do you think that is still his wish?"

Pansy nodded slightly. "We've not talked about dying since we were here last, Mr. McCarthy. I have to think my husband would have mentioned something different if he'd thought of it."

"The Reverend knew your husband well, and thought very highly of him. I'm sure you'll be pleased with his program. Ms. Collier, is there anything you'd like to say at the service?"

"No, I didn't know hi….Theodore…well," Skipper sniffed.

"All right, then, I think we're set. Is there anything else I can do for either of you today?"

"No, thank you. You've made this so wonderfully easy," said Skipper, rising.

Her mother stood unsteadily and grabbed her arm. Skipper folded her hand over her mother's.

Keeneland was becoming a distant dream, and somehow it didn't matter.

Monday night Skipper and Pansy went to a restaurant where apparently Theodore used to go regularly. It seemed as if everyone there knew of his demise, and treated Pansy with enormous respect and empathy. They barely noticed Skipper, who quickly realized that flirting or cracking even the slightest joke would probably be in poor taste.

"Ted" had been everyone's friend. The restaurant owner spent several minutes at their table explaining to Pansy how Ted had single-handedly planned a fundraiser for the Children's Hospital and had played in the dance band that evening. Three couples stopped by Pansy's table to express their shock that he was gone and report on something lovely that he'd done for each of them. Pansy's waiter, a small, rat-faced fellow with slicked-back hair and huge black eyebrows, detailed the time Ted stopped to pick him up on the other side of town, arranged for his stalled car to be towed, and brought him to work—on time. A gentleman on a walker—an old golf Buddy—nearly fell into Pansy's lap as he hugged her tight, and Skipper noticed tears on his cheeks as he inched his way to the restaurant's exit. Though quiet and still withdrawn, Pansy seemed to draw strength from each encounter. Always perfectly mannered, she managed to convey just the right degree of sorrow and appreciation when she introduced Ted's friends to Skipper.

That night, after returning home, they actually talked.

"Mother, it seems that Ted was a lovely man." Skipper poured a drink and curled up at one end of Pansy's couch. "I wish I'd known him better."

Pansy moved her pillow and sank down at the other end. "He was a perfect gentleman and an exemplary husband," Pansy said, beginning to cry. "I wish I had died first…I don't think I can stand it without him." She reached for her pillow and held it against her face, muffling her sobs. Skipper moved next to her, threw an arm around her mother's shaking shoulders and also began to cry. This disconcerted Pansy so much that she stopped.

"What's the matter, Priscilla? Why are you crying?"

"I don't know, Mother. I'm feeling bad for you and regretting that we—you and Ted and Lauren and I—were never really a family. I'm sorry that in all those years you were married to him I never once brought Lauren to visit." Skipper drained her drink and got up to make another, wiping her nose on the sleeve of her robe.

Pansy stared at family pictures across the room. "You will never regret our distance as much as Ted and I did," she said. "He could never understand it or the tension between us, Priscilla. I'm not sure *I* understand it." She smiled sadly and rubbed her eyes. "I think I'll try to sleep, dear. Tomorrow's bound to be a long day."

Theodore's obituary ran on Tuesday, a gray, chilly day filled with angry wind gusts and splatterings of showers. Skipper dropped Pansy at Yvonne's for a manicure, wash, rinse and set and returned to the big, lonely house. The gas, turned off for non-payment of the bill before she arrived in Greenwich, was back on after Skipper met with the gas company. She had found the past due bill—and others—at the bottom of the mail pile on the foyer table. Toasty and tired, she crawled between the covers of her bed in the dust-filled bedroom, cell phone in hand. She had to talk with Faith and Lauren.

✤   ✤   ✤

"Faith?" Skipper could hear the cash register in the background. Faith was the only one she knew who could talk on the phone and operate the register at the same time.

"Skipper? Hold on." Faith finished the transaction and Skipper heard the familiar intonations of delighted buyer and congratulatory seller.

"How *are* you?"

"How many customers do you have?"

"The last one just left. We're fine. How goes it?"

"I'm having some sort of meltdown, darling. I had to talk to you. This whole situation is surreal, but I know it's happening and I'm feeling weird."

"What's going on?" Faith asked, in the worried tone Skipper usually hated.

"Well, for starters, Mother can't possibly stay here. She can't get up the stairs and I'm afraid she'll try going *down* the stairs to the basement sooner or later, and break her neck. I'm not sure if her bookkeeping went to hell a long time ago, or was caused by a lack of potassium and the UTI, or if her mind's gone, but she hasn't paid a bill in months." There was a long pause. "But the thing that bothers the hell out of me, Faith, is that it seems Theodore was a lovely guy, and I never got to know him. Lauren never knew him, and he probably would have been a swell grandfather." She began to cry.

Faith was speechless. She had never heard Skipper cry. It hadn't happened eighteen years ago, when Skipper called her at 4:00 A.M. to report that her husband wasn't home; it hadn't happened four years ago when Lauren was held at the jail, caught with pot; and it hadn't happened more recently, when they both thought Mimi would die.

"Skipper? What's the matter? You've never wanted to get close to Theodore."

"I know. I think I made a mistake."

Faith started to say, "It's never too late…" and thought better of it.

"I think my mother has needed me here for months and months—maybe years—and didn't feel comfortable calling me. Do you know that Ted listed Lauren and me as his *family*? We were *it*, Faith, and we didn't even know him. It's killing me." She started to sob.

"Skipper, tell me, are you drinking?"

"No, but it's a great idea."

"It's a terrible idea. Don't do it." Faith chose her words carefully. "Listen to me, dear. We've got to look at the positives here. Think of this as a wonderful opportunity to help your mother. She needs you, and you have the time and energy and health to handle things."

Skipper was silent.

"And just think about how fortunate it is that Theodore died the way he did—in bed, not surrounded by strangers poking things in his veins or trying to force pills down his throat. He probably just went to sleep and never knew what hit him." She paused, trying to assess Skipper's reaction.

"Skipper?"

"I'm here."

"Think about how good he was to your mother, and rejoice that she had him for all those years. Think about how fortunate it is that she's on the mend, and will be better soon—if not already. Are you listening?"

"Yes."

"When are you coming home?"

"As soon as I can after the funeral, which is Friday. How is Lauren?"

"She's doing fine. She loves working, and I think she's having a good time here—she's busy every night with something or other. But I think she's missing you."

"I'll call her tonight. Tell her I love her," Skipper said. "And I love you, darling," she added, and slowly placed the phone on the nightstand, which was still covered with pill bottles. She read the labels, searching for a familiar drug, with no success.

Skipper willed memories of her childhood into her consciousness and relived a dozen incidents, used for years as examples of her mother's intolerance. Uppermost was the time Pansy refused to let her go out with Hitch Bliss, the hottest basketball player on her high school team or any other in their region. He smelled of cigarette smoke and whiskey the night he came to their door—aphrodisiacs to Skipper and red flags to Pansy. She remembered as well the night her mother followed her to a parking lot a year later. Skipper was to rendezvous with a married man—her English teacher—who had professed his love during three separate phone calls. Pansy had somehow found out and created a scene in front of the Flame Restaurant, which mortified Skipper. Skipper also recalled a meeting with the school counselor, at Pansy's insistence, to discuss the school policy that required the wearing of a bra.

Why did I hate her so?

She closed her eyes tight, stunned that it had taken the death of a man she never really knew to begin to understand her mother.

❀   ❀   ❀

"Ms. Collier?"

"Speaking."

"This is Reverend Atchison. Mr. McCarthy has arranged for me to do Mr. Edwards' service this Friday. Please accept my condolences. We are all so very disheartened at the news of his death. Ted was a wonderful friend."

"Thank you, Reverend."

"I'm wondering if either you or your mother would like to read the poem Ted picked out for his service. We often have family members either speak extemporaneously or read something that was loved by the deceased."

Skipper let the words sink in.

"Do you have a copy?"

"Yes, I do. I can either drop it off or you can pick it up here at the church."

She arranged to stop at the church on her way to pick up Pansy. To read Ted's poem was the least she could do for him.

❀   ❀   ❀

Even on Tuesday, late morning, Yvonne's was crowded. Skipper found Pansy leafing through a *Vogue* magazine in the lobby, looking much more like her old self. Her hair was gold again, the burnished knot, centered at the back of her head, was smooth. It had stopped raining. They walked next door to a small restaurant and ordered coffee.

"Mother, Reverend Atchison called this morning. He asked if either of us wanted to read Ted's poem at the funeral…I told him I would."

Pansy stopped studying her menu and began studying her daughter.

"Why?"

"I guess because I feel bad that I never did anything for him while he was alive." She watched her mother's face carefully. "Would you rather read it?"

"I can't imagine talking about Ted in public and not breaking down. You do it."

Pansy's hands trembled and her menu shook. She put it flat on the table and stared at it, unseeing. "I don't know that I can eat," she said.

Skipper moved her chair next to her mother's. Impulsively she took one of Pansy's small, delicate hands in her own. She knew the wedding band and engagement ring, hard against her palm, would never leave her mother's finger, and she now embraced their presence. Skipper squeezed the hand and its newly manicured nails tight.

"Let's share something," she said, and signaled their waitress.

Reverend Atchison, tall, dark, and almost menacing but for his smile, hugged Pansy and then Skipper as he entered the house. It was Thursday morning; the visitation would be in five hours. They sat in the kitchen and he explained the service, which would take place Friday morning. One of Ted's best friends, a golfer, would share a story about him at the funeral. The reverend would also comment on Ted's life.

"I thought it might be appropriate for you to read the poem just before we complete the service," he said.

"Mother, are you sure you don't want to say something?" asked Skipper.

Pansy nodded.

"If you change your mind, just let me know—even if it's at the service." He smiled kindly at both of them. "I'm available day or night if you need me. Call any time."

Skipper wondered idly if he did private counseling as she watched him pull out of the driveway. Somehow she had to convince Pansy that living in Greenwich was no longer an option, and she felt ill equipped for the job.

Arriving well before 3:00 P.M., Pansy and Skipper stood together at Ted's casket. He looked distinguished but much smaller than Skipper remembered him—and much thinner. Pansy began to weep and sat down on a loveseat near the entrance to the room. Skipper made sure there were tissues within reach and went looking for Mr. McCarthy. She feared it would be a long three hours.

Amazingly, McCarthy's was packed by 3:00 P.M., the start of the visitation. Pansy and Skipper, all there was of a receiving line, greeted Ted's friends and scores of people who either knew of him or had been customers over the years. From the first handshake Skipper explained her presence and her relationship as "Pansy's daughter."

Pansy, genuinely moved by the crowd of Ted's friends and admirers, managed to stand next to her daughter the full three hours, though at times she leaned heavily on Skipper's arm.

At exactly 6:00 P.M. the doors to the visitation room were closed, the sound muffled by McCarthy's thick carpeting and heavy draperies. Skipper kicked off her shoes, collapsed in a chair and curled her stockinged toes against the carpet. The room now seemed huge. The silence after all the small talk was eerie. She imagined Ted sitting up and saying to her mother, "Thank God that's over, now I can get some sleep," and she looked guiltily toward his casket where two McCarthy employees were closing the lid.

"Mother, shall we head for home?"

"Yes, dear, thank you. It's been a long day."

Pansy was exhausted. Her lipstick was nearly gone; her ankles were beginning to swell. They walked slowly to Skipper's rental car as the streetlights began to flick on.

Reverend Bruce Atchison, always pragmatic but unfailingly thoughtful, had played golf with Ted Edwards for twenty years. Each was as intimately familiar with the details of the other's family as eighteen holes of golf—several times a week in good weather—could make him. The reverend was amazed that Skipper had come to Greenwich. Ted had been very closemouthed about Skipper and her daughter. It was obvious there had been little communication among the three.

Pansy and Skipper sat front row and center at Ted's funeral. The last of his family, Theodore Edwards had outlived all cousins. A childless only child, his legacy would be a small fortune left to his second wife, Pansy, and the Nature Conservancy, as well as a code of ethics adopted by the institution he had served for thirty-two years.

Reverend Atchison spoke of the deceased's character and kindness. He mentioned Ted's enormous respect for nature and his growing concern, especially in later years, for the environment. He recalled the time that Ted took on the Greenwich city government over the cutting of trees in a certain park that harbored an endangered avian species—and won. His remarks ended with a commentary on Ted's great love for Pansy, whom he referred to as "Pumpkin". Skipper's hand tightened on her mother's. *Who would have thought?*

A deeply tanned, cadaverous man took the lectern when the reverend stepped down. His name, he said, was Dutch Johanssen, and he had played golf with Ted his entire adult life.

"Ted had a terrible habit when it came to golf. Every time he'd see a bird on the course he didn't recognize he'd whip his *Field Guide to North American Birds* and his binoculars out of his golf bag and try to find it…while we were playing. It drove us crazy, but we all loved him for it and the enthusiasm he had—both for the game and for birdwatching. I've never seen him so excited about golf as the day he saw a pileated woodpecker, and you can bet all his buddies that day learned what one looks like."

It was Skipper's turn to read Ted's poem. She surveyed the assemblage before her—ten or fifteen people, mostly gray-haired—and looked at her mother.

"My greatest regret as I stand here is that I never got to know Ted Edwards the way all of you did. We were relatives through his marriage to my mother, and I failed to develop that relationship over the many years they were together. If he were here, I would tell him that he taught me a valuable lesson, and that I will pass that lesson on to his granddaughter, my daughter, whom he also never got to know. This poem, "Carving a Name" by Horatio Alger, is one he liked and asked to have read at this final meeting of his friends and family."

I wrote my name upon the sand
And trusted it would stand for aye;
But soon the refluent sea
Had washed my feeble lines away.

I carved my name upon the wood,
And after years, returned again;
I missed the shadow of the tree
That stretched of old upon the plain.

To solid marble next my name
I gave as a perpetual trust;
An earthquake rent it to its base,
And now it lies o'erlaid with dust.

All these have failed. In wiser mood
I turn and ask myself, what then?
If I would have my name endure,
I'll write it on the hearts of men.

In characters of living light,
From kindly words and actions wrought;
And these, beyond the reach of time,
Shall live immortal as my thought.

Skipper's eyes met Reverend Atchison's. He nodded and motioned to Mr. McCarthy. The Lord's Prayer filled the room, played on an organ that sounded both somber and sweet. Ted's funeral was over.

Alger, Jr., Horatio. 1888. "Carving a Name." Crown Jewels. Rock Island IL.

CHAPTER 23

CHANGES

"Mother, are you sure you won't rethink things and come with me?"

Skipper closed the trunk of the rental car and stood looking at her mother. Pansy smiled wanly, shook her head and hugged the daughter she was already beginning to miss.

"You know I have enough here to keep me busy until this time next year, Priscilla. But I do so appreciate the offer. I'll be fine. Reverend Atchison has offered to help with bills and paperwork, and I've got Ted's attorney and his CPA to assist. *You've* been invaluable, dear." She looked up into her daughter's beautiful face. Skipper looked tired and sad. It had been a trying week for everyone. Pansy marveled at how well they had co-existed during the last week or so, and fleetingly wondered, for the hundredth time, why it had taken so many years to happen.

Skipper kissed her, slid behind the wheel and took one last look at the big house. "I'll call you when I get home," she said. "I love you, Mother."

The sedan completed the half circle in front of the house and turned toward New York. Pansy waved until it disappeared from sight, dabbing her eyes as she laboriously climbed the steps to the front door.

What a difference a week makes. She paid for the rental car and forced a smile at the same elderly man who had helped her check out the car ten days before. There was an hour to kill before her plane departed. Skipper headed for an airport bar, thought better of it, and found a coffee shop. She carried the large latte to the gate and watched the world's harried and hurried flow past, taking note, as she always did in airports, of their footwear. It was 3:00 P.M. *What is she doing now?*

Skipper's eyes fixed on a very old, hunchbacked woman who was slowly approaching the customer service desk at the gate. When the clerk asked what she needed, the old lady placed her ticket on the counter and pointed at her ear. The clerk looked aggravated and asked the woman to be seated. It was obvious that her directive wasn't heard, as the customer then tried asking the clerk something. "Just have a seat, ma'am," Skipper heard the younger woman say. Confused, the old lady stared at the directory behind the agent's back but obviously couldn't see it clearly.

Skipper had had enough. She put down her latte and reached the counter in four strides, wishing that her Stuart Weitzmans were Nikes.

"May I help you?" she asked the tiny woman, who was now standing to one side of the counter.

The woman handed Skipper her ticket. She was ticketed on the same flight Skipper was taking.

"You're in the right place, darling," Skipper said, bending down to speak in the wizened ear.

"Praise God," the woman said, and patted Skipper's hand.

Skipper glared at the ticket agent and turned back to her new charge. "Don't you have anyone traveling with you?"

"I'm sorry?" said the old woman.

"Are you alone?"

"No, my daughter lives in Atlanta. She's very ill."

"I'm so sorry," Skipper said, leading the woman to a pair of empty seats. They sat down together. Skipper pulled out her cell phone. She had an overwhelming urge to call her mother.

The plane was leaving on time. Making sure the nearly deaf woman was in the proper seat, Skipper found her own, next to a window, and performed the usual contortions settling in. Her conversation with Pansy, who began to cry almost immediately, had fueled her concern. *Should I have stayed longer?*

Guilt was a relatively new emotion for her. There had been a few times in her life when Skipper admitted she'd done something slightly unethical, but she'd never spent time regretting actions or consequences. She simply got on with things.

The plane taxied and lifted, heading for Atlanta's hub. Light, reflecting from the windows and mirrors of miniature houses and cars, flashed in the fall afternoon. A vague loneliness engulfed Skipper; her eyes filmed with tears as she watched the earth recede. Images of Pansy, solitary, silent, padding slowly through her great house and crying, assailed her. Skipper closed her eyes and finally dozed, lulled by the great plane's hum and the need for a reprieve from an awakening conscience.

Lauren heard the garage door open and flew to the foyer. Her mother had called her from Atlanta, asking about dinner, expecting to be home by 7:00. Faith was meeting them at Red Lobster later. Lauren opened the front door and watched her mother pull her huge suitcase to the steps. She stood on the second step and hugged Skipper hard. As the faint scent of White Linen enveloped her, she knew immediately something was wrong. Her mother was weeping.

"I can't tell you how much I missed you both," Skipper said, reaching for a biscuit. She smiled wearily at Faith and Lauren. "And I can't tell you how hard it was to leave. For the first time I can remember, we didn't fight."

"How was the funeral?" asked Faith.

"It was fine. He had a big crowd at the visitation, and a good group at the funeral the next day. I realized early in the trip that he was a much nicer guy than I imagined him to be. I'm sorry we never got to know him, Lauren."

Lauren raised her eyebrows. "I've never gotten to know Grandma, Mom."

"You're right. I think that's my fault, too. You didn't know me when I was growing up, but I was a handful…"

"You can't mean it," said Faith, laughing.

Skipper was too tired to retort. "Actually, you're so much nicer than I was at your age, darling," she said, looking at Lauren. "I was mean-spirited and resentful, and held a grudge forever. I never once thought about how my mother was having to cope with my dad's death, and I never gave her credit for getting on with her life. I've stayed angry at her for thirty years, for no good reason." She speared an olive and bit it in half. "Look what she sent you, honey," she said, digging in her huge leather bag.

Lauren took the slim, dog-eared book from her mother. It was actually a bird watching journal. The first entry was dated May 5, 1970, and was prefaced by a notation made with the distinctive look of a fountain pen:

> This diary, a gift from my beautiful, gifted wife, Pansy,
> begins the recording of bird sightings from the date of
> receipt—May 5, 1970—to _____.

There were twenty or so empty pages left in the journal.

"He must have just retired and decided to take up a hobby," murmured Faith.

"Apparently it was a real passion," said Skipper. "What's his first sighting, darling?"

Lauren, who refused to wear her glasses in public, squinted at the faded writing.

"A scarlet teenager?"

"*Tanager!*" said Faith. "I'll bet it's a scarlet tanager!" She peered over Lauren's shoulder at Ted's writing. "How wonderful—the males are so beautiful in the summer."

"I can't wait to show this to Henry," Lauren said. "He's a bird watcher, too. Maybe he could use this to record birds we see at Harmony Hall. Thanks, Mom."

"We'll call your grandma tomorrow and thank her," said Skipper. "It was all her idea."

Angel, wiping her hands on a hand towel, left the beauty shop in search of Terry or Dot. Eloise Brown, now under the dryer, was positive that she'd lost her glasses. Kitty McElroy, whose roll-up was nearly finished, was just as positive that Eloise's glasses were the ones lying on the table between the two dryers—and continued to tell her so. Neither customer was budging, and their voices were beginning to rise above the din of the dryers—a sure sign that each was starting to get angry. Angel headed for Dot's office, passing Mack, who was tearing something up just inside the living room. Dot's office was empty. Angel picked up the hall phone and called the employee lounge.

"Hel-ooooo, hel-looooo," answered someone, in a falsetto voice.

"Terry?"

"How did you know it was me?"

"Who else would answer the phone like that?"

"Miss Piggy!"

Angel laughed in spite of herself. "Listen, Miss Piggy, I need some help in the beauty shop. Eloise and Kitty are going at it."

"Ooooh! I love a good fight—I'm coming."

Terry was at the beauty shop door in thirty seconds. Eloise, whose only old-age challenge was her diminished sight, was ninety-four and sharp as a tack. She usually dozed off while her hair dried. Today, dimmed eyes flashing, she peered from under the hair dryer at Kitty.

"Hello gir-r-r-ls," Terry said, bending over Eloise.

"Hand her those glasses there, Terry," said Kitty. "I know they're hers."

"Here's your glasses, m'dear."

"Mister, I know my own glasses, and these aren't mine. I've lost them." Eloise practically threw the offending glasses at him.

Bertha piped up from the couch. "Would you like to borrow mine?"

Eloise rolled her eyes at Terry. "Thanks but no thanks, Bertha. Mine are extra-strong."

Terry looked at Kitty over the hair dryer and grinned. "I'll be back in a bit. No arguing over these spectacles until I return."

He started for the library, where the photo albums were kept, but stopped abruptly. Mack, tail held high, was stretched out on his belly ripping something apart on the living room floor. The whites of his eyes showed and his tail began to wave side to side when he saw Terry. Terry could hear Dot's voice and those of others coming toward her office from the lobby; it was obvious a tour was in progress. He raced into the living room, trying to grab the large white object Mack was shredding. Mack took off, dragging it by some sort of tape. Terry quickly closed the living room doors, betting that Dot would take the couple to her office before showing them the building. He ran through the dining room to the second living room entrance, cornered Mack, and took away his prize. It was a large diaper, the kind used by a handful of the residents at Harmony Hall who were incontinent now and then. This one wasn't used. Terry cleaned up the shreds and took the diaper to the garbage cans outside the kitchen, ran up the stairwell to the second floor and the library, grabbed an album, and found the picture he needed. He ran back down the front stairs, stopped at Dot's office to meet the touring couple, and entered the beauty shop just as Eloise emerged from the dryer. He whispered in her ear.

"Eloise, put on these glasses—that aren't yours—and look at this picture."

Head bristling with curlers, she took the picture and worked the arms of the glasses over her ears and under the hair rollers. It was taken at the last Harmony Hall Christmas party, and showed her hugging Santa Claus. The same blue glasses in contention now, with their unusual filigree along the sides, showed clearly in the close up of Eloise kissing Santa's cheek.

Eloise handed the picture back to Terry. Silent, she removed the glasses, examined them closely, and put them back on. He winked at her, pointed at Kitty, now under the dryer dozing, and put his finger to his lips as Angel helped Eloise into her chair, patted her shoulders and started the comb-out.

"Dot, can we talk?"

Terry stood at her door, for once slightly serious with only a half smile on his thin face.

"Sure. Want a cup of coffee?"

"Nope."

He perched on the edge of the chair facing her desk and took a deep breath. Dot smiled at him empathetically. "This must be bad," she said.

"Well, probably not in the long run." He laughed nervously. "I'm thinking of going back to school."

"Really?! For what?"

"I'd like to become a chef someday."

"That's wonderful, Terry! How long will it take?"

"About three years. There's a culinary institute in Louisville, and I've been accepted. The new term starts in January."

Dot waved at two residents outside her door and asked them to give her a few minutes. "How are we going to manage without you?" she asked.

"I've been asking myself how *I'll* manage without *this* place, Dot. You know I love it here. I just can't see myself advancing until you kick the bucket..." Terry laughed and clapped his hands. Dot snorted and giggled. He was right, of course. There was very little room for advancement at Harmony Hall.

"How soon do you need to go?"

"I'll be here until January or until you find someone and we get them trained—whichever comes first." Terry said. "I've been thinking about this for three years, and I think I've got enough money saved to tide me over for a while. Once I'm into the program, I can work while I go to school."

Dot looked at him reflectively. She loved everything about Terry. She remembered the day she'd met him, when he answered an ad for his current position. Gaunt but cheerful, he explained then that he'd moved back to Kentucky from California, barely surviving a mudslide there that killed his best friend. She had been desperate for someone to fill an unexpected opening, but had wondered if a probably gay man in an elderly, all-female community would be accepted. Camille had been the hardest nut to crack. She would sidle up to other ladies after Terry was hired and whisper and laugh about him behind her hands, pursing her mouth and raising her eyebrows in mock horror.

It took Terry just under a month to win her over. She relented at Halloween and borrowed his flapper outfit (Dot tried not to think about him in it), and won first prize for the most original costume at the Harmony Hall Halloween party. A week later, just after 8:00 A.M. when she failed to show for breakfast, he found her lying on her bedroom floor, disoriented and with slurred speech. Terry called 911, followed the EMS vehicle to the emergency room, and made sure she was in good hands immediately. Now his most ardent supporter, Camille was sure to also be the most anguished if he left.

Dot rubbed her temples. "Will you consider coming back here to work once you're a famous chef?"

"Only if you're still around to call the shots," he said, and walked around the desk to hug her.

After Terry left, Dot flipped through her foot-long Rolodex. She found the card she wanted and dialed Julie's dorm number.

❧   ❧   ❧

ANNOUNCEMENTS

*Our inimitable **Terry Glenn** will be attending culinary school in Louisville in January. We hope he will return to Harmony Hall in some capacity once he has achieved his goal of becoming a chef. **Julie Painter** has agreed to fill Terry's current position, and will be starting her full time employment on December 18. We look forward to having Julie here to train on a part-time basis on November 1. We'll let you know the date of Terry's good-bye party when we have plans finalized.*

Don't forget our trip to **Bluegrass Mall** *this afternoon at 2:30. We have room for two more residents. Let Dot know if you're interested in going.*
10/16/98

❦   ❦   ❦

Mimi threw on her old, ragged jean jacket, double-tied her sneakers and exited the building. It was 2:00 P.M. Late October was a bittersweet goodbye to summer. Cool, clear and cerulean, the sky belied what lay ahead in coming months. Vivid leaves, no longer at their peak and proclaiming autumn from the trees ringing Harmony Hall, crackled underfoot in the parking lot.

Henry, silver head gleaming in the U-pick garden, was pulling up summer's last zinnias, cutting the long stems in half and stacking them neatly in the yard waste receptacle.

"Hey!" he said, handing her a pair of gloves. "What do you know?" He grinned at her delightedly.

"I know it's getting cold out here!" said Mimi, zipping her jacket and putting on the gloves. "How are you, Henry?"

"Better now," he said, shaking soil from a thick brown stem. "You showed up just in time—I was getting anxious."

Mimi laughed. "It would be awful to have to do all this alone."

They worked alongside each other for an hour. The breeze picked up, whipping around the still standing zinnias, rustling their brown leaves.

"Henry, I can't take it any more. I'm cold," said Mimi. "I'm sorry."

"We'll finish this when it's warmer," he said, flipping the top down on the receptacle. "How 'bout a cup of coffee on the balcony?"

They stashed their gloves and pruners in the shed, and carried their coffee in Styrofoam cups from the dining room to the balcony. Mack followed them and flopped at their feet, enjoying the sun that heated the still, quiet ledge overlooking the courtyard.

"It's so much warmer here," said Mimi, watching the sparrows sip from the fountain. "Like another world."

Henry took a sip of his coffee and studied Mimi's face. Her eyes, always arresting, looked liquid in the fading sunlight. He swiveled his chair toward her. "I feel I've been in a different world since we met."

Mimi blushed. "Isn't it interesting how life turns out?"

Henry put his coffee down and took her small hands in his. He leaned forward and shyly kissed her. Mimi felt the bristly pressure of his moustache momentarily—just under her nose—before she realized what he was doing. It was over immediately. He picked up his coffee and took another sip. "Interesting doesn't do it justice," he said.

Mimi could still feel his moustache against her lip. She squeezed his big, calloused hand. "You're right, Henry. It's amazing, isn't it?"

Behind them, watching from the laundry room windows, Minnie gasped. *Wait 'til the girls hear about this.*

Virginia Wilhoite had lost her husband thirty years before she moved to Harmony Hall. Now dependent on her sister (whom she despised), childless and nearly friendless, deaf and incontinent, Virginia had been a challenge for Dot and her staff since the day she arrived. Extremely intelligent but totally self-absorbed, she had once possessed a keen wit. She remembered where every penny she ever spent had gone and held a grudge forever. The more forgiving residents overlooked her unfortunate traits and catered to her out of sympathy. Those she had maligned ignored her.

The Halloween party was over; it was 5:20. Harriett, hunched and hurting, sank slowly into the chair at the end of her dining room table. The magician had performed for an hour, and then the kindergarten kids had sung for ten minutes—the whole program had been too much for her back. She tried to get comfortable, and it struck her that she was not in her usual chair. This one was lower and lacked the special pad her daughter had given her last Christmas. The chair she now sat in was heavy and unforgiving—it suited a larger, stronger woman.

Minnie breezed in, this week's wig centered over her left ear. It gave her a wing, or flip, of sorts, directly over her nose.

"Minnie, do you mind looking around for my chair?" asked Harriet. "I imagine it was used in the living room during the party, and someone returned it to the wrong table."

Harriett's face glistened with the perspiration pain creates when one is trying too hard to ignore it.

"What color is it?" asked Minnie.

"What?"

"What color is your chair?"

"The pad is blue with strawberries on it, I think," said Harriett.

Camille sat down and smiled as Julie poured her coffee.

"What's up?" she asked Harriett.

"Minnie's looking for my chair." Harriett watched the tiny figure go table to table. "It was taken back to the wrong table after the program."

"I'll help her, honey," said Camille. She jumped up and headed for the back of the dining room.

Mimi sat down at the other end of the table. Her eyes were sparkling and her cheeks were flushed. "It's getting cold out there," she said. "How are you, dear?"

"I'm suffering a little tonight, Mimi. My chair is gone, and this one's not too comfortable."

"Let me go look for it," said Mimi, getting to her feet.

"Camille and Minnie are hard at it," said Harriett. "Don't worry, Mimi, they'll find it."

Mimi sat down and passed Harriett the salad. A commotion was going on at the other end of the dining room, but it was impossible to make out the words.

They both watched Dot rush through the dining area to the source of the noise, Julie right behind her. Cookie, the Harmony Hall evening chef, delivered their sandwich platter and glanced worriedly at the other end of the dining room. Voices were being raised, always a bad sign. Suddenly they saw Virginia, steel gray hair slicked back, leave her table at the opposite end of the dining room. She brandished her cane at Minnie and said something insulting to Camille, who stepped back a foot or so to let her by, and then gave the finger, high and emphatic, to Virginia's retreating back. Julie and Dot, unable to make Virginia hear, followed her from the dining room.

"Virginia…wait just a minute."

Chin jutting forward and talking to herself in an angry mumble, Virginia continued down the hall to her room.

"*Virginia!*"

Stopping at the door, she pulled on the long metal chain around her neck. Her keys, at the end of the chain, were hung up on something under her blouse.

"Shit," said Virginia, still unaware of Dot and Julie.

"VIRGINIA!!" Dot placed her hand on Virginia's arm.

"Eh?" She turned around, still pulling on the chain.

"We need to talk."

"Eh?"

Dot bent over, directly in Virginia's face. "We have to talk about what happened in the dining room."

Virginia squinched her face and glared at Dot.

"Let me help you with your keys," Dot said.

"What?"

"DO YOU NEED HELP WITH YOUR KEY?"

"It's stuck," said Virginia, unbuttoning her blouse.

Behind Dot, Julie started to giggle.

The chain with its set of keys had been put on before Virginia's bra. Virginia, blouse now unbuttoned, grabbed the room key from below her bra and managed to open the door. The bra, old and loose and stretched by the pulled chain from beneath it, allowed both breasts to escape. Dot heard Julie snorting behind her, desperately trying not to laugh.

"Come in," Virginia finally said. She put down her cane, adjusted the bra, and rebuttoned her blouse. Julie tried to hold her breath. Virginia smelled bad and so did her room.

Dot flipped on the light and wished she were elsewhere. Piles of envelopes and magazines were stacked on old, worn furniture. Dresser drawers were crammed full of something—hopefully clothes—and none were fully closed. The contents of a large plastic bag, open at the top, were visible in the small bathroom.

Lord! Used diapers!

Dot sat on the edge of Virginia's bed. Virginia plopped down in her old brown recliner, worn bare on both arms where she grasped them to help her rise. Julie stood in the doorway, poking her head in the hall every few minutes to gasp.

"Virginia, why did you shake your cane at Minnie?" Dot had to mouth the words slowly. She took Virginia's old carved cane in her right hand and pretended to wave it at someone.

"I had that chair first. She had no right to it."

"We can't have you threatening people with your cane, Virginia. That's just not acceptable behavior. I'd like you to apologize to Minnie."

Virginia fiddled with her hearing aid.

"Virginia?"

"What?"

"Let's go down to my office and we'll talk with Minnie."

"Why?"

Dot sighed. She looked at Julie, who was now standing outside the door to Virginia's room.

This was going to take a while.

Dot set the font on her computer to Arial, size 26. Virginia, Julie, Minnie, and Camille sat on her two office chairs and the small couch. A topnotch secretary in her early twenties, Dot's fingers flew over the keyboard now. For everyone's benefit, she read the message aloud as she typed:

Virginia:

We all must talk about what happened in the dining room. It is not permissible to threaten another resident, and it is also unacceptable to swear in the dining room within earshot of other residents. I understand you did both. Minnie and Camille were simply trying to find Harriet's chair, which had been placed mistakenly at your table.

She handed the note to Virginia, who read it and then glared at Minnie and Camille.

"Nobody's going to take my chair out from under me," she said.

They would have given you your regular chair to exchange with Harriet's, if you'd let them.

Dot wished her printer were faster.

"They never said that."

"She never gave us a chance, Dot. She called me a bitch and told Camille to screw herself," said Minnie.

Virginia, did you call Minnie a bitch, and did you tell Camille to screw herself in the dining room?

"Yes, and I don't care where she does it. They're not going to push me around."

Julie rolled her eyes. Dot persisted.

Minnie and Camille were simply trying to help Harriett, Virginia. She is in pain all the time, and that chair is the only one she's found that's even slightly comfortable.

"Then she should come over and ask about it."

She was in too much pain.

Virginia was silent.

I'd like you to apologize to Minnie and Camille for making a scene in the dining room.

"No."

Then *I'll* apologize to them for your behavior.

Dot shoved a copy of the Harmony Hall "Policies" at Virginia.

You signed this when you moved here. It says you will be cordial to other residents and that we have the right to ask you to move if you create a disturbance. I want you to understand that this behavior can't be tolerated, and that if it happens again, you'll have to find another home.

Virginia read the paragraph and narrowed her eyes. "Fine," she said, struggling to get on her feet.

"Just a minute," said Dot, standing up. She walked around the desk and stood between Virginia and the door. "You two can go, and thanks for coming," she said to Camille and Minnie. "I'm so sorry this happened, and we'll try to see that it doesn't occur again. Julie, you and I need to talk further with Virginia."

Virginia said, "Eh?"

Camille took Minnie's hand and they left Dot's office.

You still aren't disposing of your diapers properly, Virginia, and your room smells like urine. I'm also worried that you're not bathing regularly.

I'm going to call your sister and see if we can get someone to come in and help you once or twice a week. This situation also can't continue.

Virginia was furious. "Leave my sister out of my affairs!"

She's your only living relative, and your power of attorney. I have to ask her for help because there's no one else.

"I'll find someone to help me—I don't need her help or yours."

She grabbed her ancient, carved cane, rocked several times and got to her feet. She stomped from Dot's office, leaving a large wet spot on the cranberry chair facing the desk.

"Why don't you just tell her to leave?" asked Julie.

"I keep thinking we can make her relatively happy here, and I know she would be more miserable somewhere else," said Dot. She sprayed Resolve on the chair. "Virginia's not a bad person. She's deaf, which is probably a worse handicap than blindness, even, and she's losing her sight, and she's incontinent and she has trouble walking. She is also virtually friendless. I'd be miserable too. She can't afford anything else. Imagine being in that position."

"She's got everyone on edge, Dot. I know she's unhappy, but I doubt that we can change that. I just worry about the effect she's having on everybody else."

"Let me work on her a little longer. I think I've got someone who can help turn her around. I'm going down to her room."

Dot got up slowly and looked at her watch. Twenty minutes 'til bingo. Maybe Virginia would be so anxious to get rid of her that she'd agree to some home health care.

"Virginia?" She knocked on the door as loud as she could. Two residents in nearby rooms poked their heads into the hall. Dot waved at them. She heard a shuffling sound beyond the locked door. Virginia opened it an inch.

"What do you want?"

"We need to finish our talk."

"Eh?"

"WE NEED TO FINISH OUR TALK."

"I'm going to bingo."

"WE'LL TALK FAST."

Virginia stepped aside and let Dot in. Dot gestured to the bed and sat down on the very edge of it. Virginia, feet planted, refused to sit down. Dot stood up. She spoke slowly and into Virginia's better ear.

"Virginia, I have someone I'd like you to meet. She's a lovely girl, and helps ladies with their rooms and their baths. I can't let you continue living in this condition at Harmony Hall. Your room is a mess. You can't seem to take proper care of your incontinence pads, and you and your room smell of urine. Why don't I introduce you to her tomorrow, and we'll take it from there?"

Virginia looked at her watch. It was 1:45. *What the hell!* "OK," she said, and stomped off to the upstairs activity area, hoping that no one had settled into her favorite chair there, and forgetting her quarter.

"Myrtle?" Dot pressed the phone to her ear. Virginia's sister was ninety-eight. No telling how her hearing was.

"Speaking," said the voice on the other end.

"This is Dot Turner at Harmony Hall. There's no emergency here."

"Ms. Turner! How good to hear from you. How is Virginia?"

She's meaner than a junkyard dog.

"She's OK. I'm worried about her personal hygiene and the condition of her room. Can she afford to have someone in to help her once or twice a week? It may cost her thirty or forty dollars."

There was a slight pause.

"Yes, she can."

"It won't be a hardship?"

"No. Call me if she puts up a fight."

"OK. Thanks."

"Thanks for your concern, Ms. Turner. I don't know what she would do without you folks."

"Maria?"

"Just a meeneet."

Dot signed checks while she waited for Maria Alonso to come to the phone.
"Hello?"

"Maria?"

"Yes, eet ees."

"This is Dot Turner at Harmony Hall. I got your name from Faith Green at Boutique Magnifique."

"Yes?"

"Faith tells me you are a caretaker and might be able to help one of my ladies here once or twice a week."

"Yes?"

Nuts, she doesn't speak English.

"Comprende?" Dot asked.

"Si—yes."

"Maria, could you come to our home and let me introduce you to a lady who needs help here?"

"Yes. I come there when?"

"Today? 4:00?"

"Yes."

"Do you know how to get here?"

"'Yes."

"I'll see you at 4:00. Muchas gracias."

"Thank you," said Maria.

Dot checked the time. It was 2:30. If Maria showed at 4:00 she'd have an hour or so to work on Virginia and convince her that Maria's services were necessary. Fortunately, Virginia couldn't communicate with anyone very well, so Maria's limited English might not be a problem.

"Virginia, there's a lady coming by today at 4:00 to meet you. I think she can help you with bathing and keeping your room in order."

Dot sat gingerly on the edge of Virginia's bed. Bags of napkins—new and used—poked from beneath it. Dot tried not to think of what else might be there.

Virginia scowled. "I can't pay her," she said.

"This lady charges less than everybody else, Virginia. You can afford twenty dollars a week, which is just ten dollars an hour. She'll only be here twice a week for one hour. You've got to have some assistance—or you'll have to leave here, and I don't want you to leave. Just try her for a week, OK?"

Virginia's right hand curled around the head of her carved cane. Her knuckles, red and swollen, drew Dot's attention to her ragged, dirty nails. Virginia ground her teeth and fell backward into her old recliner. Her crusty feet, in worn, frayed slippers, were several inches off the floor.

"One week," she said.

Dot sighed. "I'll be back at 4:00." She left the foul smelling room and its grimy occupant.

Oh, Maria, please come through.

❧   ❧   ❧

At 3:50 Maria Alonso, tall, lithe and dark haired, pushed the door bell at Harmony Hall. An exchange student working on a nursing degree, she realized that America was indeed a land of opportunity. Maria, industrious, loving, respectful and insightful, usually gleaned her income from the families of very elderly women. At ten dollars an hour she sometimes made hundreds of dollars a week—more than her contemporaries in Mexico made in months. Half of what she made was sent home, and a small part of what was left she sometimes spent at Faith's consignment shop, where she had first learned of Harmony Hall.

"Maria?" Dot shook Maria's hand. They walked together back to Dot's office with Mack gamboling at their heels. Once Maria was seated, Dot closed the door; a rare occurrence and clear signal to anyone who saw it that something serious was going on.

"Maria, my resident's name is Vir-gin-ya." Dot spoke slowly and enunciated each word clearly.

Maria nodded and said, "Veer-geen-ya."

"Virginia is deaf," Dot said, pointing to her right ear. "She cannot hear."

Maria nodded.

"She is incontinent. She needs help with her Depends. Comprende?"

"Yes. Wee or poo?" asked Maria.

"Wee," said Dot.

"OK."

"Her room is a mess. She needs someone to help her keep it neat."

Maria nodded.

"Comprende?"

"Yes."

"Virginia needs someone to mak—help—her bathe—two times a week. She is not clean."

Maria nodded.

"Once a week, Virginia needs help with her laundry. It is not clean, either."

"Ees no problem," Maria said, smiling.

Dot stared hard at the attractive, pleasant girl across the desk, and tried to remember something appropriate from high school Spanish.

"Virginia is very difficult—muy dificil. She does not want you here, but I am making her get help. She says for one week only."

Maria laughed. "Ees OK," she said. "I help many ladies. Some ladies are not so nice, but we are happy."

Dot wasn't sure what that meant, but figured she'd given Maria sufficient warning. "Well, let's go meet your new lady," she said. Dot pounded on Virginia's door. It opened slowly, and Virginia looked up into Maria's dark eyes. She glowered at Maria and said, "I can only pay you for one week."

Maria smiled and took one of Virginia's hands in hers. "Ees OK." She turned to Dot and said, "Thank you, Meeses Dot; we are fine."

The door closed as slowly as it had opened, and Dot walked back toward her office, imagining poor Maria trying to convince Virginia that it was time for a bath.

❋   ❋   ❋

Maria stifled the urge to choke and looked around. Across the room, atop the cluttered dresser, was a single sepia photograph, whose subjects smiled within the confines of a plain wooden frame. She walked to the dresser and examined the picture. A young couple, holding hands, stood before an antique car. The girl, slim and beautiful, was laughing at the photographer. Her parasol was held above dark curls. Her partner, a head taller and light-haired, was grinning.

"Mees Veergeenya," said Maria, turning back to her charge, and smiling, "ees your parents?"

"Eh?"

Virginia joined Maria in front of the dresser.

"EES YOUR PARENTS?" Maria asked, louder.

Virginia snorted. "That's my husband and me. We were leaving for our honeymoon."

Maria's eyes widened. "Ees you?"

"Eh?"

"Mees. Veergeenya, you are *beautiful!*" Maria pointed to the man in the picture. "Your husband ees *very* handsome."

Virginia reached up and took the picture. She studied it closely.

"This was taken in 1923 when we were both twenty years old. He was a salesman for Underwood Typewriters. He was a perfect gentleman. We were very happy for many years."

She handed the picture to Maria.

"Look at your hair, Mees Veergeenya—so preety!" Maria studied the faded photograph. She turned to gaze into Virginia's cloudy eyes, wondering about the life of the ninety-five year old woman whose gray, greasy hair was so unlike what she saw in the picture. Returning it to the dresser, she surveyed the room. Small and cluttered, it was double the size of what she'd left in Mexico, but had half the usable space.

"May I look een the bathroom?"

Virginia nodded.

Maria opened the cabinet doors under the lavatory. The usual collection of lotions, soap, shampoo and over the counter medicines were jumbled beneath it.

"Mees Veergeenya, you have curlers?"

Maria pointed to her own hair and then pretended to roll it.

Virginia moved to her closet and pulled one of its sliding doors open to reveal shelves crammed with bags. She rummaged around, finally pulled one out and handed it to Maria.

Inside the bag were bristly rollers of various sizes.

"Ees perfect!" Maria exclaimed, laughing.

Virginia smiled at her enthusiasm. She looked at her watch.

"I have to go to the dining room—it's almost time for supper."

"Ees OK. I come tomorrow. Ees OK at 3:00?"

"Yes."

"Goodbye, Mees Veergeenya."

Maria bent down and hugged the small, thick, aged body. Taken aback but pleased, Virginia hesitated and then hugged Maria back with her one free arm.

"Good-bye," she said, and watched as Maria's long legs quickly covered the distance down the hall and turned toward Dot's office.

❀   ❀   ❀

At 5:10 Maria knocked on Dot's doorframe.

"Mees Dot?"

"Come on in, Maria."

Dot rose and pointed to her loveseat. Maria sat down.

"How did it go?" *I'll bet she's turning this assignment down.*

"Great!"

"Great?"

"I come tomorrow for the bath at 3:00, ees OK?"

"Sure. Any time you can make it is good. Was it OK with Virginia?"

"Yes." Maria paused.

"Mees Dot, ees a beauty shop here?

"Yes."

"Ees a dryer?"

"Yes. Let me show you."

They walked next door to the room that served as Angel's shop and Dot flicked on the overhead lights. Maria's eyes sparkled.

"Ees OK eef I use tomorrow for Mees Veergeenya's hair?"

Dot hesitated. Angel was adamant that only she operate out of the beauty shop because of licensing regulations. She wouldn't be in tomorrow, though.

"Maria, if you use the shop, leave everything just as you find it. We're not supposed to have anyone in here except our beautician. Comprende?"

"Si."

They returned to Dot's office.

"Do you need anything else?"

"Beeg bags."

"Maria, if I give you some money, can you buy what you need and bring me the receipt?"

"Yes."

"Just a minute."

Dot walked to Julie's office. Julie, working on her computer, eyes wide, mouthed, "How's it going?"

"Good, I think," said Dot. She rolled her eyes, looked heavenward and put her hands together as if she were praying. Julie giggled.

"I'm giving Maria a twenty out of the slush fund to buy some supplies. She'll bring us receipts."

"Is she going to do it?" Julie whispered.

"That's what she says." Dot grinned at Julie. "She's supposed to be back tomorrow at 3:00. Say a prayer or two."

Julie nodded, her face serious. She prayed about everything, and adding Maria to her list was no problem.

❦   ❦   ❦

CHAPTER 24

GIVING THANKS

NOVEMBER, 1998

Maria knocked on Virginia's door promptly at 3:00 on Friday afternoon. Amazingly, the door opened immediately; Virginia had obviously been sitting next to the door on a small chair.

"Hello!" Maria said. She had a small bouquet in a vase in one hand, a huge shopping bag in the other. She handed the vase to Virginia.

"Ees a present for you!"

Virginia beamed. "How pretty...thank you...uh, uh,..."

"Maria," said Maria.

"Thank you, Maria."

Maria walked to the dresser.

"They go here, yes?" She pointed to the back corner, near the old picture they had looked at together the day before. Virginia nodded. Maria took the vase and positioned it near the photograph. It seemed suddenly newer and brighter with the flowers nearby.

"Ees time for a bath, Mees Veergeenya. We do your bath, your hair, your feengernails, OK?"

She opened the door to the bathroom. Virginia followed her inside. Maria turned the water on and tested it. She gently helped Virginia undress, and positioned her on the shower chair. She unhooked the handheld sprayer from the cradle on the wall and let the warm water flow over Virginia's body, lathering liquid soap into the folds of her skin. The warm water and perfumed soap and Maria's gentle touch were all soporific. Virginia actually dozed in the soft-seated chair as Maria washed her hair and massaged her scalp. Maria dried Virginia's body, rubbed lotion on her flaking skin, and helped her dress.

"We go to the shop now," she said, and grabbed the bag of rollers. The transformation was underway.

❧   ❧   ❧

Angel's Salon, next to Julie's office, was as comfortable as an old shoe. Maria helped Virginia into the well-worn styling chair, reached into her huge shoulder bag and pulled out a pair of scissors. "I treem just a leetle," she told Virginia. The damp, gray hair collected at her feet and on the towel she'd spread across Virginia's shoulders. She laid the bristly rollers out on the counter, sprayed Virginia's hair with a mixture of water and setting solution, and deftly rolled the trimmed hair, securing everything with a hairnet.

"What time is it?" asked Virginia.

"Ees early—3:30."

Maria settled the old lady under a hair dryer and pulled up a chair. She took Virginia's left hand and began cutting the nails. Virginia dozed off—barely opening her eyes when Maria finished with that hand and moved on to her right.

"Mees Veergeenya? *Mees Veergeenya!*"

Virginia's eyes flew open. Maria was bending over and smiling at her.

"Stay here. I weel be back, OK?"

Virginia nodded and closed her eyes.

Maria dashed back to Virginia's room. She pulled on a pair of disposable plastic gloves and began throwing old papers, napkins and used diapers in large plastic bags. She carried the bags to the garbage containers outside the building, returned to the room, sprayed it with air freshener and then installed another one in an outlet near the door to the room. At 4:15 she returned, woke Virginia, checked her hair and turned off the dryer.

"We comb, OK?"

Virginia rocked four times and staggered back to the styling chair, slightly stupefied by the heat and her nap. Maria removed the rollers and began to brush through the thick, gray hair, exclaiming to Virginia all the while how wonderful she looked. The new do was sprayed and Virginia's glasses were arranged on her nose. Maria stood behind her new client, and they both gazed at the results in the large wall mirror.

"You like?"

Virginia nodded. She then noticed that her nails were rounded and now a pale pink.

"Mees Veergeenya!" Maria grabbed Virginia's chin and laughed, "Leep-steek!"

"Uuh!" said Virginia.

Maria quickly outlined the thin, dry lips with a pink liner and filled them in with a lighter shade. She applied blush and powdered Virginia's nose, stepping back to catch the whole effect. Delighted, she raised her right hand for a high-five, and waited until Virginia's hand met hers. It was official. Mees Veergeena was *perfecta.*

❦   ❦   ❦

Mimi, Camille and Minnie were always first at their table for supper. Harriett, who had a hard time getting down to the dining room, always put it off 'til the last minute, and Eloise generally came with her. Bertha often needed reminding that it was time to eat. Tonight, Friday, was wine night. All three were taking their first sip when Virginia walked by them to her table. Minnie, her wig sideways, stopped in mid-sip. Her eyes, wide, met Camille's over the rim of her wineglass. Camille had lowered her glass—and her jaw. Her tongue, slightly pinker than usual thanks to the red wine, was thoroughly visible from where Mimi sat, across the table. Mimi, her back to the dining room entrance, turned around to see what it was that had left her tablemates thunderstruck. The retreating figure of a fairly stout woman with curly gray hair moved toward a table in the far dining area.

"Do you know her?" asked Mimi.

"Is that who I think it is?" asked Camille, looking at Minnie.

Minnie lowered her glass. "It can't be."

"Who is it?" said Mimi.

"My God…what's happened?" said Camille.

Minnie squinted at the distant table. The volume of chatter at that end of the dining room was turned up to high—she could hear squeals coming from Virginia's table. Suddenly, a resident at the noisy table raised her wine glass high. It was obvious a toast was being made. Minnie was dying to find out what was up.

"I'll be right back," she said, and pulled her wig off over her right ear. She laid it in her chair, as if saving her place from some unknown diner, and began working her way through the dining room, back to the scene of Wednesday's altercation. As she drew nearer, she confirmed that it was, indeed, Virginia who had passed their table just minutes earlier. This Virginia had bouncy, curly hair, manicured nails and—wonder of wonders—*lipstick*. Virginia's tablemates were patting her on the back and exclaiming over her new look. She was looking slightly dazed, but was smiling and pretending to hear what was being said. Minnie acted lost and made a right turn out of the dining room and into the living room. She circled back to her own table, and grabbed her wig off the chair seat.

"It's Virginia, alright," she said. "I think she's had a facelift."

"Well, maybe she'll be nicer now," said Camille.

"I doubt it, but when she's bitchy she'll look a *helluva* lot better," said Minnie. Grinning at Mimi, she finished the interrupted sip of Chillable Red.

Maria wrote her invoice on a yellow pad Dot gave her the first day she visited Virginia at Harmony Hall:

For general assistance:

Friday, November 6, 1998–1.5 hours @ $10.00/hr.	= $15.00
Friday, November 13, 1998–1.0 hours @ $10.00/hr.	= $10.00
Total due:	$25.00

Payment is due when invoice is received. Please remit to:
Maria Alonso
174 Westerland Way
Lexington, KY 40503
277-3443

She slipped the bill in an envelope and dropped it in the mail. Hopefully, she would be paid by the next time she saw Virginia, who now seemed to look forward to Fridays and her bath.

On Wednesday afternoon Maria received her pre-addressed, stamped envelope. Inside was a ragged twenty dollar bill and a printed note:

YOU KNOW WE AGREED ON $10 AN HOUR. I CAN'T HELP IT IF YOU
TOOK LONGER. THIS IS ALL I HAVE.
    VIRGINIA WILHOITE

Maria's hands shook. She replaced the note and the bill in the envelope and
stuck it in her purse. She dialed the Harmony Hall number.

"Good afternoon, Harmony Hall," a young voice answered.

"Mees Dot, please."

"Just a moment."

Lauren dialed Dot's extension. "Dot, I think it might be Maria on line one
for you."

Dot bit her lip.

"Dot Turner," she said.

"Mees Dot, eet ees Maria. Please, to tell Mees Veergeenya I no can work for
her."

Dot gazed out her window, eyes narrowed. "What's the matter, Maria?"

"She no can pay my fee," said Maria. "I am sorry. I weel help other ladies eef
they can pay, Mees Dot."

"OK, Maria. Comprendo. I will call you soon. Gracias."

Dot felt her face flushing. She saved the computer file she'd been working
on and called Virginia.

"Virginia? This is Dot. May I come down and talk to you for a minute?"

"Eh?"

"IT'S DOT. I'M COMING TO SEE YOU."

"OK."

Dot turned off her office lights. She pounded on Virginia's door a moment
later, and took a seat, uninvited, on Virginia's bed when the door opened. The
room smelled fresh. There were no newspapers stacked in corners; no bagged
napkins protruded from beneath the bed. Virginia looked happy and
clean—Dot caught a whiff of cologne when she turned to sit.

"Virginia, I just wanted you to know that Maria called me this afternoon."

Virginia looked surprised. "Is she all right?"

"Yes. She's fine. She told me she cannot come back, though, and she wanted
me to tell you."

"What?"

"You heard me," said Dot.

"Why not?" asked Virginia.

"You tell me."

"I'm sure I don't know," said Virginia, tremulously.

"Well, it's a shame, Virginia. She's a wonderful girl, and you've never looked better. You still need a bath every week, and I'll see if I can find someone else. I'll try to get them here by Friday. They'll probably charge fifteen dollars an hour, so be prepared. Do you understand?"

The hot flash hit her like an instant sauna. Dot wiped her brow, her upper lip and her neck, in one fluid, practiced motion, and wiped her palm on her skirt. Without waiting for Virginia's reply, she fled the room for cooler air.

From her recliner Virginia stared at the pre-honeymoon photograph across the room but could not make out the figures. The room was dark, but through the blinds a lemon moon created white light slivers that streamed across her carpet. The invoice lay in her lap. Painfully, she turned the switch on her night-stand lamp and reached for her address book. It took several minutes to find "Maria," a new entry.

"Hola, Mees Dot!"

Maria stood in the doorway, radiant.

"Maria! What are you doing here?"

"Mees Veergeenya call me—ees OK now. I geeve bath again today!"

"Wonderful! I'm so glad you're back on the job, Maria. I don't think we could replace you."

"She knows ees good price and I do good job, Mees Dot. No problema!"

Dot smiled and waved as Maria left for Virginia's room.

She's had an epiphany at ninety-five. Thank you, Lord—I owe you.

"Lauren, have you seen Jim?" Minnie leaned against the little lobby desk and grinned at Lauren, who was sorting mail.

"I think he's in the dining room, mopping," said Lauren.

"Well, guess what!"

"What?"

"I've got a mouse in my room!"

"Really?" Lauren stopped sorting. "How do you know?"

"He got into my crackers and left his calling card."

Lauren looked puzzled. "What do you mean?"

Minnie leaned toward Lauren and whispered, "He pooped."

"Yeech," said Lauren. "Let's go find Jim."

Ben Briden, from Prevent-A-Pest, who sprayed the group areas at Harmony Hall every month, confirmed the presence of a mouse in Minnie's room. He set out poisoned bait and told Minnie that the mouse would likely eat it, crawl away and die. Just to be sure, for a week she set out her own bait to confirm the mouse was gone. It wasn't.

"Jimbo, that little rascal is still in my room."

Jim, replacing light bulbs in the hall, looked down at Minnie from his ladder. "Are you sure?"

"Yep. He ate one of my Oreos last night."

"I'll get Ben back over, Minnie. He'll have to try something else."

"Ms. Potter, I've put out some sticky paper in the corners of your room. What happens is, the mouse will run across it and get stuck, and then you can have Jim dispose of it. I'm sorry the bait didn't work."

Ben left Minnie's room in search of Jim. There seemed to be a small opening behind a corner cabinet in Minnie's room. Once that was covered, and the current critter killed, all would be well.

Minnie felt better about the paper. Being poisoned had to be a terrible way to die. That night, late, she heard a squeek and scrambled for her glasses. It was nearly 2:00 A.M. She checked the corners and found it, near the bathroom. Was it a baby? It was the tiniest mouse she'd ever seen. All four feet were stuck to the paper and it stared at her, terrified. She stared back for only a moment, then picked the paper up and gingerly walked to the parking lot door. As she started to turn the handle, the door opened and she found herself face to face with Mimi. The taillights of a car pulled away from the door and disappeared down the exit driveway.

"Minnie! What are you doing?"

"Ha! What are *you* doing?"

They both burst out laughing; then Mimi saw the mouse.

"Oh, no. The poor little thing."

"I know. I wish we'd never called that guy. What can we do?"

"Let's try to get him off the paper and let him go."

They sat together on the old iron bench under the portico. Mimi put her purse down, got out her glasses and pulled a toothpick from her coat pocket. Minnie held the mouse's body off the paper with a twig once both hind feet were free—Mimi worked with the toothpick on the front ones. Suddenly her finger got too close, and the mouse bit her.

"Ouch! Calm down, Buddy, we're almost there."

When he was free, the mouse took off in the night, running under the shrubs along the building. Mimi squeezed her finger, trying to make it bleed. She looked at Minnie and grinned. "I feel a lot better now, don't you?"

"Yes," said Minnie, in her hoarse voice. "And so does the mouse. Thanks, Mimi. It was a miracle that you were here."

"Life is full of them," said Mimi, and opened the door to the building.

❦   ❦   ❦

"Mother?"

Skipper was lying in a tub of hot water and bubbles, trying to soak away the dirt and depletion of a four-hour stint at the arboretum.

"Hello! How are you?"

It had taken Pansy seven rings to get to the phone. *Was she sleeping? It's 3:00 P.M.!*

"Great. I've been outdoors working in a garden all day—I'll sleep tonight. How goes it there?"

"Things are coming together. Reverend Atchison has been a huge help, of course. I think we've managed to identify and pay most of the outstanding bills. I'm still on an anti-depressant, and I believe it's helping. Not too many awful days of late."

Pansy paused, and Skipper heard her say something to someone in the room—it was obvious that she'd covered the phone.

"Is this a bad time to call, Mother?" Skipper took a sip of her drink and tried to hear the other party's voice in the background.

"It's just Bru…Reverend Atchison. He's on his way out."

Skipper heard the front door slam. "Did you get your ticket?" she asked.

"Yes, dear. Are you sure you can afford this, Priscilla? It's awfully expensive to fly these days."

"I've got a million frequent flier miles, Mother. It didn't cost a thing."

Thanksgiving was Thursday. Tomorrow her mother would visit them for the first time—ever. Skipper stared at her toes, above water, scarlet nails shimmering behind a mountain of bubbles. *What in the world will we do?*

❧   ❧   ❧

"Are you cooking Thursday?"

Faith, scurrying between clothes racks and fitting rooms for three customers, could barely remember what was planned for Thanksgiving.

"Let me call you back, Skipper. Where are you?"

"Home."

"Bye."

For the last three years they'd all gone to Mimi's duplex. Skipper pictured Mimi's room at the retirement home. *Hell, she doesn't even have a microwave.*

❧   ❧   ❧

Faith locked the front door at *Magnifique* and whistled softly at Babe, who was beginning to point at a pigeon. She fished in her bag for her cell phone, dialed Skipper's number, and rolled down the window on the front passenger's side of her aged Toyota. There were few days cold enough to dissuade her from giving Babe an open window on the way home.

Skipper answered with her usual, "Darling!"

"What's up?" said Faith.

"I'm scared stiff. Mother's coming tomorrow, and I have no idea what we're going to talk about—much less where we're going for Thanksgiving. What are you doing?"

"Mom's having us over to Harmony Hall Thursday for lunch. Why don't you come with your mother? I'll check with Julie, but I'm sure they've got plenty of room."

Skipper hesitated. *What will she think of eating with a bunch of old women?*

"What time?"

"The usual—12:30. Oh, come on, Skipper. It'll be fun."

"Let me know if they've got room for us. I'll check with Lauren. It really snuck up on me this year."

Pansy awoke, startled, when the plane's wheels dropped. Bluegrass Airport, surrounded by manicured horse farms and home to the private jets of their owners, magically emerged from the middle of a field. It was Tuesday morning. Horses grazed in pastures adjacent to runways, coats gleaming in the bright November sunshine. *If only Ted were here.*

"Mother!"

She heard Priscilla's voice, sharp and distinctive, before she saw her. Pansy turned toward the voice and was suddenly wrapped in arms—both her daughter and granddaughter were hugging her. "Oh, m-m-my! Oh, m-m-y!" she stuttered, trying to get a look at both of them.

"Hi, Grandma!" said Lauren.

She was tall and had a short, spiky haircut. Her boots, with three-inch heels, looked terribly uncomfortable, but she was smiling, as if they were the last thing on her mind.

"Lauren, dear, how wonderful to see you," said Pansy.

"Hey, Mother," said Skipper. "You look pretty darn good." She grabbed Pansy's carry-on and all three walked together toward the baggage area, each trying to get a word in.

The red Mercedes, top up, snaked out of the parking lot. Lauren was squeezed in somehow behind her mother and grandmother, along with the luggage.

"Mother, I can't wait for you to meet Faith's mother, Mimi," Skipper said. "I think we'll have a chance to see her tonight—we've been invited to the entertainment this evening at Harmony Hall—a group of Hawaiian dancers. What do you think?"

"You'll love her, Grandma."

"I'm sure I will, dear. Honestly, anything you'd like to do is fine with me." Pansy reached for Lauren's hand, squeezed it, and smiled at her beautiful daughter as they sped toward Skipper's townhouse.

❧   ❧   ❧

Julie had arranged for Tuesday's entertainment through word-of-mouth. The activities director at a local nursing home had referred her to a group that performed authentic Hawaiian dances for forty-five minutes. Anxious to please Dot, she volunteered to stay late Tuesday evening to ready the living room and introduce the performers. Most programs took place at 4:00—it was a special treat to have something after supper…especially something as unusual as hula dancers.

As her ladies began to file into the living room at 6:00 for the 6:30 performance, the doorbell rang. Julie rushed to the lobby and opened the door to admit two very heavy older women, each pulling a large overnight bag on wheels.

"May I help you?" she asked.

"We're part of the Hallelujah Hula show," said the larger of the two, glancing around the lobby.

"I'm sorry?" said Julie. *Surely she's joking.*

"We're part of the hula group," the woman said. "I'm Ada Rambone. This is my friend, Cora Hathaway."

"Oh…well, how nice to meet you. I'm Julie Painter, the Assistant Director. The residents are so excited about seeing you."

Ada gave Julie the once-over. "Do you know where we'll be dancing?"

"We're in the living room," said Julie. "Just follow me." She headed down the hall, followed by Ada and Cora.

"How long have you been doing the hula?" asked Julie.

"Not long enough," said Cora. "We can't practice very often, but we're getting better every time we get together…aren't we, Ada?"

She adjusted her glasses and peered at the larger woman.

"You bet your booties," said Ada.

They inspected the living room and asked if there was a place to change. Julie led them to the beauty shop and ran back to the lobby to answer the doorbell again. Three more elderly women, one with a cane, stood under the portico. They were all carrying large mesh bags—one also carried a boom box.

"Hello," said Julie, breathlessly. "I'll bet you're part of the hula group."

"You got it," said one of the three. "Have our other members shown up?"

"Ada and Cora are here," said Julie.

"That's all there is," said the first woman.

They followed her to the beauty shop and Ada gave her a crumpled sheet that detailed their act and which, she explained, could be read as an introduction:

The Hallelujah Hula dancers are the brainchild of Ada Rambone, who fell in love with Hawaii during several trips there with her husband. After he died, Ada felt called to bring the beauty of the island dances to people who could not travel, and later began to choreograph her favorite hymns. Her partners in this celebration of dance and music are Cora Hathaway, DeeDee Jones, Anita Campion and Mabel Guthrie, all bridge players and members of their church choir.

The doorbell rang again. Julie left the beauty shop for the foyer, and saw Skipper, Lauren and a slight blond woman standing at the door.

"Sorry, Julie, I forgot my key," said Lauren. "This is my grandma, Pansy," she added.

"I'm so pleased to meet you," said Julie, trying to usher all three to the elevator and away from the living room.

"We're here to watch the Hawaiian dancers," said Lauren. "Mimi's meeting us in the living room."

Oh, no. "We've never had them before," whispered Julie. "I hope they know what they're doing."

"We'll critique them for you," laughed Skipper. "I've been known to do a few hula dances myself, in younger years."

Lauren rolled her eyes, but grinned at Pansy. "Let's go meet Mimi," she said, and all three started toward the living room.

Julie cut through the nearly deserted dining room and entered the living room from the side door. Nearly all the residents were present—there were only a few empty chairs. She saw Mimi jump up and greet Skipper, Lauren and Pansy, then lead them to seats she'd obviously been saving. Suddenly, Ada was at her elbow. It was 6:30.

"We're ready if you are," said Ada.

"Great! I'll introduce you," and Julie read the introduction with all the enthusiasm she could muster.

"Blue Hawaii" began to play from the boom box tape, and suddenly the five dancers formed a line in front of the gathered residents and guests. They were in grass skirts and colorful flowered halter tops. Julie watched, horrified, as their bare arms and midriffs jiggled uncontrollably during the first dance. Rolls of white skin hung over the waistbands of the skirts. The woman with the cane managed to dance with it in one hand and used her other to balance herself, at times waving wildly, out of rhythm with the other dancers. As they warmed to the music all five women began to move their hips with greater zeal—especially Ada, who now and then would bump into either Cora or the woman on her left, nearly knocking each off her feet.

When the first song finished, Julie recognized the familiar strains of "The Old Rugged Cross." The dancers were moving to the music, waving their arms in some mystic Hawaiian way, looking sanctimonious. She stole a quick look at Skipper and Lauren. Skipper had her hand over her mouth and had put her sunglasses on. Lauren was looking at the clock. Pansy was watching all five women intently—as if fascinated by a strange native ritual. The rest of her residents were transfixed, but Julie couldn't tell if it was the dancing to Christian hymns or the sight of five jiggling, overweight women that held them captive.

This can't be happening.

At the end of the program, weak with embarrassment, she thanked all five dancers profusely, in front of her residents, who clapped politely. She slid an envelope containing the check Dot had written earlier that day into Ada's large, perspiring hand. Too discomfited to speak to anyone assembled in the living room, she went to her office and called Carmen, the security employee, and told her she was leaving.

That night, sleepless, Julie decided it would be best for her to resign. She would never be able to live this down—and it wasn't fair to ask Dot to keep her on board. Finally, early the next morning, she cried herself to sleep.

❧   ❧   ❧

"Dot?"

"Hey! How goes it?" Dot was flipping through the previous day's mail, pitching most of it.

"Can we talk?" Julie's face was drawn and pale.

Dot stopped her mail review, got up and closed her office door.

"What gives?" She sat back down and motioned for Julie to do the same.

"I think I'd better resign, Dot." Julie started to cry.

"What? Why?" Dot sounded rattled.

"Last night was horrible. I know these ladies were mortified, and we even had guests. I've probably ruined our reputation." Julie held a Kleenex over her nose.

Dot slowly let go of the breath she'd been holding.

"What happened?"

"Oh, Dot, they weren't really Hawaiian dancers. They were big, fat old ladies trying to act thirty years younger—and on top of that they were trying to dance the hula to *hymns.*"

She blew her nose and looked at Dot with red, swollen eyes.

"They *what?*"

"They had choreographed the hula to Christian *hymns*—it was awful!"

Dot laughed. "Julie, don't tell me that's why you're quitting."

"Well…I just can't see anyone ever taking me seriously around here…".

"Julie, a third of our ladies probably thought it was a spoof and another third were probably wishing they could be dancing in a grass skirt. Anybody else probably got a good laugh and will forget it in twenty-four hours. Don't take this stuff too seriously—honestly, this is nothing."

Julie looked unconvinced.

"Did I ever tell you about *my* worst booking?"

"No."

"It was some guy who called from Oklahoma. I can't remember his name, but it was something like, "Singing Joe from Oklahoe"—except worse. He knew all the names of the big for-profits in town, and told me he had appointments at all of them to sing. I arranged for him to be here one night, and he walked in with some guy—his pianist, he said—who looked like a bum off the street. When Joe started to sing, I knew we were in trouble. He was either drunk or on drugs, and halfway through his show his accompanist went to sleep *on the piano* while he was playing!"

"What did you do?"

"I got them out of here, somehow, and decided from then on to get references from someone whose opinion I respected. Unfortunately, everyone has their own idea of what constitutes good entertainment."

Dot winked at Julie. "Don't sweat the small stuff, kiddo."

Julie got to her feet.

"Thanks, Dot."

"Hang in there," said Dot, and continued sorting her mail.

"Mother, did I tell you I'm working tomorrow?"

"What?"

Lauren was trying on earrings that Pansy had brought her from Connecticut. "I'm helping Evie and Cookie get Thanksgiving dinner out, and I'm helping bus tables and wash dishes so they can get out early and have Thanksgiving with their families."

"Will you be able to eat with us?" Skipper sounded miffed.

"Sure—I just might have to get up and serve somebody coffee or something."

"That's so nice of you, to volunteer your services, Lauren," said Pansy.

"Uh…I'm getting paid for it, Grandma."

"Well, there you are, then," said Pansy.

"Julie's working tomorrow, too," said Lauren. "She's celebrating Thanksgiving on Saturday in Pikeville; and since she's working, Dot can go home to South Carolina to be with her family."

"How's Julie doing?" asked Skipper.

"She's the best," said Lauren. "She always knows exactly what to do."

Thursday, November 26, broke clear and cold but sunny. Lauren awoke early, her internal clock insuring that she had plenty of time to get to work by 11:00 to help Cookie set the tables for Thanksgiving. She could hear the murmur of voices downstairs—her mother and grandmother were probably sitting at the kitchen table, drinking coffee and watching the birds flutter down to the backyard feeder. It was hard to figure why Grandma had never been here before and why her mother seemed so nice to Grandma now, after saying bad things about her over the years. With time to kill, and snug under Faith's comforter, a gift last Christmas, Lauren mused on that relationship and wondered how she'd do at lunch—her first day working as a kitchen assistant.

Julie arrived at Harmony Hall at 10:00 on Thanksgiving morning. It was the first time she would actually be in charge for an extended period. Evie had been at it since yesterday, making yeast rolls and getting things ready for fixing today. Dot had set out yesterday afternoon for Beaufort—a ten hour trip. She would probably stay overnight in a motel, and get to her mother's house by noon. Jim had promised he'd be on call to help her if she needed it, all the way from Richmond, and Julie had taken the Harmony Hall cell phone home with her Wednesday so that Carmen could reach her that night in an emergency. It was a huge responsibility taking care of Harmony Hall at Thanksgiving, but Julie knew she could do it.

❧   ❧   ❧

At 12:15, those residents who had elected to stay at Harmony Hall for the holiday meal began entering the dining room, some with family members, some alone. Faith had called Dot Wednesday morning to confirm that Skipper and Lauren could eat at Mimi's table, and Dot had said there'd be plenty of room. About half the residents would be gone, leaving only about seventeen to eat at home with friends and family—and there were forty-two seats. Faith found out when she told Mimi about Skipper and Lauren that Henry was also joining them, unsurprising news that was somehow comforting to Faith, who had begun to accept Henry as an extended family member. Henry, always comfortable in his skin but historically cautious of the all-female environment, was now a frequent caller at Harmony Hall, and no longer felt required to distance himself from the ladies. His link with Mimi was accepted, celebrated, and discussed at length by nearly everyone, so it was no surprise when he joined Mimi's family at her table.

Lauren moved smoothly through the throng now entering the dining room, and kissed her grandmother, her mother, and Faith. She eyed Henry and gave him the thumbs up. Her apron, green with the Harmony Hall logo in white, was several sizes too large, but it was evident she enjoyed wearing it. Smiling, she took their drink orders, and moved quickly to the next table.

Faith looked at her mother, who was holding hands with Henry under the table, and patted her knee. She followed Lauren with her eyes. *Who would have imagined?*

Skipper and Pansy watched diners file into the room; some chatting with strangers, others talking with friends from the home. It was a surprisingly jovial group, and wine was being served, which seemed to affect everyone by heightening the decibels at each table. At the table across the room a short, squat woman with lovely gray hair sat next to a Spanish-looking girl, who spoke animatedly to the middle-aged couple across the table from them. Minnie, without family, was trying to discuss something with the gray-haired woman, who kept looking at the Spanish girl for translation.

"I hear you've come all the way from Connecticut to have dinner with us," Henry said to Pansy, who was looking slightly frayed.

"Well, I mainly came to see my family, but this is certainly an added benefit—none of us has to spend all day in the kitchen." She looked at Skipper. "The last time my daughter and I had a Thanksgiving dinner together was nearly thirty years ago, so this is a real treat."

Mimi flashed a look at Faith. "This is Henry's and my first Thanksgiving together, so we've all got something to celebrate." She raised her wine glass and they toasted.

In the far dining room, above the muted Tony Bennett CD, laughter erupted and spread to the adjoining table. Faith felt a warm glow, surprised at the comfortable atmosphere and gaiety in an environment housing women whose average age was nearly ninety. She seemed transported to a gentler era. *Magnifique's* predominant clientele, busy young career women and middle-aged workers looking for a great deal, had no interest in much of anything but a sale. Harmony Hall's customers, double the age with careers and deals behind them, were apt to ask anything, spend time discussing anything. *How will* **we** *be at ninety?*

The swinging **Employees Only** door opened, and Cookie pushed a metal cart, laden with bowls and platters, through it, followed by Evie with a second cart, her face glistening with perspiration and a huge smile breaking as she looked around at the guests. She waved at returning family members who knew firsthand that hers was one of Lexington's best Thanksgiving meals, and started placing turkey and dressing, mashed potatoes, green beans, yeast rolls, cucumber and onion salad, sweet potato pie, and cranberry sauce around each table. As she began serving, normal conversation ceased and guests began to pass the food, some bowls to the right, some to the left, some straight across, until everyone had a full plate. Pandemonium reigned for a few minutes; then, intent on the meal and aware of its magnitude, those seated at each table fell silent.

From the kitchen, Lauren peered through the small, square window in the kitchen door. Everyone in the dining room looked content. Even Virginia, seated next to Maria, seemed delighted with the meal.

Cookie brought in the last cart from the dining room. "Wow! That's a full house." She and Evie high-fived, and Cookie began arranging the pies to cut. Before you knew it they'd be going back out with the dessert cart.

"Evie, may I go eat a few bites of your great meal with my family?" asked Lauren.

"You go, girl," said Evie, sitting on the kitchen stool, trying to cool off. "I'll call you if we need you."

Henry stood up as Lauren approached the table, and she flushed, surprised by his formality. Her hand brushed an empty wineglass as she slid into her chair, and it flew to the floor, shattering, and breaking the room's relative silence. Mortified, she sprang to her feet and then heard someone clapping. It was Minnie who was applauding her, thin arms raised high in front of her little face, wig askew, but on. Suddenly, everyone was clapping and laughing, and Julie rushed from the kitchen with the broom and dustpan. Lauren bowed in the direction of Minnie's table and sank bank into her chair.

"I'm sorry, guys," she said, looking at her grandmother.

Pansy winked at her. "You remind me of your mother, Lauren. Anything for a little attention."

"I would have made a lot more noise in my day, darling," said Skipper, raising an eyebrow, and passed the turkey in Lauren's direction.

Evie and Cookie were gathering the dishes, making room for pie. Lauren was pouring coffee. Julie stood in the middle of the now noisy dining room and tapped a fork against a glass, asking for attention, and finally getting it from those who could hear. Those who couldn't hear were nudged by those who could, and finally the room fell silent.

"Hello, everyone, and thank you for joining us today. I understand there's a tradition at Harmony Hall on Thanksgiving. If you have something you're especially thankful for, and would like to share it, please stand up and let us know. We'll start at Myra's table."

At the end of the far dining room an elderly, courtly gentleman, sitting next to Harriett, rose slowly to his feet, looked out at the assemblage and placed his hand on her shoulder.

"I am thankful to have survived the war, when so many of my peers did not, and I am thankful to have been raised in the South." He sat down carefully.

Harriett immediately stood, tiny and hunched over, and looked at her brother. "I am thankful to have been born in this country, and I am thankful for people like my brother, who insured that it has survived this long."

Applause erupted in the dining room, drowning out the next speaker's first words. He was a thin, serious-looking young man, dressed in jeans and a wrinkled tee shirt. His long brown hair was loosely pulled back in a ponytail. He began again, "I'm thankful that my great-grandmother invited me to join her today. It's the best meal I've had this year." Murmurs of assent ran through both dining rooms.

At Maybelle's table, Carl stood up, impeccably dressed, gelled hair slicked straight back, reminding Julie of male models she'd seen in magazines. He raised his water glass and said, "I'm thankful for Evie and Cookie, who have managed to turn out a fabulous meal." More applause, and both cooks, who were bringing the dessert carts back into the dining room, beamed.

Maria jumped up, looked at Virginia, and said, "I am thankful for theese place, for Mees. Veergeenya and all the ladies."

Once Maria was seated, Minnie, her wig now sideways, turned to face the room and said, with great seriousness, "I'm thankful some of us can't hear everything that goes on and some of us can't see everything that goes on, which just goes to show everything works out."

Camille was next. She put on her eyeglasses and read from a notebook she'd brought to the table. "I had to cross out a few things that some of my predecessors mentioned, but here goes of what's left: Having a beauty shop on the premises," she waited for the laughter to die down. "Having that sweet Mack as our mascot. Being so close to Kroger that we can walk if we have to, and never having to cook again." She sat down with a grin.

Mimi's table was the last to profess thanks. Skipper rose first, green eyes moist, and in a husky voice, said, "I'm thankful that Harmony Hall was desperate enough to hire my daughter, who has gained so much insight and humanity since she's worked here."

Faith, seated next to her best friend, squeezed Skipper's hand before she stood. "I'm thankful that someone, years ago, established an endowment so ladies with limited resources can live here with dignity and grace. Thank you, whoever you are."

Lauren was last. "I'm thankful that my grandmother is with us this Thanksgiving from Connecticut," she said, looking at Pansy. "And I'm thankful there wasn't any wine in that glass I broke."

Julie made a mental note to check with Dot about the endowment. She knew it involved money, but wasn't quite sure how it worked. "Enjoy your dessert, everyone," she said, and went into the kitchen to fix herself a plate.

❦   ❦   ❦

CHAPTER 25

BEARING UP

DECEMBER, 1998

"Julie, what do you have on your list for Eileen McKenny?" Dot was sitting cross-legged on her living room Oriental rug, surrounded by bags of unwrapped gifts. It was December 19, a cold and overcast Saturday morning. The Harmony Hall Christmas party was Monday night. Santa would distribute a gift to every resident.

"She's getting a framed picture of her and Mack—we took it in July."

Dot drained her coffee cup and started digging through the bags. She found the picture. Mack was doing his usual butt-in-the-air, front-paws-horizontal stretch, looking up at Eileen with his bottom teeth slightly visible. Eileen was grinning back at him from behind her walker.

"She'll love this," said Dot.

"We have six ladies getting a personal framed picture with Mack. You'd think he was a VIP."

"That's VI*D*," said Dot, reaching for the wrapping paper, and looking at Julie over her reading glasses.

"Look Dot! Can you believe I found this for two bucks?" Julie opened a large bag and pulled out a plastic mannequin's head. Julie had painted a Raggedy Ann face on the blank surface, its smile black and bisected by a red circle, a red triangular nose below wide black eyes.

"It's perfect! Minnie will never lose her wig again! Where'd you get it?"

"Faith had it. I spent about three hours in her shop looking for stuff, and we started talking about Minnie. This was back in her storeroom."

The gas logs were on, giving Dot's living room a festive feel despite the darkening day. They wrapped and chatted, glad to be getting things in order well before the party, thankful to be working without interruptions. By 2:00 every resident had an individually wrapped and tagged gift, as well as a Harmony Hall tee shirt rolled up in a Christmas gift bag.

"I can't **wait** for the party, Dot. Won't it be great?!" Julie's enthusiasm was contagious.

"It's always a ball—even when some ladies get ticked because they think someone else's present is nicer. Invariably, someone will start flirting with Santa, and before you know it everyone in the room is trying to kiss him. You won't believe it." Dot threw the last of the wrapping paper scraps in the garbage. "I'll bring this stuff with me Monday—early—and we'll sneak it under the tree. Thanks so much for all the work you did to make this happen, Julie." Dot hugged her. She had never expected to find anyone to fill Terry's shoes, but Julie was doing it. *How blessed we all are.*

A shotgun blast outside the bedroom window woke her at 2:00 A.M. Sunday. Confused, Dot lurched to the window and opened the blind to look out at her backyard. Beneath the window her small garden, put to bed in late November, was filled with a gigantic branch from her beloved Red Sunset maple. She walked to the front of the small house and flicked on the porch light—or tried. The power was off. Outside, gleaming and sparkling when an incidental car drove by on the treacherous but still navigable street, was the ice. An inch thick on every blade of grass, every twig, every tree branch, every telephone line and cable, it had transformed the city overnight. Years later, in cold, rainy weather, Dot would recall the beauty and the destruction of the ice, and pray that it not return.

Carmen heard the generator kick on at 2:10. An old 10K, it had always been noisy; tonight it was deafening. In the dark, she slipped on a tee shirt and pants and found her running shoes. Too small to provide light in the resident rooms, the generator would keep the lights on in the group areas, as well as the kitchen. It would insure that the sump pump worked, along with the fire alarm and monitoring system. The phone system, on a back-up battery, would operate for three hours without electricity. Carmen knew that the longest they'd ever been without power at Harmony Hall was thirty-five minutes. She headed upstairs to check things out.

❦   ❦   ❦

Dot's flashlight frantically scanned the garage door opener, a system of chains and pulleys that seemed extremely complicated in the cold, dark garage. She leaned against her old car, suddenly aware that the garage door was frozen to the concrete. She couldn't make it to work in her car. Outside the garage she heard the cracks and snaps of limbs breaking and plunging to the icy ground, and on her front steps, returning to the house, she stopped to watch a transformer across the street light up the sky with a blue flash. Inside, she grabbed her address book and dialed the cell phone number of Len Lester, Harmony Hall's neighborhood policeman and a frequent parking lot drive-through visitor. He picked flowers for his wife every summer in their garden, at no charge, and had twice eaten lunch with the ladies. *Come on, Len, answer the phone.*

"Lester."

Dot began to breathe again. "Len?"

"Yes."

"It's Dot from Harmony Hall. Have I got you at a terrible time?"

"It's a terrible night. Are you at the home?"

"No, I'm at my house. I need to get there, Les—Carmen's by herself. I can't get my car out of the garage. Is there any way I can get a ride with you?"

There was a brief silence.

"Hold on a second."

Dot heard a siren over the phone, and muffled voices. Les was gone a full minute.

"Dot?"

"Yes."

"Where do you live?"

"I'm at 1755 Doe Run, between Bluegrass and Secretariat."

"I'll be there as soon as I can. If the streets aren't blocked, I should be there in thirty or forty minutes."

"Bless you, Les."

She rushed to the bedroom and began throwing overnight necessities into her gym bag. The flashlight, its battery low, began to wane.

"Damn!"

She raced to her office, as well as she could in the dark, and clawed through the top desk drawer. Batteries were there, somewhere. Her hand curled around a package of small batteries, and she cursed again, knowing that there were no larger ones in the house, and that the flashlight took D's. She threw them in her bag, pulled her telephone charger from the outlet behind her desk, and returned to the front door. She stood there, watching for Les, and realized that the house was already beginning to get cold.

❧   ❧   ❧

Les's cruiser pulled into her driveway at 3:30, its headlights revealing the early destruction of the neighbors' trees. Dot gingerly made her way down the front steps to the driveway, ice crackling beneath her running shoes. She carefully opened the door of the police car. Les looked at her over his cell phone. He wasn't smiling. She heard him say, "I'll meet you there as soon as I can…right." He put the phone down and smiled wearily at her.

"Les, I can't thank you enough," Dot said, putting her bag on the floor as she slid in.

"We're not there yet, Dottie," he said, throwing the car in reverse. "I've had to drive all over town to find streets that aren't blocked. Keep your fingers crossed."

Theirs was the only car moving on the street. Through a window several houses down from her own, she saw the erratic movement of a flashlight, and wondered about her neighbor, a young woman who also lived alone.

"Most of the city is without power," Les said. "The streets are actually in great shape—thank God—but there are so many trees down that you can't get to where you're going." He drove in silence for a moment.

"*Nuts!*" Les said. Dot jumped at the exclamation. A truck, abandoned, blocked the road, its hood crushed under the weight of a huge branch. "Sit tight."

He flicked on his cruiser's revolving red light and walked to the driver's side of the truck, shining his service flashlight inside the deserted vehicle. Les returned to the car.

"He got out—somehow. Let's try another route."

Harmony Hall, built in the sixties, was surrounded by mature trees. As Les made his way there, Dot tried to remember when she'd last had them pruned. *Was it this year? Will that huge pine that's leaning slightly toward the building be lying on it when we get there?* She was dizzy with dread. Every yard they passed looked decimated in Les' headlights; showers of ice flew up each time an over-burdened limb exploded on the ground. They both held their breath as they passed beneath the maples lining the road to the Harmony Hall driveway.

"Oh, no!" whispered Dot.

The driveway was blocked. Much of the enormous bur oak that had served as a landmark in the neighborhood for years lay across the street, the jagged remnants of its trunk pointing skyward. Les backed the cruiser into a driveway across from Harmony Hall and tried circling to get to the exit driveway on the opposite side of the building. That side street was also impassable.

"Les, I'll walk from here," she said.

"Do you have a flashlight?"

"Yes." *The dang batteries are about dead, though.*

Something in her voice bothered Les.

"Here's a spare. Don't tell anyone where you got it."

She turned on the heavy, substantial flashlight he handed her. The glow was strong and wide.

"Watch for downed lines," he said. "They're everywhere."

"Be careful, Les." She grabbed her bag and stepped back from the car. Its taillights turned the ice into ruby sparklers momentarily, and then she was alone in the black night, picking her way between ice-encrusted branches, toward the sound of the generator.

❧   ❧   ❧

"Miss Dot, you made it!" Carmen appeared in the low, generator-powered lights of the hall, cheery, slightly breathless, and obviously relieved.

"Are you OK?" Dot asked.

"Yes, we are all OK."

They walked to the living room, one of the few areas well lighted by the chugging generator. Carmen had the gas logs on in the ventless fireplace; they were creating enough warmth to make a difference.

"Is there anyone else here?" Dot asked.

"No, just you and me," said Carmen. "Mees Julie called. She cannot get out of her driveway. Mees Evie called—she cannot get down her steps."

Dot checked her watch. It was 5:15. "Let's figure out how we're going to handle breakfast," she said, and they walked back to the kitchen. The gas stove was working. The same gas line that fed the generator would insure they ate—as long as the food lasted. In the dry goods storeroom, Dot found paper plates. They had plenty of Styrofoam cups.

"Carmen, we'll have to serve most of the second floor residents upstairs. Let's set them up in the parlor."

They reviewed the resident list. Four of the twenty-two second floor residents could make it down the stairs to the living room. Fourteen of the remaining eighteen could eat in the upstairs parlor. Four could sit at the bridge table in the upstairs foyer. They could handle it.

❦   ❦   ❦

At 7:00 Dot set out the paper plates and plastic ware she'd found in the storeroom. Carmen was heating water on the stove. She would make the coffee by pouring it through the ground coffee and filter into a large pot, then ladling it into carafes.

Dot began racing through the upstairs hall. Mimi's door was open.

"Mimi?"

"Dot! How did you get here? I thought all the roads were blocked."

She was listening to her tiny battery-operated radio, probably circa 1975. It had been maintained perfectly, as she maintained everything.

"I had our trusty neighborhood police officer come fetch me," Dot said. "We owe him big time, Mimi."

"What can I do to help?" Mimi asked.

"Would you mind letting the rest of the folks on this floor know they'll be eating in the parlor upstairs? I can only think of four people who can get down the stairs to the dining room—you, Minnie, Kitty and Camille. What do you think?"

"It sounds like a good plan," said Mimi. "I'll have everyone else up here go to the parlor—and I'll go downstairs with the other three."

"Thanks, Mimi, you're a lifesaver." Dot hugged her and went downstairs to check on the thirteen ladies there, who were just beginning to wake up to a world without electricity, telephones, hot water, heat and the morning newspaper. When she thought about it, Dot's knees grew weak. Surely the power would come on by lunch.

❧   ❧   ❧

Her ladies began entering the upstairs parlor at 7:45. They greeted each other happily, faces alight with the excitement of eating upstairs with new tablemates. Most of them were in their robes and slippers. The sun, bright through the east facing parlor windows, created a wonderland of sparkling light off the ice on the trees just outside. Dot was amazed when she entered the parlor with her carafes, and poured coffee into Styrofoam cups. Everyone was smiling.

❧   ❧   ❧

The generator sputtered to a stop at 2:00 P.M. on Sunday. In the kitchen, Carmen, trying to prepare for her third meal of the day, prayed for a miracle—or, just as acceptable, a resumption of their power. Without light it would be much more difficult to fix a meal and by 5:30, the usual dining time, it would be almost dark.

"Carmen?" Dot stood at the kitchen door. Her face, grim, seemed thinner than usual. Her eyes were deeper.

"Si?"

"I'm handing out flashlights. Do you have one?"

"I have three," said Carmen.

"I think we'd better move supper up to 4:30," said Dot. "They can get back to their rooms by 5:00 or so, and we'll have enough light to clean up. How are you fixed on food?"

Carmen, as organized as anyone Dot had worked with in her thirty years as an administrator, smiled. "We are good until supper tomorrow."

Tonight they'd have stew, served in Styrofoam cups, with biscuits. Breakfast was no problem. Cereal reserves were fine, and there were eggs and sweet rolls. Lunch on Monday was sliced ham and canned sweet potatoes with pineapple rings and cottage cheese. After that, they'd be out of milk and bread; but God willing, they'd have electricity well before then.

❧   ❧   ❧

At 5:45 the emergency lights began failing, and Dot started policing the halls. She and Carmen had placed lighted flashlights in all the halls, but the effect was minimal. There was no light in the residents' rooms, no light in the living room, dining room or parlor. Though each woman had a flashlight, Dot knew half would be misplaced. Other residents, trying to conserve their batteries, would try to make it to the bathroom without light. Mack joined her as she knocked on apartment doors and poked her head in to insure no one had yet fallen. He checked under every bed, then joined her back in the dark hall—a silent, comforting presence.

She stopped for a moment and stared through the glass veranda doors at the surreal scene outside: Still no lights in the street, still no traffic, transformers still exploding in the distance. Huge ice-coated branches littered the Harmony Hall property. She flicked the flashlight at the large, round thermometer on the wall outside the living room. It was twenty-nine degrees. Tomorrow morning it would be chilly inside, by Monday night it would be cold.

Before climbing the stairs to check on the rest of her charges, Dot dialed the emergency rescue center for the eighteenth time. This time the call went through.

"Emergency," answered a deep male voice.

"This is Dot Turner calling from Harmony Hall Retirement Home at Second and Julep. I've got thirty-five very elderly women here with no heat and no light. Half these gals are on walkers. Is there any way you can put us on your priority list?" She could hear phones ringing in the background.

"I can try, Ms. Turner. Do you have a medical emergency?"

"Not yet, but it's likely we will by morning. Our generator's out and my cell phone is about shot. Our regular phone service is dead." *Why do I sound so whiney?*

Visions flew through her mind…someone stumbling on the way to the bathroom and hitting her head on the way down, breaking a hip or a neck; someone already sight impaired and confused by the dark, tumbling down the parlor stairs; Bertha or another forgetful resident, unused to using a flashlight, lighting a candle, turning it over and setting the whole place on fire. The possibility of a disaster was increasing by the minute.

The deep voice broke her reverie.

"We'll do what we can, Ms. Turner."

"Sir," Dot heard her voice breaking slightly, and corrected it. "Most of these ladies can't see or can't hear or can't walk or have problems with all three of those things. This really is an emergency."

"Yes, ma'am."

She persisted, hating the fact that she was powerless.

"Can't you give me some idea when they'll get to this neighborhood?"

"No, ma'am."

"Can you have someone stop by as soon as possible? We're without a fire alarm or monitoring system."

"I'll see what I can do, ma'am."

For some reason the "*ma'am*" made her furious. The guy was probably thirty years old and didn't know what it was like to have thin blood and arthritis.

"Thanks," said Dot, and turned off the phone. She flew up the stairs, convinced there would be a problem waiting, charging into her first sleepless night at Harmony Hall.

❧   ❧   ❧

"Minnie?"

It was nearly midnight. All the residents were asked to leave their doors open, but several, Minnie among them, had forgotten. Camille tapped on Minnie's door and whispered her name a second time. She tapped louder and stuck her ear up against the cold wood. Inside the room she heard a bed creak, a crash, and she heard Minnie say, "Shit!" Then there was silence.

"*Minnie!*"

The door opened slightly. "What's up?" Minnie croaked, nonchalantly.

"Did you fall?" Camille asked.

"No, I turned over that dang lamp next to my bed."

Camille tried to turn on her flashlight but couldn't find the button in the dark. "How do you get this thing to work?"

"Hold on, I've got one in here somewhere," Minnie said, and turned back into the room.

"I'm looking for Mack," Camille whispered. "Have you seen him?" She tried to follow Minnie inside, but thought better of it when her foot met something on Minnie's carpet. There was no telling what might be between the door and the bed.

"Heck, I can't find anything in this room. Let's just go hunt him down."

They started down the long, nearly black hall, each clutching the handrail. Camille's thumb finally made contact with the flashlight's switch.

"Wait a minute!" She turned the light on Minnie's face, momentarily blinding her. "Now we'll find that sweet pup."

They continued down the hall, softly calling Mack's name. As they rounded the corner a dark figure suddenly appeared through the upstairs parlor door.

"Wheeeee!" screamed Minnie.

Camille held the flashlight out in front of her like a sword, playing it on the intruder.

Dot shielded her eyes with her left hand. "What are you two doing up?" she asked. "It's midnight."

"We can't find Mack," said Camille.

"Why do you need him?" asked Dot.

"I usually take him out about this time," said Camille, a confirmed night owl.

Dot imagined Camille in her house slippers walking Mack on ice among downed trees.

"Camille, it's a war zone out there. We can't walk him outside, and we can't go around waking up everybody at this hour. Why don't you go back to bed. I'll be up all night—I swear I'll let him out in the courtyard when he shows up."

Camille pursed her lips. "That poor little dog is probably scared to death without light, Dot. There's no telling what's going through his head right about now, wherever he is." She looked hopefully in the direction of the parlor.

"He's not in there, Camille. I've just combed the place."

"I sure hope he finds you before he goes in one of these halls."

"These are desperate times," rasped Minnie, and grabbed Camille's hand. "Come on," she said. "He'll show up."

They turned back toward Minnie's room, Camille's flashlight beam ricocheting off the walls.

"'Night," Dot said, hoping Camille would give it up, but knowing better. Once something got on Camille's mind, it stayed there. Dot turned the corner. The glow from the flashlight Carmen had placed in the north hall was nearly gone. It was eerily quiet without the hum of the incidental noise from late night television programs. Her ladies, under every blanket they owned, were snugged in. Conserving her own flashlight battery was paramount, and she resisted the urge to check her watch. There were four or five hours left to patrol the halls, sniff for smoke from banned candles, and listen for cries of help. Then it would be time to work on breakfast.

Out of habit, she stuck her head in Harriett's room. Tiny Harriett, her most frail resident, always left her door open. Dot could barely make out her silhouette against the glass of her window.

"Harriett?"

"Yes? Hey, Dot. Why aren't you sleeping? It's late."

"Just checking on things. Are you O.K.?" Dot flicked on her flashlight. Harriett was wrapped in a blanket that covered the sides of her walker. *An accident waiting to happen.*

"Oh, yes. Just tired to death of staying in that bed. My back hurts and I had to stand for a few minutes."

Outside Harriett's window, on the street, gleaming in the dim light of a full moon, lay the huge oak. Dot felt her throat tighten. Harriett was probably mourning the tree—she had always loved it.

"How old do you suppose that tree is?" asked Dot.

"It was full grown when I was a girl, long before this building was here," said Harriett. "I can't believe it's gone, can you?"

"No." Dot was at a loss for words.

"It was my favorite tree in the city," Harriett continued. "I feel like I've lost a family member." She sighed and began to move toward the bed. "It's getting chilly, isn't it? Go to bed, Dot. We'll all be fine."

❧   ❧   ❧

At 6:45 A.M. on Monday Carmen started boiling water for coffee. Upstairs, Dot began setting the tables with Styrofoam plates and cups. It was another clear, cold day. None of the ice, still an inch thick on every twig and power line, had melted.

Mimi awoke to low voices in the hall outside her open door. She shivered as she put on her heaviest robe and slippers and poked her head out into the hall. It was dark in the hall, but she recognized Minnie's voice. "Minnie?"

"Howdy," said Minnie.

"Morning, Mimi," said Camille.

"Hi, gals," said Mimi. "What are you two up to?"

"We're looking for Mack," said Camille. "That poor baby's been gone all night and I know he needs to go outside."

"Have you been downstairs?" asked Mimi.

"We've been everywhere. I'm worn out."

They began walking toward the elevator landing where there was more light. Suddenly Minnie stopped at the door to Maybelle's room. Her eyes widened. Inside the room Maybelle lay in bed under several blankets, her eyes closed.

"Get Dot," Minnie said hoarsely. "Maybelle's having convulsions."

"I'll find her," said Mimi. She reached the parlor door quickly and saw Dot. "Dot—can you come to Maybelle's room? Minnie thinks she's having a seizure."

"Oh, no!" cried Dot. She raced past Mimi. Camille and Minnie were just inside the door, watching the covers rise and fall.

"Maybelle!" Dot said, grasping her arm under the covers. Maybelle's eyes opened wide, then focused on Dot. The lower part of the bed continued to shake.

"Morning, Dot," she said.

"What's the matter?" Dot asked.

"Nothing. Is the power on?" Maybelle threw back the covers. At once the shaking stopped and Mack, lower teeth showing, stuck his head in Dot's face.

"Mack!" exclaimed Camille, with delight.

"He kept me warm all night," said Maybelle.

"I thought you were having a fit," said Minnie.

"Is the coffee ready, Dot?" asked Maybelle.

Dot's knees were weak and her eyes itched. She watched Camille and Mack head for the parlor door and the courtyard. "I'll go check, Maybelle. If it's done, I'll bring you a cup." She met Mimi's gaze and smiled. "How 'bout a cup, Mimi?" They walked together to the kitchen, both wondering how Mack would spend his next night.

At 7:30 the whine of chain saws wafted through the upstairs parlor. Dot put her tray down, flew to the windows facing the street and looked down at a city work crew dismantling the huge bur oak. Ice and sawdust sprayed from the blades, covering the street. Eloise, the first to arrive for breakfast, joined Dot at the window. Her nearly sightless eyes widened. "What is it?" she asked Dot.

"Eloise, they're cutting up that huge tree that's been blocking Julep since early Sunday morning. Before long cars will be able to make it to the parking lot." She stopped, so tired from her night's vigil that it was impossible to talk and think of the ramifications at the same time.

"How lovely!" said the ever-gracious Eloise. "Maybe you can get some relief."

"You're so sweet," Dot said, and put her arm around Eloise's shoulder. There were so many layers under the now tight robe that Eloise's arms were slightly extended from her body. "At least the utility trucks can get through—and maybe get our power back on," said Dot. *And if we need one, an ambulance can make it to the door.* She helped Eloise get settled and decided to talk to the emergency folks one more time before things got too hectic. Her cell phone needed charging; this would likely be the last call she could make. An older woman answered "Emergency," and Dot's spirits lifted.

"Hi, this is Dot Turner at Harmony Hall at Second and Julep."

"Dot! This is Miranda!"

Her mind foggy, Dot tried to place the voice and connect it to a face.

"Miranda…" Dot said.

"My Aunt Jo was there years ago, Dot. She used to play the piano before supper."

"Miranda!" A full-time volunteer even then, Miranda was now obviously helping out at the emergency center. "I think of her often—she was such a live wire," said Dot.

"Are you without power?"

"Yes. I hate to bother you, but we've got all kinds of accidents waiting to happen here—especially at night."

"I guess you *do.* Dot, I'll do all I can. We've still got 180,000 people without power—some of them in nursing homes—but I'll get you on a priority list."

Dot's voice shook. "Bless you, Miranda. Come see us when this is all over." She turned off her cell phone, started toward the kitchen and Carmen's waiting trays, and nearly ran over Jim, who had somehow made it in to work, all the way from Richmond. "Jim!" She realized suddenly that her hair hadn't been washed since Saturday morning and was beginning to flatten against her skull. Dot wondered if she smelled as bad as she looked.

Jim said, "It's a mess out there. How's everybody here?"

"We're great," said Dot, hoping it was true. "How's Richmond?"

"The ice storm missed us. We're fine. What happened to the generator?"

"It conked out yesterday afternoon," said Dot.

"Have you checked the basement?"

My God! The sump pumps!

"No—would you?"

"Sure."

"Jim?"

"Yes?"

"Have you got a cell phone charger in your truck?" She held her breath.

"Yes. You need charging?"

"Yes, in more ways than one."

He laughed, took her phone, and she flew back to the kitchen for Carmen's waiting trays, renewed by his presence.

※   ※   ※

It was their fourth meal upstairs. In the parlor at 8:30, morning sun streamed through the windows and illuminated the faces of fourteen residents. Most now wore something over their ears. Several were eating with gloves on. In the dining room downstairs, Mimi and Camille were helping Carmen serve the fifteen first floor residents. Both the upstairs parlor and the dining room were filled with conversation. Mack drifted back and forth between them, somehow knowing that the rule barring him from the dining room had been temporarily lifted. His schnauzer moustache was matted with bacon and butter. After breakfast, everyone began shuffling back to their rooms or to the living room and the gas logs. It was now 58 degrees in most of the house; 28 degrees outside. Amazingly, no one had complained of being cold.

※   ※   ※

The sump pump pits are filling up fast," Jim said.

"What do you suggest?" Dot asked, trying to remember what they'd done the last time the basement flooded.

"I've got a friend in Richmond with a small generator. We can hook it up to the pump."

"Oh, Jim, that's such a long drive."

"You're not going to find one here," he said.

She pictured the thirty-five lockers in the basement, stuffed with the memorabilia of her residents. "OK," she said, "Go for it."

※   ※   ※

By 3:00 P.M. a thaw had begun. As each ribbon of ice lost its grip on a tree branch it fell on the ones below, creating an aerial avalanche. Now, throughout the neighborhood, there was a chorus of chain saws.

"Where do they plug them in?" asked Bertha, watching men across the street attack a huge pine.

"They're gas powered," said Kitty. She had Bertha's upper plate, wrapped in a napkin, deep in the pocket of her robe. At mid-afternoon almost no one was dressed in street clothes. The ice storm had created one long, uninterrupted pajama party, though Kitty doubted there'd ever been one quite like this before.

Kitty and Bertha turned away from the fireplace to a commotion in the hall. Mimi's family had dropped in. Faith walked toward them with a fearful look on her face.

"Hello, ladies," she said. "Are you all doing OK?"

Kitty thought they were doing great, and said so.

"Have you been eating?" asked Lauren.

"Three squares a day," said Kitty.

"How?" asked Faith.

"Carmen is cooking and Dot's helping—they're getting it done just fine. We've got a gas stove, you know." Kitty watched as Mimi's red-haired friend, Skipper, walked to the fireplace and held her hands to the flame. She looked tired and stressed. Kitty joined her at the fire and put her hand on Skipper's arm. "Set down, dear. I'll find a blanket and you can wrap up for a few minutes."

Skipper gave her a wan smile. "Don't you worry about me, darling—I'm trying to figure out how to keep *you* warm."

Lauren left to look for Dot, and Faith went searching for Mimi.

"Most of Lexington is still without power, and it may be another week before it's restored," said Skipper.

Kitty's eyes twinkled. "We really don't need much here. I'd be more worried about folks with young babies."

Skipper looked around and sighed. The couches had been converted to beds in the living room. A stack of blankets lay on the piano bench, neatly folded.

Mimi appeared, napkins in one hand and a long tube of Styrofoam cups in the other. Faith followed with Lauren and Dot.

"Skipper! Are you doing OK?" Mimi dropped the napkins and cups on the puzzle table and hugged Skipper hard.

"We're swell now, Mimi. It took two days for us to get out of our street and four hours to find a room with heat and hot water—but we did. We've got two rooms reserved in Versailles, and we're sneaking Babe in with us. We came to pick you up and anyone else who needs to warm up."

"I know," Mimi said. "Faith asked me to join you. I think I'll stay here, but you're so dear to think of me."

Skipper was speechless. Faith rolled her eyes.

"Mother, honestly, it may be days before you get power—it's freezing in here already."

"It's not so bad," said Mimi. "We just get under the covers and stay put. You all go on and give us a call now and then."

"Your phones aren't working, Mother."

"Try Dot's cell phone—or mine. Or I'll call you." She glanced at Bertha, who was rubbing her hands together on the couch. Mimi draped a blanket over her lap and shoulders and picked up the napkins and cups. "Give me a kiss," she said, and pecked Faith, Skipper and Lauren each on the cheek.

They left her and walked toward the parking lot doors, longing for a hot shower and some way to convince Mimi she was being foolhardy. Lauren slid in the back of Faith's car, joining Babe.

"Don't worry, Faith," she said. "Dot's got it under control."

"I'm afraid Mother Nature's in control this week," said Faith, and pulled out of the newly cleared "Entrance Only" driveway.

Jim, his stubble adding ten years to his sixty, snaked the 150-foot extension cord down the basement steps. Light outside was waning, and the basement was pitch black. Once he managed to plug in the sump pump to the generator, if all went well, and until the gas gave out, they'd stave off a flood. The thought of digging through the wet contents of 35 storage compartments made him shudder. This would be a long night.

At 8:00 P.M. on Monday Carmen stretched out on her twin bed, exhausted. Since the ice storm had hit on Saturday night she had fixed, help serve, and cleaned up after 210 meals. The Kroger store, only a half block away, was still without power, its doors closed. Jim had managed to find bread and milk in Richmond; they were now OK through tomorrow. The kitchen was now the warmest place in the house, and refrigerated food had been moved outside and stacked under plastic bags in a shady corner of the courtyard. She shivered, wondering how much longer they could last.

❦   ❦   ❦

Dot began her continuous hall walk at 9:00 Monday night. Three residents were now with their families, out of the city at hotels or the homes of friends with electricity. That left thirty-two women to watch over. All had turned in for the night. It was warmer in bed, hunkered down under blankets and clothes—than it was in the living room in front of the fire. Images crowded her mind. She thought of Eloise rubbing Virginia's hands, lending her a hot water bottle filled by Carmen, wrapped in a towel; Mimi, always cheerful, always positive, bending over someone in the dining room, smiling as she helped pour coffee; Camille and Maybelle at peace, clambering into Maybelle's bed together with Mack between them, Dot's last view of Mack his tail, heading south; Kitty, her large body now huge under layers of clothing, gently putting Bertha's teeth in before supper; JoAnne, their only cat owner, lovingly covering Amelia, her Siamese, with a heavy robe in her recliner. These were the scenes she loved to revisit. They kept the *what if* images away, those of cold blue lips, bones jutting through thin skin after a horrific fall, flames birthed by a candle racing through a bedroom. Her thoughts turned to the garden, and as she circled the building, she imagined it was April, her favorite month, with tulips still blooming beside the garden walkway. She pictured her beloved Siberian iris, their buds ready to burst open, their lance-like foliage moving in the spring breeze. In her mind's eye she saw the lovely lavender scilla and marveled, as she did each year, at the sudden appearance of the daylily foliage.

At midnight she stood before the fire for a moment, then turned to look out the veranda doors and gasped. The traffic light, a block away, was on. She could see the utility trucks clustered at the intersection, their yellow lights raking the neighborhood.

Surely to goodness we'll get power tonight.

At 7:00 A.M. on Tuesday she checked the thermostat they'd moved from the now empty kitchen cooler to the dining room. Dot's vision was blurry, but Carmen confirmed it was 47 degrees in the house.

"I'm going to start delivering hot water and coffee door to door," Dot said, her hands trembling as she filled a pot with water and turned on the burner below it. "I'll haul a cart upstairs and then carry trays up there. When we've finished upstairs I'll start down here. You OK?"

"Sure, no problema," said Carmen.

Upstairs, Dot pushed the cart to each open door, poked her head in and checked for signs of life. A few of her residents were awake, delighted and thankful for a hot cup of anything to wrap their hands around. Suddenly Carmen was next to her and exclaimed, "Miss Dot! Ms. Evie is here!"

The ice on her steps must have melted.

Dot leaned against a doorjamb, eyes closed, silently giving thanks for another set of hands.

At 8:30 she noticed that Harriett was missing from the parlor table. Everyone else, bundled like Eskimos, was there, nearly motionless. Now and then Dot would see a resident's breath as she exhaled. She poured a cup of coffee for Harriett and headed toward her room. Harriett, blue eyes sparkling, peered past the covers at Dot. She was wearing a bright red toboggan, over which she'd wrapped a long wool scarf, tied under her chin.

"Harriett, are you all right?"

Harriett's lips were white.

"Yes, dear," she whispered.

"How 'bout some coffee?"

Dot sat on the edge of the bed and set the coffee on Harriett's nightstand. Harriett smiled at her in the dim light. Suddenly, amazingly, the room was bright. Down the hall they heard a huge cheer.

"Oh Lord," said Harriett, beginning to cry. "Oh Lord, thank you Lord, thank you Lord."

It took Dot a few seconds to realize what had happened. She heard Harriett's room heater kick on and the sound of excited voices in the parlor. She squeezed Harriett, turned toward the door, and noticed a short gray body flash past. It was Mack, scratching out in response to the cheers and applause.

Carmen and Dot arrived in the parlor at the same time. The ladies were toasting each other with their Styrofoam coffee cups, headgear already coming off. The lights flickered, then went out. The room hushed, the lights came back on, and cheers again filled the parlor. Jim fairly flew up the stairs to report that the phones were working. Behind him, Dot saw Julie, in sweats and running shoes, and they high-fived.

"Do you have power?" Dot asked.

"No, I'm staying here tonight," said Julie. Take the car and go home, Dot. We'll be fine."

Dot's knees shook as she walked one last time down the stairs to her office. Sleepless and on edge for fifty-five hours, she now could barely hold her head up. The drive home was dreamlike and distressing. Trees and huge portions of trees still littered the yards of her neighbors, whose homes, like her own, would be without power for three more days. Dot cleared a path to her door and entered her freezing house. She dropped her overnight bag in the foyer, turned on the gas logs in the fireplace and made a bed in front of it. Early on Wednesday, seventeen hours later, she awoke, chilled, trying to recall a Christmas party that had never happened.

Terry, staying with his mother in Lexington over the holidays, rang the Harmony Hall doorbell.

"Terry!" screamed Julie. They hugged, both delighted.

"I came by for a cup of hot water," he said, lifting Mack high in the air, "to bathe in."

"We've got all you need," said Julie. "Dot's taking a bath right now, in fact. You can be second." She waved her hand in front of her nose. "And none too soon!"

"Ha!" said Terry. "You haven't changed a bit, Buzz." He sauntered into the kitchen, and Evie's welcoming shriek could be heard as far as the second floor. Now *everyone* was home for Christmas.

On Thursday, Christmas Eve morning, Julie stood at the living room entrance watching Harriett, who was seated near the fireplace, comb in hand, with Mack on her lap. Harriett would dip the comb in a glass of warm water and carefully work on his matted moustache, slipping him a dry treat every thirty seconds or so to insure he stayed put. Terry was helping Evie in the kitchen, while Jim and Dot pulled branches out of the pond and off the exit driveway. Most of the city was still blacked out. The Christmas bags, stuffed with gifts she and Dot had painstakingly selected and wrapped, would be hung on each resident's doorknob during lunch. Santa, a police officer in his real life, had his hands full and couldn't put in an appearance after all. A stream of visitors had been in and out already this morning, most of them well-wishers. Some were in need of help, like the neighbors who were sleeping in the Harmony Hall living room until their electricity returned. Julie sighed, wishing they could have had a real Christmas party. From the end of the hall, Maybelle McCardle was moving toward her slowly, a scowl on her face.

"Hi, Maybelle. May I help you?"

"My son's on his way over to pick me up—I have to sign out."

"How nice!" said Julie. "You'll be spending Christmas with your family."

"It will be a zoo at their house—all my sister's grandchildren and great grandchildren are in town." Maybelle signed her name in straggly script on the sign out pad. She seemed a bit morose.

"Wait! I have something you need to take with you," said Julie. She ran to Dot's office, found Maybelle's Christmas bag and presented it to her. "Merry Christmas!"

"Oh, Julie…"

"It's from Santa. He couldn't be here because he's out helping people who need him more than we do," Julie said.

"Tell Santa our Christmas is already perfect, but thanks for the icing on the cake," said Maybelle. "I'll miss you all today." She hugged Julie, wistfully watched Mack and Harriett for a full ten seconds, and headed for the lobby and her son.

❦   ❦   ❦

Another year nearly gone. Dot replaced the pages in her desk calendar. It was December 28. She flipped back through the 1998 pages, remembering the year's high and low points. Somehow the postman had managed to get through the neighborhood with the Harmony Hall mail, and she began opening the few envelopes he had delivered. Suddenly her neck tightened and her letter opener stopped mid-slit. The return address of the envelope in her hand was a large, well-known legal firm in town. Dot sighed and closed her eyes, thinking back over the year. *What individual or group have we offended?*

She pulled the expensive stationary from the envelope. The one-paragraph letter simply read:

> Our client, who has elected to remain anonymous, wishes the enclosed donation to be applied to the existing Harmony Hall endowment fund, to be used as needed and as determined by the Board of Directors.

The second sheet, computer generated and perforated, was a trust department check for $100,000.

CHAPTER 26

MY OLD KENTUCKY HOME

APRIL, 1999

"C'mon, Camille, they're about to pull out."

Camille pursed her lips, glared at Minnie and slammed her dresser drawer. "If some people would leave me be I *might* have time to be on time."

"Oh, crap," Minnie said, and started for the elevator. Her Jackie Onassis sunglasses covered half her face; her blonde wig poked from her huge handbag. Her sneakers didn't match. She reminded Dot, who passed her in the hall, of a tiny, bald, homeless alien.

"C'mere, I need some help," yelled Camille.

Minnie looked out the upstairs windows at the line of women getting on the new van. She hit the *Down* elevator button and turned back, unsteadily, to lend a hand to Camille, who was now walking toward her shaking her right pant leg.

"Here's the elevator," Minnie gasped. "Get on, quick! That darned Julie will leave us if we're not down there at 10:00."

Camille, breathless, forgot about her pant leg momentarily, and charged into the lobby when the elevator door opened at the first floor. Julie was on the lobby phone—calling Camille's number—and frowning. "There you are—we're all ready," she said, forcing a smile.

"I'll just bet you are," Camille said, under her breath. She walked to the van behind Minnie, and sat across the aisle from her, a row back from the driver's seat.

"Everybody have a seatbelt on?" asked Julie, looking at Camille in her rear-view mirror.

"Yes," rang out, and Julie closed all the doors, settled in, and adjusted the side mirrors. "We're off!" she exclaimed, and the van pulled out, headed for *Boutique Magnifique.*

Camille dug around in her purse and pulled out her glasses. Once they were on, she identified the thing coming out of her pants leg as the foot of a pair of pantyhose, obviously dried with her pants and caught inside them. *Damn!*

"Minnie," she growled.

"Eh?"

Camille extended her right leg. "Pull that out."

Minnie, nearly sightless in her big black sunglasses, was no fool. "What is it?"

"My hose."

"Ha-ha," snickered Minnie.

The girls in the back fell silent for a moment as they watched Minnie pull on the pantyhose.

"It's not coming," she said, and gave a great tug.

"Pull it harder!"

The offending hose was now stretched taut across the aisle. Kitty, next to Minnie and the window, began pulling on the end of the hose, her shoulders shaking, breathless with laughter.

"Whoa!" said Camille. "You're killing me!"

Julie, eyes on the road, felt sure she'd heard wrong. Unable to turn around, and blissfully unaware of the activity taking place behind her, she missed Camille's next move, which was to unzip her pants, grab the bulky section of the pantyhose caught in front, and start pulling on the leg.

"Pull harder," Minnie said to Kitty, unaware that Camille was now pulling, too.

"Let go!" Camille screamed at Minnie. She firmly pulled the offending leg free and stuffed the pantyhose in her purse.

The six residents behind them were weeping with laughter. Kitty said, to no one in particular, "I'm glad I have a diaper on, because I'm gonna wet my pants!" This set everyone off. But for her seatbelt, Minnie would have fallen out of her seat.

Focused on the traffic, Julie giggled and shook her head. She loved it when her ladies laughed like schoolgirls.

❧   ❧   ❧

The **CLOSED AT 4:00 P.M. ON SATURDAY** sign on the door as they entered did not go unnoticed. Faith had offered to lend a hat appropriate for the Kentucky Derby, three days away, to anybody needing one, and Julie had a list of names in hand. Spring clothes were on sale. Skipper and Faith were there to help the residents try on 75% off items. Saturday was the annual Harmony Hall Derby party, an especially important day for those raised in Kentucky, and a perfect opportunity for everyone to dress to the nines.

❧   ❧   ❧

"Hi! Come on in," said Lauren, opening the door to an elderly couple standing under the portico at the Harmony Hall door. "May I help you?" she asked, smiling.

"We're here to see Ms. Turner. I'm Mildred Stafford and this is my husband, Paul."

"I'm Lauren Collier." The Staffords both had gray hair and looked extremely ill at ease. "Have a seat, if you don't mind, and I'll let Ms. Turner know you're here. May I get you coffee or iced tea?" Lauren had watched Julie go through this routine a dozen times.

"Thank you, dear, we're fine," said Mrs. Stafford.

Lauren used the intercom, and Dot came to the lobby to meet the couple.

"Come on back," said Dot. "We'll talk for a few minutes, and then Lauren will take you on a tour."

Dot and Julie had been coaching Lauren all spring. Julie was out with the ladies, and this would be her first time at conducting a tour all by herself. She stepped inside the lobby restroom, checked her hair, tucked her shirt in tighter, and then went back to the desk in the lobby to wait for Dot's call. The phone rang almost immediately.

"Hey, Dot," said Lauren.

"Who is this," the voice on the line demanded.

"Uh…this is Lauren."

"Who?"

"It's Lauren," she said, louder.

"Oh, Lauren. This is Harriett. Is Julie in?"

"Hi, Harriett. She's taken everyone to the consignment shop."

"Get Dot. There's a snake in the hall up here, just down from Bertha's room."

"What?"

"Hurry—I think it's going under Bertha's door."

The phone clicked.

The snake, a common garter, had entered Harmony Hall curled up in the bottom of a hatbox. Looking for a dark, cool hiding place, it had found access to a basement, and entered the hatbox through a small hole chewed in the corner. The hatbox had been delivered at lunchtime to Maybelle McCardle's room by her daughter-in-law, Betty, who tried to avoid contact with her mother-in-law whenever she could. She set the box in a corner of Maybelle's room and left a note in Maybelle's mailbox. The snake, sensitive to temperature changes, left the hatbox in the too warm room through the small corner hole, and slipped under the door to the hall.

"Tell me about your mother," Dot said to Mildred Stafford, smiling.

"She'll be ninety-two on Sunday. She broke her hip and her collarbone in late March, and can't manage any longer in her apartment, though she won't admit it."

"What's the problem?" asked Dot.

"She's unable to get up and down the steps where she lives," said Paul. "She's on a walker."

"She was having a terrible time cooking, and she wouldn't let us send anyone in to help. My mother is at our house now, and we're all unhappy," said Mildred. "Paul and I still work, she's alone all day, and we're afraid she's going to burn the house down."

"Have you talked to her about a retirement community yet?"

"No, not really. We wanted to get an idea of what's available first."

"Let me give you a rundown of our services," Dot said, "and then you can look around."

❦   ❦   ❦

Lauren ran toward Dot's office but stopped in front of the linen closet. She whipped open the closet door and grabbed a hand towel, raced to the stairwell, and darted up the stairs. Twice last summer she and Henry had rescued a snake from Blackie, the outside cat. Henry had shown her then how to hold a snake behind the head, and she had held the second rescued snake by herself. It was sleek and smooth; a young garter snake that Henry thought had probably just shed its skin. "They'll bite," Henry had said, "but they're not poisonous, and they only do it when they're scared." Lauren saw the snake crawling next to the baseboard, searching frantically for a hole or nook. As she approached it, the snake coiled up and stared at her. *Chill out, Buddy. Chill out, chill out, chill out.* She quickly dropped the hand towel on the snake and put both hands on top. Underneath, the snake tried valiantly to escape, but was trapped. Lauren managed to get her hand and the towel around its head, and wrapped the rest of its two-foot-long body in the towel. She ran to the elevator, prayed it would be empty, and hit the *"Down"* button with her elbow. It *was* empty, but when the door opened to the lobby, Mimi stood in front of her, waiting to go upstairs.

"Mimi!"

"Lauren!"

"Can you watch the phone for me for just one minute?"

"Sure!" Mimi never looked at the towel.

"Thanks!"

Lauren sped out the door and across the parking lot to the koi pond. Under the huge cedar tree at the pond's edge she carefully released the garter snake who slowly disappeared from sight. "Whew!" she said, aloud. Racing back to the door, she grinned at Mimi, who opened it quickly. "Thanks, Mimi, you saved my life." The lobby phone rang.

"Hello, Lauren speaking," she answered, breathless.

"Lauren, can you take Mr. and Mrs. Stafford on a tour?"

"Sure, Dot. I'll be right there." She brushed her hair with her hands and walked the short distance to Dot's office, casually stopping on her way to pitch the hand towel in the dirty laundry bin inside the linen closet.

Julie pulled the van up to the curb and cut the motor. Behind her, hats on, nine women chattered unceasingly as she jumped from the driver's seat and began unloading walkers from the van's storage area. Once everyone was out of the van and back in the lobby, Julie followed with a stack of brightly colored extra hats, just in case.

At *Magnifique*, Faith and Skipper reviewed the hat list, laughing over the reactions of the ladies to each other's hat selections.

"I wouldn't miss this party for a date with Donald Trump," said Skipper.

"Yeech! I would hope not."

Skipper, always the belle of every ball, would be absent from the Derby in Louisville for the first time in a decade, in order to attend a retirement home Derby party in Lexington. Faith chuckled, imagining what Skipper's other friends would think.

On Saturday, Pansy and Bruce stepped off the plane at Bluegrass Airport and walked the short distance to the baggage claim and rental car area. Unknown to Skipper, Lauren had invited Pansy to the Derby party and Pansy had invited Bruce.

"Mother, it's just a little party."

Georgia, trembling at the effort it took to button her blouse, shook her head. "Why are we going?" she asked, petulantly.

"I thought you'd like to get a look at this place, and the director invited us. You haven't been to a party in ages."

"Hrummph."

"You ready, girls?" asked Paul.

"Where are my pearls?"

"I'll get them," said Mildred, leaving the room.

"Mom, how are you feeling?" asked Paul, kindly.

"Like a sick old lady," she said, and reached for her walker.

❦   ❦   ❦

Lauren sat behind the name tag table just inside the lobby doors at 4:30 on Saturday, black Flair pen poised. Faith had found her a bright blue hat, complete with trailing feathers. Lauren felt like an idiot in it, but *everybody* was wearing a hat today. She watched her mother, Faith and Pete cross the parking lot and met them at the door.

"Wow! You look gorgeous," said Pete.

"Oh, c'mon," said Lauren, blushing. She tried to kiss Faith, but their hats got in the way.

"Go on in, the party's in the living room." She beamed as she handed them their nametags.

"Will you be able to join us, honey?" asked Faith.

"Yeah, in a few minutes. Behave, Mother."

"Sure, darling," Skipper said.

Thank God, they got here before Grandma.

Minutes passed. A car pulled up to the door, and Lauren recognized Mildred Stafford, who got out, pulled a walker from the back seat, and rushed to the front passenger's side. A small, thin woman, hair flipped up, slowly and carefully exited the car. They both turned to wait for Paul to park. Neither was wearing a hat. As they entered, Lauren greeted them and was introduced to Georgia.

"Welcome to the party!" said Lauren. "How 'bout a hat?" She pulled two that looked suitable from under her desk and proffered them to Georgia and Mildred.

"Oh, no—thanks anyway," said Mildred.

"I'll take one," Georgia said, sharply.

"Great," said Lauren. "This one?"

It was a gorgeous hat, violet with a huge cloud of lavender tulle at the back.

Georgia nodded. Lauren placed it carefully on the silver hair. "It's perfect," she said.

"Thank you Lauren," Georgia said stiffly, reading Lauren's name tag.

The Staffords and Georgia began walking toward the living room, where Julie, Dot, and especially Terry, who *never* missed a party, would put them at ease. Lauren glanced at the clock. It was 4:40. *Is Grandma lost?* They had talked briefly on the phone earlier in the day. *Did I give her the wrong directions?*

A long black car pulled slowly into the lot and parked. Lauren held her breath. Her grandmother's blonde knot gleamed as she emerged from the car. A nice-looking older man, who Lauren knew must be Reverend Atchison, held the door for her and looked around. Her grandmother took his hand and they walked to the koi pond for a moment. Lauren wanted to yell, "*Come on! Come on!*" but stifled the urge, and waited quietly at the door until they reached it. She opened it quickly, screamed "Grandma!" and lifted Pansy off the ground.

"Lauren, you look so beautiful!" laughed Pansy. "Bruce, this is my beautiful granddaughter, Lauren."

Bruce looked into Lauren's eyes. "Thank you for inviting us, Lauren. Your grandmother and I are delighted to be here."

"Grandma, do you want me to bring Mom out here, or should we just go in and surprise her?"

"Let's go in," said Pansy.

Terry was bartending, pouring drinks and sticking fresh mint from the garden in everything—mint juleps, Coke, Sprite, bourbon and iced tea. The living room was a sea of hats. Lauren peered into the crowd, looking for Skipper's huge hot pink concoction. She finally found it—and her mother—deep in discussion with Dot by the fireplace. She wove her way past groups of residents and family members and came up behind her mother, grinning at Dot.

"Mom?"

"Yes, darling?"

"Look who came to the party!"

Skipper turned, saw Pansy and Bruce, and cried, "Mother!" Dot, in on the plan from its inception, gave Lauren a thumbs up, as Skipper and Pansy hugged. Skipper stood back and gave Bruce the once-over. "Are you now the chauffeur or the new beau?" she asked, looking from him to Pansy.

"He's chauffeur and best friend," said Pansy.

"That's even better," said Skipper, and took Bruce's hand, leading him across the room to Faith and Pete.

From the drink table Julie watched Camille and Minnie talking to Georgia and her family, and saw Minnie lift her hat off her head. Her wig, which was always loose, lifted with the hat and stuck in its dome, revealing Minnie's pink scalp. Julie could see Camille make some risque' remark to the wide-eyed Georgia, then slap the wig back on Minnie's head. Her eyes moved to the veranda, where Lauren was talking animatedly with Mimi and Henry, all three suddenly doubling over with laughter. She looked at Terry, his straw hat set rakishly on his head, cracking jokes with those who made it to his little bar. Everyone was engaged and smiling, when suddenly Dot started striking a spoon on a glass and called for quiet.

"Ladies and gentlemen, we're happy to have Paul and Mildred Stafford as guests today, for the first time, and honored to have Georgia Todd, Mildred's mother, here on the eve of her ninety-second birthday. Pansy, can you start us off?" Pansy nodded, and slid to the middle of the piano bench. She began playing the *Happy Birthday* song, and everyone joined in. Terry lit a candle, stuck it in a cupcake, and presented it to Georgia, who, astonished, blew it out. Everyone clapped, and in front of Georgia a short line of well-wishers formed. Bertha, seated on the couch with Eloise, was sucking the chocolate off peanuts and spitting the nuts in a cup. Mack, who gained a half-pound or so at every party, was grinning and licking his chops as he went from group to group.

At 5:30 Dot turned up the volume on the big screen TV, and everyone who could stand, did, to sing "My Old Kentucky Home." Skipper, overcome by Lauren's initiative and her mother's presence, aided and abetted by several mint juleps, cried. The race, over in two minutes, yielded a total pot of $68 dollars. Maybelle had pulled the winner's name and she was ecstatic at her good fortune, joyfully hugging her son and daughter-in-law. Carmen placed second. Virginia's horse was third. Skipper and Faith divided the money, and Dot doled it out amid cheers and applause. No one looked ready to leave at 6:00, when Cookie began serving dinner and the party had to break up.

Faith and Skipper collected the hats and carried them, with Pansy's help, to their cars. Dot and Julie rearranged chairs and tables, cleaning up as they went, while Georgia and her family gazed out the veranda doors, mesmerized by a squirrel who scampered effortlessly past the baffle to the bird feeding station. When the Staffords began moving toward the living room door, Dot and Julie joined them.

"Georgia," Dot said, "we're so glad you and your family could make it. Will you come back and have lunch with us sometime?"

"When could I come?" Georgia looked at Mildred.

"Anytime, Mother."

"Come Monday, about 12:00, and stay for bingo," said Julie.

"*Bingo!?*"

"Bring a quarter."

Dot smiled and walked the Staffords to the parking lot. It was a perfect May evening. She hugged Georgia good-bye and started through the garden, mentally measuring the height of each perennial, comparing it to yesterday's growth. In the bulb garden the spiderwort was flourishing—it would take over soon, and need thinning by mid-June. Low voices broke her concentration. On one bench facing the pond, Lauren was sitting with Bruce and Pete. They were poring over Lauren's bird watching journal. Next to them, on the second bench, Faith and Skipper and Pansy sat, gazing at the waterfall, exclaiming now and then as the koi, slow moving in the still-chilled water, put in an appearance. Mimi and Henry, on the swing in the hummingbird garden, were laughing quietly at something.

Dot strolled back to the building and the rest of her diverse, extended family, grateful beyond words, wholly content in the moment.

978-0-595-37104-4
0-595-37104-3

Printed in the United States
51696LVS00006B/67-75

9 780595 371044